Shadow Lane Volume 8

The Spanking Libertines

by
Eve Howard

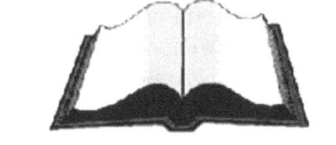

CCB Publishing
British Columbia, Canada

Shadow Lane Volume 8: The Spanking Libertines
A Novel of Spanking, Sex and Romance

Copyright ©2009 by Eve Howard
ISBN-13   978-1-926585-53-6
Second Edition

Library and Archives Canada Cataloguing in Publication
Howard, Eve, 1953-
Shadow lane : volume 8: the spanking libertines, a novel of spanking, sex and love /
written by Eve Howard – 2nd ed.
ISBN 978-1-926585-53-6
Also available in electronic format.
I. Title.
PS3608.O82S538 2009   813'.6   C2009-905337-3

Cover and interior artwork by Tarsis: www.briantarsis.com

Shadow Lane Volume 8 was originally serialized by Shadow Lane in *Stand Corrected* magazine, Copyright © Eve Howard 1999-2000, and was first published by Blue Moon in 2003, Copyright © Eve Howard.

Publisher: CCB Publishing
               British Columbia, Canada
               www.ccbpublishing.com

Dedicated for

Keith and Arthur

Lupe Freeman on one of her adventures in the city

Shadow Lane

Volume 8

The Spanking Libertines

Contents

Susan Ross and Anthony Newton

Chapter One

Lupe Freeman Meets Her Match

During the week of her matriculation at college, Lupe Freeman felt no need of a student advisor, but since one had been assigned to her she visited that young woman's room in the east tower of her dorm at the appointed hour.

Prepared to meet a politically correct senior, harried in her selection of a grad school, Lupe was charmed by the small, striking Diana Stratton, clad in a tweed skirt, satin-backed waistcoat and crisp white shirt, her nut brown page boy smooth as a mink. Lupe knew that she too looked heavenly, in a black and white checked sundress that clove to her own petite torso and set off her waist-length black hair.

Diana was pleased to usher Lupe into her lair, which appeared to have been furnished by Oscar Wilde.

"Where are you from Beauty Girl?" Diana asked, offering her tea.

"L.A., but I've been back east for several years at school." Lupe was flattered by Diana's civility. She had often wished that her day-to-day existence could be as pleasant as one long, on-going Jane Austen novel, only with sex. That lifestyle never seemed more within her grasp.

"Where did you go?" Diana asked her.

"Braemar in Massachusetts."

"In Random Point?" her hostess cried.

"That's right."

"I know the place quite well." Diana said, not setting too much store by the coincidence.

"I loved it there," admitted Lupe wistfully.

"Me too," agreed Diana, "but probably for different reasons. Well, this is your first day at school. Do you have any questions?"

"Actually, I was wondering whether there was anything like a B&D support group on campus," Lupe murmured.

"Not at the moment," replied Diana with the greatest astonishment. "Perhaps you and I should start one!"

Two weeks later, after the posting of a flier campaign, Vassar's first B&D support group met in the parlor of Cushing, the beautiful Tudor style dorm in which the girls resided.

Lupe and Diana arrived a few minutes early to fill bowls with chocolates and nuts while Diana's other protégé, a handsome junior named Carl-Adam Johanson, carried in a keg and tapped it. His trim waist, remarkable shoulder spread and chiseled profile caused Lupe to stare, but Diana whispered, "Alas, he's submissive."

"All six foot four of him?"

"Oh, Lupe, look who just walked in," Diana whispered, "that gorgeously eccentric Clarence Gerard. I've suspected for quite some time that he might be in the Scene!"

Lupe had already learned to admire that absurd creature. He wasn't precisely gothic, had no long fingernails or deadly pallor. But he would affect breeches, top boots and waistcoats over shirts most days. He wore his light brown hair long and though it suited him, Lupe found it difficult to resist the impulse to pull off the black grosgrain ribbon that bound his elegant ponytail.

He was a history major, music minor, captain of the fencing team and avid devourer of two hundred year old novels. On set crew at the Powerhouse Theatre, Lupe had been watching him rehearse one of the lead roles in The Rivals for the past two weeks and was already fixated on the flamboyant junior.

She murmured to Diana, "His dad is a Silicon Valley magnate yet he himself won't even pick up a mouse. He writes out everything in long hand and pays some scholarship kid to key it in."

"I'm becoming more charmed by the moment. Wouldn't he be perfect for you?"

"Bet you he's a sub," guessed Lupe.

"You're probably right," Diana sighed, "though in all probability he's a switch."

"I hate long hair on boys. It only serves to me remind me that my parents wore bell-bottoms," the girl from Los Angeles reflected with a shiver.

"But what hair, he's looks like the lead singer from The Cult."

"You mean to say you admire his affectations?" Lupe demanded.

"He's very appealing."

"At least he doesn't seem to be pierced or tattooed," Lupe granted.

"And mar that flawless skin?"

"He's noticed us looking at him."

Diana waved at the young man, who immediately crossed the room to them.

"Hello," she said. "I'm so glad you could join us! My friend Lupe and I were just trying to guess your orientation."

"Really!" This was pronounced with such irony that Lupe waited for him to produce a quizzing glass to scrutinize them through. Instead he merely asked in the same haughty tone, "And what was your conclusion?"

"Submissive!!" Lupe cried, causing Clarence's eyebrows to jump.

"I was going to say it was too early to tell," Diana chided her friend.

"Submissive!" Clarence rounded on Lupe, a fine color rising in his face.

"Not submissive?" Lupe replied innocently. Clarence glared at her and stalked off to take a seat behind the piano, whereupon he began to play jagged airs from Kurt Weill's German period with excessive violence.

"He looked like he wanted to slap your face," Diana murmured to Lupe. "I wish he had!"

"Thanks!"

"I'm sorry, but that kind of thing turns me on."

Diana chaired the meeting while Lupe took the minutes, Clarence remaining at the keyboard to accompany Diana's opening remarks with the overture to Peter and The Wolf.

Nearly thirty students had arrived, with an even number of men and women. When Diana observed that they were numerous enough for a party, she received a roomful of blank looks, yet the word germinated in all of their brains as she spoke in practical terms about the dungeons and sex clubs of Manhattan.

Then the concept of a party was revived. They wondered with one voice whether they could have a party on campus?

"Out of the question," Clarence snapped, abruptly ceasing to play.

"And why is that so?" Lupe demanded.

"The noise would disturb the other students," he pointed out.

"Any boom box will drown out a whipping," Lupe observed.

"The feminazis will prevent you," he warned.

"Really, Clarence, in spite of what you may choose to believe, we're no longer living in the 18th century," Lupe casually remarked, flushing his fair complexion for the second time. Instead of retorting, however, he simply narrowed his eyes at her, subsided on the piano bench and fell to playing something gloomily Russian.

"I quite understand Mr. Gerard's concerns," said Diana judiciously, "and I believe they may be minimized by holding the proposed party in one of the townhouses facing the woods."

"I live in a townhouse," Carl-Adam volunteered.

"Would your roommates object to a party?" Lupe demanded.

"Certainly not!" replied the flaxen haired youth with conviction.

"What might occur at such a gathering?" queried one thoughtful girl.

"Well, what would you like to occur?" Diana threw out.

There followed a period of quiet reflection as the sexually disenfranchised of Vassar decided how best to articulate their most private obsessions. Meanwhile, the muted rumble of Scriabin provided a suitably dramatic backdrop. A thunderstorm had commenced as well and presently the noise of a heavy downpour augmented the emotion charged atmosphere of the wood beamed common room.

"A bondage demonstration," suggested a pale boy with blue-black hair.

"I own six yards each of the finest white and black nylon rope, and will happily volunteer to be a subject," Diana assured the enthusiast gravely, rendering him speechless with enchantment. "What else?"

"A piercing demonstration," a heavily pierced girl suggested.

"That shouldn't be hard," mused Lupe, "students seem to get pierced on a daily basis around here."

"More's the pity," Clarence mused with a shudder, hoping the impertinent brat taking the minutes would never do so.

"You mentioned whipping before," said another brave coed, nodding towards Lupe, "I'd be interested in that."

"Nothing can be accomplished more easily," Diana promised.

"I wonder why no one has mentioned spanking," said Lupe.

"Are you volunteering to be demonstrated on?" asked Clarence casually.

Lupe's chin came up but then she rather saucily replied, "Why not?"

After that Lupe and Clarence seemed to run into each other everywhere. And after the unifying support group meeting, they were also beginning to share the same friends. But Clarence persisted in returning Lupe's friendly smiles with perfect sheets of ice, making it clear that she would not be soon forgiven for assuming him to be submissive.

Then a small incident occurred that gave Lupe to understand that he was not indifferent. She was studying art history in one of the library's most remote basement carrels while chain-smoking cigarettes when Clarence poked his aristocratic head into her cubicle.

"Oh, it's you. I might have known," he remarked, taking her by the forearm and pulling her out of her seat, into the aisle and down to the wall that prominently bore a "no smoking" sign. "I was under the impression that admission to Vassar was largely contingent upon the ability to read," he declared as he released her.

"You know, nine out of ten Vassar women would take serious umbrage at being manhandled," she commented, rubbing her arm as though he had hurt her.

"Yes, but nine out of ten Vassar women don't deserve to be put across someone's knee!" he told her before turning to stride off.

Lupe watched him go with a fluttering heart.

5

Frustration, anxiety, jealousy and pique were a few of the emotions aroused in the bosoms of our principals during the course of the first Vassar B&D party.

Martin, the ardent bondager and Carl-Adam, the fledgling submissive, suffered varying degrees of anguish from the capricious machinations of Diana Stratton, who first tormented Carl-Adam by allowing Martin to tie her to a whipping post, then virtually crushed Martin's soul by prettily begging Clarence for a whipping while thus restrained.

Taken pity on by Lupe, who was then sleekly clad in skintight PVC capri pants and a halter top of the same material as well as stiletto heels, Carl-Adam was offered the opportunity to serve as her pony and carry her on his broad back through the split level town house as he vigorously traversed it on all fours.

While this athletic exhibition temporarily distracted Carl-Adam from brooding on Diana's reprehensible lapse into simpering submissiveness, the arrant display of Lupe's dominant side had only succeeded in infuriating Clarence, who had been dreaming for many days of subjecting the half-Latina girl to his own will.

He really had thought Lupe submissive and was not entirely convinced that he had been wrong, but the sight of her in stiletto heels struck all the wrong chords with the arch traditionalist, which Clarence then fancied himself to be. He had become accustomed to admiring her slender charms set off to innocent advantage by adorable wool skirts, retro cardigans, penny loafers and pearls. The sight of her sleek curves so boldly revealed by the cleavage enhancing, midriff baring outfit was shocking and made him wanted to shake her for daring to look so sophisticated.

But he was in for greater shocks from Lupe Freeman before the clock stuck twelve.

The moment that Lupe dismounted from Carl-Adam's back and that in which Clarence ceased to crop Diana Stratton's pantied bottom so exactly coincided that they found themselves suddenly face to face in the basement, which had been transformed into a make-shift dungeon composed of steamer trunks and ropes thrown over beams. It was then that Clarence recalled those famous words of Jane Austen about the foolish postponement of pleasure and decided to act at once on the impulse to master this girl.

"Are you ready to go?" he demanded.

Her eyes opened wide but she nodded.

"Then I'll see you home."

He ushered her out.

"It's such a beautiful night," she remarked, tightly clad in polyvinylchloride and impervious to the chill in the air. "Do you want to take the long way back?"

"And which way would that be?"

"Around by the lake?"

"You expect to do that much walking in those shoes?"

"If I got tired you could carry me," she suggested blithely. This almost made him smile, but instead he suddenly frowned.

"I should have thought you'd been carried enough for one night!"

They had already begun down the winding wooded path that lead away from the townhouses and back to Raymond Ave. when she stumbled on the uneven ground and was forced to lean on him.

"Why didn't you play with me at the party?" Lupe asked as he slipped a firm arm around her waist to steady her.

"In front of anyone and everyone?"

"You did it with Diana."

"That's different. She's a little vixen. And a senior."

"Oh."

"Although you look far more the hellcat than Miss Stratton tonight," he gazed at her shining curvature with disapproval.

"Can you actually not like my outfit?" she cried in acute disbelief.

"I'm sure it's extremely becoming, but to me it's an impenetrable suit of armor."

"Not really. The pants unzip in the back," she pointed out the zipper.

They did not resume their conversation until they had crossed the street and walked onto the main campus.

"I've been meaning to ask you since you showed up at the support group meeting, what exact facet of B&D are you into, Clarence?"

"The same one you're into, I think."

"I never said what I'm into."

"Didn't you?"

As they walked past the Gothic library they both remembered their last encounter in the basement. Lupe's heart pounded and Clarence's face flushed.

"You seemed to crop Diana masterfully," Lupe murmured several minutes later, as they were crossing the wooden bridge that spanned Vassar Lake. "I envied the attention she was getting. But I suppose that I wore the wrong outfit."

No sooner had these mildly wistful words issued from her lips than Clarence seized Lupe around the waist, lifted her to eye level and kissed her resoundingly. When he set her feet back down on the bridge she wobbled slightly. This gave him the excuse to sweep her up into his arms.

"What are you doing?"

"Carrying you home."

"You can't carry me all the way like this."

"How much do you weigh? A hundred pounds?"

"Yes."

"Besides, if I get tired of carrying you this way I can always put you over one shoulder," he threatened.

"No!"

"I've been wanting to kiss you for weeks."

"But you've been so aloof," she reminded him.

"You needed to be punished."

"You're horrible," she cried, gripped by a spasm of pleasure.

"Oh, you have no idea."

"Why? What are you into, Clarence?"

"What do you think?"

"Could be anything from vampirism to cattle prods."

"Oh, don't be silly."

"Rope bondage, hot wax and nipple clamps?"

Clarence snorted his derision.

"I know! Cross-dressing! With your alter ego being Mrs. Siddons!"

Clarence put Lupe down and gave her a shake. "You brat!" He

kissed her again. "I don't think I'll wait to get you home before I spank you!" He pulled her off the lake path to the first fallen log he saw and turned her over his knee. Then holding her fast to his lap he brought his palm down vigorously on her shiny, PVC wrapped bottom a dozen or thirteen times. The spanking was delivered so rapidly that she hardly had time to kick before it was over and he'd set her back on her feet.

"There!" he told her. "Now you know for a certainty what I'm into!"

Lupe walked along beside him, still feeling the impact of his hand on her bottom. She wondered why in the stories she'd read on the subject, girls always rubbed their bottoms after a spanking. She herself would never attempt to disperse that exquisite sensation of just having been spanked. Meanwhile freshets of pleasure coursed through her as she pondered what Clarence had just done.

By the time they walked up the hill to the golf course and around the terrace apartments he felt it necessary to seize and firmly kiss her again.

"You're a little character," he said. "In fact, you're just my type."

They reached their dorm. Clarence being an upper classman possessed the larger, grander room. He invited her to visit him there as soon as she had changed into a more accessible costume.

When she joined him in his third floor corner aerie he had cracked the latticework windows to let in the spicy autumn air. Now clad in a fitted long sleeved dress of olive corduroy and chestnut brown riding boots Lupe pleased Clarence much more and he took her on his lap the right way around to kiss her and squeeze her 23" waist.

"Much improved," he commended her, nuzzling her silken throat. But Lupe ached for more spanking, not necking and jumped off his lap. She strode around the room, examining his books and things. There were cobwebs on his computer. She sat down at the keyboard and stroked it on.

"Can I check my e-mail?" she asked, logging on without waiting for permission but adding earnestly as she saw him bristle, "There was a message from my dad on my machine when I went to change and it said to check my e-mail right away."

"By all means," he replied, meticulously filling a pipe with tobacco.

"Oh!" she cried, reading her message.

"What's the matter?"

"I have to go home this weekend!" She pressed her small hands to her face.

"I hope nothing is wrong."

"No. Nothing is wrong."

"Then why do you look so shaken, dearest?"

"I have to go home to help my dad," Lupe announced dramatically.

"Help your dad do what?"

"Increase magazine sales!"

"Increase magazine sales? Is your father in publishing?"

"Yes. He's a publisher of men's magazines. Ron Freeman."

"Oh my god, you're Ron Freeman's daughter?" Clarence physically recoiled.

"Of course I am."

"How hideous for you."

"Why do you say that? Are you porno phobic?"

"No, but I've always found your father's magazine particularly offensive, as must every person of sensibility. Including yourself, I should hope."

"Yes, of course. Anyway, sales have been flat since the spring and Ron won't be able to meet my college expenses for the next semester unless I come home this weekend and help."

"You call your father by his first name? I don't approve of that. It's very confusing. And how in the world can you help?"

"Ron says if I pose for a photo spread in the magazine he can vaunt it on the cover and book lots of expensive alcohol and cigarette ads for the issue."

"If you do what?"

"If he can put on the cover of American Lust: 'First nude photos of Ron Freeman's 18 year old daughter' it will be a big selling point and earn enough advertising revenue to pay for two or three terms here at school."

"Lupe you can't possibly dream of letting your father exploit you in that way!"

"He's not exploiting me, Clarence. He's just suggesting a way to keep me here at school. He's not a multi-zillionaire tycoon like you're dad. He's just a struggling pornographer trying to run his business, pay for his lawsuits and provide his daughter with a refined education."

"Lupe! Am I hearing you correctly? You mean to say you actually don't resent your father's making such an obscene suggestion to you?"

"It's not obscene. It would only be a nude photoset, not an explicit one. Anyway, I always planned to go into the business after graduation."

"Going into the business is one thing, though I can't imagine why a young woman of your character could want any part of that sleazy concern, but performing for it is quite another, young lady. After all, you don't see Christy Heffner posing nude."

"Maybe she's shy. I'm certainly not," said Lupe negligently. "My mother is Saturnia X, you know."

"The sexual performance artist from the 80's?" he asked faintly.

"Yes," Lupe cheerfully replied, causing Clarence to shudder.

"I still can't believe your own father would ask such a thing of you. How I'd love to tell him off!" Clarence paced.

"That wouldn't be very nice."

"Lupe, tell me the truth, has your father abused you?"

Lupe laughed and shook her head. "I can understand you despising the tone of his magazine. I do also. That's why I plan to go into the business, to affect the necessary upgrades."

"Well, be that as it may four to six years from now, this minute we're discussing the ridiculous notion of you posing for American Lust. And I tell you, I won't permit it."

"But Clarence, it's too late to apply for financial aid for this year. Would you have me take a semester off?"

"Can't you get a loan?"

"For next year, yes."

"Damn it, Lupe, I'll give you the money myself if it will prevent you from taking this horrifying step!"

"You have that kind of money?"

"Yes."

"Why would you do that for me? You scarcely know me."

"I won't have my girlfriend flashing her charms for American Lust magazine, even if she is the publisher's daughter."

"Your girlfriend?"

"You heard me."

"And what do I have to do in return?"

"In return for what?"

"You rescuing me."

"If you feel under some slight obligation," he shrugged mildly, "you could of course be my slave all year."

"But where in the world would you get that kind of money?"

"I have investments," the multi-millionaire's son who had almost become a math major modestly revealed.

"Clarence, I'm so touched. You make me want to cry," she murmured, laying her head against his chest and hugging him hard.

"You make me want to make you cry," he growled, shaking her by the shoulders again. "I'm still stunned that you could even consider such a rash act."

"Do you have anything besides tobacco to smoke?"

"Of course." He sat down at the desk and pulled out the top drawer. While he was feeling around towards the back for a small tin his gaze fell upon the freshly activated computer monitor with the e-mail from Lupe's father still up on the screen. Scanning it rapidly, then re-reading the brief note several times, Clarence felt his face redden. Forgetting to look for his weed he slammed the drawer shut and turned on Lupe with sparks in his blue eyes.

"You made it up."

"I beg your pardon?" she politely asked, attempting to repress a smile, for she had certainly noticed him reading the screen.

"You made up the entire story about posing for American Lust."

"Really?"

"This e-mail from your father merely informs you that he will be in Manhattan for Thanksgiving and promises to take you shopping at Barney's!"

"Listen, Clarence, don't get mad," Lupe said, attempting to edge away from him but finding the room too small to put much distance between them.

"Mad isn't the word," he warned her, seizing her by the ear lobe and dragging her over to the bed whereupon he turned her over his knee for the second time that night. "How dare you tell outrageous lies to shock me?"

Lupe cried out in surprise as his palm came down hard on the back of her skirt and commenced spanking her resoundingly.

"Why was that necessary?" he demanded, pulling up her skirt to reveal slim bare thighs and a neat, round bottom snugly encased in white silk panties. "Weren't you getting enough attention as it was?" Smack! Smack! Smack!

"No, not nearly," Lupe cried between gasps and whimpers.

"Well you'll be getting it now." His hand came down hard again and again, warming her so thoroughly that he began to feel a tangible heat rise from the thin fabric. He pulled the panties down to examine the pinkest bottom he had ever held across his lap.

"It hurts!" she cried, attempting to shield herself with her hand. He caught her wrist and slapped her on the back of the hand.

"It's going to hurt a good deal more before I'm through with you, young lady!"

"I was only playing a joke on you, because you're such a prude!"

"I'm nothing of the kind." He whacked her hard.

"Ow! You certainly are. You didn't even want us to have a spanking party!"

"Never mind that. We're discussing your character flaws, not mine," he pointed out, paddling her firmly with his very hard hand until she squirmed.

"Ow, that really stings! I've had enough for now. In fact, I'll be good," she cried, really attempting to wriggle off his lap in earnest now.

"Hold still," he ordered, mitigating the severity of the spanking by vigorously rubbing her bottom.

"Mmmmm," Lupe intoned appreciatively while grinding against his lap.

"I'm glad you seem to like this position," he observed, "because you're going to be spending a great deal of time in it from now on!"

In spite of meeting a female bondage enthusiast (who subsequently became his girlfriend) at the townhouse party, Martin never forgave Diana for allowing Clarence to crop her while she was restrained in his own beautiful bondage.

Less resentful but more deeply affected by Diana's merry submission to Clarence was Carl-Adam, who had adored the small, sophisticated coed for the past several weeks and had envisioned serving her for the rest of the school year. The sight of his lovely little mistress whimpering with pleasure and apprehension as Clarence's crop punished her divine bottom filled Carl-Adam with confusion and unhappiness.

As he fell into step beside Lupe the next morning on the way to the dining hall her smile cheered him. Though she had recently supplanted him as Diana's best friend, he liked her only slightly less than his goddess.

"Diana has become bored with me," Carl-Adam reported.

"Carl-Adam, never think it. She adores you," Lupe reassured the formidable young man.

"No. She didn't pay me the slightest attention at the party. She cared for your Clarence much more. When all he did was hurt her!"

"Oh, Carl-Adam, he did not hurt her."

"She flinched as he struck her. I saw her. And heard her cry out."

"But cropping can be quite enjoyable. Surely you can empathize, or does your interest lie only in servitude?"

"What do you mean?"

"Don't you realize that corporal punishment can be a powerful aphrodisiac?"

"You mean spanking?"

"Spanking, whipping, strapping, caning," Lupe recited the litany reverently.

"Can that be what Diana really likes?"

"You know, Carl-Adam, there's a lot you can do with a girl when she's across your lap."

"My lap?" He was taken aback.

"You're such a big young man and she's such a little girl. Hasn't it occurred to you that her being your mistress is incongruous?"

"No, but I'm in love."

"Well I assure you it's occurred to her. And if you really are in love, you'll drop this submissive nonsense and start behaving like a man with that girl."

Diana had become accustomed to Carl-Adam carrying her golf clubs every Sunday morning when she took her exercise on the lushly landscaped course. But that morning he was so late in arriving to meet her that she assumed he had completely forgotten this cherished obligation and was sleeping off the effects of the previous night's revelries. But going out the door of Cushing at eleven, with her neat golf bag over one shoulder and delightfully attired in a pleated skirt, matching sweater set and oxfords, she bumped directly into Carl-Adam.

"Did you remember our appointment at the last minute?" she smiled up at him with her usual charm but was startled to note the stern resolve in his slate-blue eyes.

"I remembered," he answered shortly, shouldering her clubs and ushering her out into the golden autumn day.

"Well, aren't you going to apologize for keeping your mistress waiting?" she asked in all good humor, in spite of his foreboding expression.

"You forfeited that title when you behaved like a whimpering submissive in front of everyone last night!" he informed her severely.

"Oh?" she slowly replied, feeling her heart contract as she realized that Carl-Adam was angry with her.

"Yes, and in my very own house," he continued, "after I'd arranged everything for your pleasure. You were so busy genuflecting to that silly Clarence that you couldn't spare a moment for me. Did you think I threw a party to watch you play with him?"

"Carl-Adam, are you giving me a scolding?"

"You behaved very badly last night!"

"Mistresses don't need to behave well. They only need to please themselves."

"And did you please yourself last night?'

"Apparently not as much as I displeased you," she smiled ruefully as they reached the golf course.

They continued to converse as she played her nine holes, Carl-Adam's demeanor becoming stiffer and grimmer by the moment as he followed her across the emerald grass. In this manner ninety minutes passed quickly, Carl-Adam's fascination growing for her with every frown.

She finally said, "If I have been mistaken in your character, you have only yourself to blame. I never asked you to dote on me. You took it upon yourself to behave as though you were here for my convenience. Now you seem to be angry about it, almost jealous. It's really quite absurd."

"You're a spoiled brat!" he snapped. "And as soon as we get back to your room I'm going to turn you over my knee!"

All too soon Diana and Carl-Adam stood before the locked door of her room.

"Thank you, Carl-Adam, I'll take the clubs now."

"Open the door, Diana."

"I don't think I will."

"Afraid?"

"Only of you humiliating yourself."

"I beg your pardon?"

"How do I know that if I let you in you won't simply fall to your knees as you normally do?"

"Key."

Diana sighed and opened the door, unwilling to attract attention by arguing in the hall. He closed and locked the door behind them and stood looking at her for a moment with his hands clasped behind his back.

"Carl-Adam really, you just can't change roles in midstream like this!" Diana flushed with embarrassment as she saw how very serious he was.

"Why not? Come over here, young lady," he took her by the wrist, led her to the bed, sat down and deftly turned her over his knee, which wasn't much of a challenge, given their respective sizes.

"Carl-Adam, you're terrifying me!" Diana cast him an imploring but mischievous look, putting back one tiny hand to shield her bottom. Unmoved he took her wrist and pinned it to her side then tentatively raised his hand and firmly brought it down on the seat of her skirt. She gave a little wriggle. Again he smacked her, a little harder now. When she made no move to escape he spanked her five or six more times. She caught her breath as the slaps became harder. Carl-Adam had a very large hand and huge, muscular thighs to support a girl luxuriously.

"God," she sighed, in heaven. "You do this well, Carl-Adam."

His anger melting in the glow of her compliance, Carl-Adam began to realize that this could be a pleasure for them both. Again and again he brought his palm down on her pleated skirt until she couldn't help but grind against his thighs in a state of arousal. He could feel the heat that the spanking produced though the fine wool of her skirt. No amount of kissing her tiny feet would ever bring this sort of response, reflected Carl-Adam.

Without a word he pulled her skirt up to her waist to behold the sheerest white nylon panties he had ever seen. Her creamy skin, already deeply tinged with pink, glowed alluringly through the nearly transparent material. It was all he could do not to cover her exquisite bottom with kisses. He had of course imagined her bottom to be flawless, but he hadn't guessed how much lovelier it might appear while disposed across his lap and pinkened by his own relentless hand.

Reading his mind, Diana softly teased, "Aren't you going to tell me how pretty I am? You used to be full of compliments when I was dominant and allowed you to glimpse far less of me!"

"Your head has been turned by too many compliments," he told her sternly, continuing the spanking with great resolve. Lupe's advice had not fallen on inattentive ears and he was already feeling the good of it.

"Oh? Are you implying that I'm vain?" she demanded, twisting on his lap to avoid his hand. Firmly righting her and holding her fast he spanked her six or seven times soundly.

"Not vain perhaps, but so over-confident that you've forgotten the importance of good manners."

"Really! Now you're going too far," Diana bristled. This inspired him to pull her panties down. "No! Don't you dare! I never agreed to a bare bottom spanking!"

"How pink you are."

"Let me see!" Diana craned her neck to view herself. He pushed her back down.

"Later," he told her, delivering additional vigorous smacks. Diana bit her knuckle so as not to whimper aloud. As a submissive, Carl-Adam had been endearingly absurd, as a dominant, he was remarkably daddy-like from the big lap to the heavy hand and Diana could have kissed him for it.

The spanking became harder and her perfect bottom redder. His hand began to produce a sting very nearly past bearing. She found herself gripping the bedclothes and making a great effort not to cry out. The spanking was beginning to hurt, but at the same time, it felt more exciting by the moment. Carl-Adam was quite the inflexible dom, punishing her as sternly as a strapping Swedish country minister of the early 1900's might have disciplined a naughty village sweetheart.

Finally Carl-Adam removed his mesmerized gaze from her squirming bottom long enough to notice the great effort she was making not to cry out or complain. He dropped his hand abruptly and then deliberately and respectfully set her to rights, pulling up her panties and pulling down her skirt before lifting her from his lap.

Her hand going back to rub her bottom, she murmured, "Why did you stop?"

"That's enough to give you something to think about," he told her over folded arms.

"Aren't you going to comfort me, Carl-Adam?"

"Why should I?"

"It felt so real that I was about to get tears in my eyes when you stopped. But I would have let myself cry rather than ask you to stop."

"I'll make you cry. With a switch out in the woods," he promised unsmilingly. She was startled when this caused her butterflies and began to wonder how Carl-Adam had managed to pick up so much dominant polish overnight.

"Carl-Adam, you're being very harsh with your Diana," she

reproached him mildly. This being more than even Carl-Adam could withstand, he took her in his arms and kissed her deeply.

"From now on," he said, sitting her on his lap like a child, "instead of issuing me orders, you must ask me politely for whatever you want or need."

"Carl-Adam, I always ask you politely," she smiled.

"You understand what I mean. As you may have noticed, I'm no longer you're possession. Instead, you are mine."

"And when you do mean to take possession of your possession?"

"On the first day you want me."

"What makes you think I don't want you right now?"

"That naughty smile. It makes me realize that you're much too sure of me." Carl-Adam chastely kissed her brow and took his leave, causing her to marvel at his sudden and inexplicable metamorphosis. How smart of him to make her wait! Now she would think of nothing but Carl-Adam and the next opportunity she might give him to spank her.

Diana managed very easily to enrage Carl-Adam the following night by inviting to her room and playing spanking games with a boy named Rudy Wolfe who had homed in on Lupe and herself at the orientation meeting. Although in love with a Manhattan attorney and fast developing a tendre for Carl-Adam, the flirtatious Diana was unequivocally willing to play with virtually anyone on campus who took the trouble to ask, at least once.

Rudy was enjoying his hour of glory in Diana's room. The shy, dark haired boy was only a sophomore and barely three inches taller than herself, but he had a friendly hand and a comfortable lap. Moreover, he spanked effectively while causing very little pain. He'd confided he had spanked his girl cousins as well as his high school girlfriend. Diana was pleased by his unassuming manners and used him for her pleasure unabashedly.

When Carl-Adam approached Diana's door at around ten on that Saturday night and heard the spanking noises issuing from within, he was very nearly wounded into turning on his heel and walking away. But a desire to assess his rival caused him to instead rap smartly on the door. After an audible scramble within, the door was opened by a flushed Diana, who nonetheless calmly smoothed her navy wool jumper back into perfect pleats.

"Oh, Carl-Adam. Are you early? Do you know Rudy Wolfe?"

"No!" the towering Carl-Adam growled at the boy in such a way as to expedite his departure.

"So!" he accused as soon as the door had closed behind Rudy, "you sub to dweebs now?"

"Physical beauty isn't everything, Carl-Adam I value sensitivity and expertise as well. The young man's style was at once refined and robust. Therefore how could I help being charmed?"

Carl-Adam was about to seize and shake her when she airily announced, "I'm going down to the Vault tonight with Lupe. Would you like to drive us?" Diana went behind a wooden screen to change clothes as they continued to talk.

"Yes," he replied calmly, though inwardly thrilled. She emerged in an open-collared black leather cat suit that clung becomingly to every dainty curve. She sat on a Windsor chair and opened a large box to withdraw a pair of brand new black thigh-high boots from London.

"Will you help me put them on?" she taunted Carl-Adam, knowing that to kneel to her and help her on with her shoes had as recently as two days before been enough to give him a raging erection.

"Of course," he replied matter of factly, kneeling before her and deftly lacing up the leather dream boots. Expecting him to nearly swoon with pleasure at this divine duty, Diana was puzzled when he signaled the completion of the job not by covering her size five feet with the usual kisses and sighs, but by giving one shapely calf a squeeze and a smack through the skintight pant and boot leg that clad it.

"Looking like that, it's good you'll have me there to protect you," Carl-Adam commented.

"But not serve me, Carl-Adam? Even while I'm dressed like this?"

"As far you're concerned that part of me no longer exists." He got up.

"You sound so firm, Carl-Adam."

"You're smiling, but some day you won't."

"This masquerade is very amusing, Carl-Adam, but how long can you keep it up?" He was left to brood on this impertinent question as Diana e-mailed Lupe to meet her in the lobby immediately.

They were standing in the lobby deciding whether to take Diana's car or Carl-Adam's when Clarence entered the dorm, laden with books. He stared at Diana in her cat suit and Lupe in her long sleeved, sweetheart cut black leather dress.

"What's going on?" he demanded.

"We're going to the Vault," Lupe revealed casually, delighted that he had chanced by.

"Don't you think that Lupe's too young for that hellacious den?" asked Clarence, reluctantly admiring Lupe's beautiful little shape.

"Nonsense, Clarence," said Diana. "Don't be stuffy. Go put your books away and come along with us."

"I think I'd better," he agreed, marching off at once.

"Let's leave him here," said Lupe mischievously. "Make him chase us in his car!" She jumped up and down excitedly in spite of her four inch heeled pumps.

"No. It's going to take both of us to make sure you two don't get into trouble," Carl-Adam decided maturely, causing Lupe to stare at him in fascination.

"Carl-Adam seems somehow different today," Lupe remarked to Diana as their pet Viking went to warm up the jeep.

When Lupe begged Carl-Adam to let her drive he handed her the keys without hesitation. Sitting in the back seat with Diana for ninety minutes seemed much more enjoyable than driving, especially if she was naughty enough to give him an excuse to pull her across his lap again.

Clarence wasn't pleased but didn't argue. Lupe set off down the lush Taconic Parkway hell for leather. Vigorous protests from both Clarence and Carl-Adam slowed her to the speed limit, though not uncomplainingly, for the road was quite open at that hour. Clarence made a mental note never to let her behind a wheel again while Carl-Adam thought hard about a way to get Diana into his arms.

"Fucking move!" Lupe cried, thumping her horn at a sluggish motorist in front of them as she wove in and out of lanes.

"Really, Lupe, I'm sure you know better words," Clarence scolded, earning a sidelong glance of indeterminate meaning.

"Clarence, do you realize you're a walking, talking anachronism? I mean, will you fucking look at yourself?"

In the ten seconds of silence that followed even Carl-Adam momentarily forgot his own objective and waited agog for Clarence's reply. That his classmate was boiling was obvious. It was quite possible, thought Diana exchanging a look with Carl-Adam, that the brief affair of Lupe and Clarence had just come to an end.

Finally Clarence tuned in the radio to an underground station and in moments the desolate sounds of the Damned filled the awkward silence.

Shame and guilt at having spoken so brusquely to the one that she loved caused a lump to constrict Lupe's throat. She brushed away the sudden tears that over spilled her eyes while Clarence affected indifference. "I'm sorry," she murmured, in deep misery. He handed her a clean handkerchief then ignored her for the rest of the ride, deciding he might never talk to her again.

Yet Clarence couldn't help commenting acidly on the environs of the Vault when they debarked in the meatpacking district of lower Manhattan at around midnight.

"I'm not thrilled with this neighborhood," he muttered to Carl-Adam.

"You should have brought your sword," Lupe commented, not quite chastened enough to wholly curb her tongue.

Clarence fought the impulse to slap Lupe hard as they proceeded down the stone steps into the premiere B&D club of New York. They paid their admission to a burly doorman in a Harley Davidson vest, $25 each for the boys and $5 each for the girls, though the girls' fees were waived.

Upon entering the play rooms Carl-Adam's eyes widened and Clarence muttered, "What the hell goes on here?" for neither young man had been warned about what to expect from Diana, who alone of the group had been there before.

Carl-Adam observed with fascination as a handful of mistresses strutted around the rooms in command of a small army of obsequious males, on their knees to a man, with their cocks in their hands. 'There but for the counsel of Lupe,' thought Carl-Adam, 'might have gone I.' Not that he would have dreamt of getting down on his knees on that floor! But when he turned to share this revelation with Diana, he found her already securely mounted on the back of the club's chivalrous mascot, Danny the Wonder Pony. She cheerfully waved at Carl-Adam and disappeared around a corner on the veteran centaur's back.

"This is no place for Lupe," Clarence scowled.

"She tried to make us leave without you, so you'd have to chase us in your car," Carl-Adam blithely informed on the girl who had done him the biggest favor of his life. He felt it important that Clarence see the big picture with Lupe and not judge her feelings for him solely on the basis of the one unkind remark she had made in the car. Since Lupe had helped him with Diana, he felt he had to help her with Clarence.

"Oh, she did, did she?"

"Do you really think you ought to let her wander around by herself in here?" Carl-Adam asked, noticing that Lupe had slipped out of sight. Clarence sighed and went looking for her, his mouth set in a grim line. He hadn't forgotten her incivility, but somehow the steamy, anything goes atmosphere of the Vault was beginning to work like a tonic on his overwrought nerves. If there was any place that one could grab a naughty girl and thrust her across one's knee without raising the slightest demur, although fifty persons looked on, it was here.

And he did find Lupe, allowing a slave to worshipfully kiss the seat of her leather skirt as she leaned forward with her hands on her knees and thrust her slim bottom into his face. She looked exactly as though she were posing for her father's unspeakable magazine, just as she had teased him she might.

"Intolerable!" Clarence said to himself, striding across the room to his sweetheart and straightening her up.

"I won't allow you to make this kind of spectacle of yourself," he informed her, taking her by the wrist and leading her away from the disappointed slave. "Didn't you notice that that man was masturbating?"

Lupe contrived to look meekly chastened as he found a wooden bench against a wall for them to sit on. Her submissiveness aroused him acutely, though he still felt that she should be punished for insulting him so gravely two hours before.

"I wish you would forgive me," Lupe murmured, reading his mind. "I'm sorry I was rude. You can spank me if it will help."

Clarence's organ throbbed at this winsome invitation. "If I do it won't be playfully," he warned her. Lupe lowered her eyes so compliantly that he almost went to pieces and took her in his arms. Instead he pulled her easily across his lap and began to spank her rather hard.

Lupe could feel Clarence's pique in every resounding smack that descended on the seat of her tight leather skirt, and there were scores. As Clarence was young, strong and tireless, this went on for some time. A semi-circle formed around them, which Clarence greatly resented but contrived to ignore. Remembering again the ease with which a vulgar epithet had rolled off Lupe's tongue, he redoubled his efforts to impress upon her that manners still count.

Pulling her leather skirt up to her waist wasn't easy, so he made her get up off his lap and hike it up herself before being summarily pulled back down. As she did this she bestowed upon the breathless crowd a Giaconda smile, which it was fortunate that Clarence did not see.

Needless to say being spanked by an outrageously handsome boy in front of dozens of players in the legendary Vault when she was scarcely eighteen and a half years old figured as one of the crowning moments of Lupe's life, the other two being: her first whipping from a leather man at the age of sixteen in Hollywood and the caning she'd received from Mr. Lawrence, her Senior Lit teacher at Braemar the previous Spring. To say that she was excited would have been a vast understatement. But she was also moved, almost to tears, by the notion of her young man spanking her indignantly for verbally devastating him earlier on. This was exactly what she wanted out of the Scene, drama and passion!

Clarence kept smacking her hard, while considering the possibility of utterly humiliating her by pulling her panties down. He felt she needed it, but did this ocean of B&D zombie-voyeurs really deserve that thrill?

"Are you learning a lesson?" he asked her, reminding her very much of her divine Mr. Lawrence as he yanked her sheer black panties down to reveal her rounded, rosy bottom to the crowd of spell bound on-lookers, one or two of whom were not chronic masturbators, but rather serious corporal punishment practitioners, who viewed the exquisite demonstration with even more appreciative eyes.

As the spanking proceeded on Lupe's bare bottom word seemed to fly though the rooms of the club that a beautiful young couple were enacting a perfect spanking scene. Within a minute a ring of fascinated B&D players, including several attractive couples, supplanted the penis pullers in the choicest viewing spots and watched with rapt enjoyment as Lupe squirmed and kicked across Clarence's lap. Male masters put their female submissives up on their shoulders to look on approvingly while corseted dominatrixes and their harnessed, collared slaves paused to be charmed. The next time Clarence raised his eyes to his audience he glimpsed not one wagging penis, but instead a well-behaved circle of actual players offering silent encouragement in the form of subtle smiles. This change cheered him and he returned to his job with renewed vigor.

Meanwhile Lupe was on the brink of tears for the spanking had continued long enough to become very painful. She tried to shield her bottom but Clarence caught and slapped her hand until she pulled it from his grasp and tucked it under her bosom. Then his palm continued to sharply sting her soft skin, which had already borne more spanking than she could have imagined possible in one session. She longed to cry mercy, but forced herself to endure. After all, she was being punished, which in itself was sexy. But how it had begun to hurt!

"Oh, please!" she cried at last, "I'll be good!" She turned her large, dark eyes toward him appealingly.

"Very well, I'll let you up, but it's not over!" he promised, pulling her up off his lap and getting to his feet. Without allowing her to lower her skirt, Clarence took Lupe by her bare forearm and led her to the closest corner. "Stand there just like that until I come back for you," he ordered sternly, forcing her to leave her skirt up and her panties pulled down, with her freshly spanked bottom turned towards the room. It was a horrible thing to do to Lupe, but it made Clarence very happy.

Lupe was aware of how angelically naughty she looked, standing in the corner, with her hands clasped together in front of her and her straight, black hair flowing to her waist. She could also imagine how adorable her bottom looked as well, so pink above the lace tops of her sheer black hose. But these aspects of her situation did not completely comfort her. She wondered how long Clarence planned to leave her there. The club didn't close until four. Every minute or so she would hotly decide to break her position and tell Clarence off. But then it occurred to her that this might be some sort of test, and that if she balked at it, he might not want her for his girl friend after all. And she wanted very much to be his. So she didn't move. She didn't turn around either, terrified that if she did she would confront a full battalion of masturbating males, all fixated on her backside.

Only once was her reverie disturbed and that was when someone came up beside her and slipped a card into her hand. Startled she turned to look into the eyes of a bold, young Latin male with collar length black hair and a moustache. He was dressed all in black and was obviously dominant. She looked down at the card. On one side his name was printed: Xavier Duarte. On the other side there was a phone number. When she looked up from the card he was gone. Lupe turned back to face the wall, and this was how her friends found her moments later.

"Poor girl!" Diana cried, changing mounts as Danny's strong back yielded her to Carl-Adam's sturdy shoulders. Enclosing his neck between her thighs she grabbed a hank of straight blond hair for balance and was transported closer to the scene of Lupe's humiliation. Carl-Adam held her steady with one hand on each of her leather-clad thighs. "Should we rescue her, Carl-Adam?"

"Don't you dare!" Clarence cried, coming up beside them with a faint smile on his face. "I've never enjoyed myself so much in my life," he added, admiring his handiwork while glancing at the clock on the wall. She had only been standing there for eight minutes.

"Well I think you're a horrid brute!" Diana charged while

continuing to gaze with fascination at her beautifully exposed friend.

"Oh, all right," Clarence said, going to fetch Lupe out of the corner, which was indeed becoming surrounded with the masturbating males she had anticipated.

Walking briskly up to Lupe he pulled her panties back up into place, worked her skirt back down over her slim hips and turned her around to face him. Lupe's big brown eyes reproached him for his cruelty while her full red mouth pouted for a kiss. Instead he took her by the wrist as though she were a child and led her back to Carl-Adam and Diana. Clarence noticed she refused to meet their eyes and took pleasure in her embarrassment.

"Lupe, would you like to go back now?" Diana asked, putting her arm around her friend's shoulders and hugging her. Lupe nodded and they all left the club.

The night air was bracing above ground. This time Carl-Adam got behind the wheel, with Diana beside him, while Clarence and Lupe took the bench seat in back.

For the first half hour on the road back Carl-Adam, Diana and Clarence held an animated discussion on what they had seen at the club. Lupe curled up in her corner and pretended to doze. Eventually the conversation fell off, with Carl-Adam and Diana now and then murmuring soft comments to each other.

Observing her tensely curled posture, Clarence pulled Lupe out of the corner and made her stretch out with her head in his lap. When she shivered he covered her with his jacket. Lupe fell fast asleep, only to be woken once they were back at the dorm.

Pulling her up the stairs by the hand he waved at Carl-Adam and Diana, who together headed off.

Lupe was very nearly awake when they arrived at Clarence's room. She allowed him to unzip her and take her out of the dress, revealing to him for the first time her saucy bosom. This he covered with kisses as he took her down to his bed, stripping off all of her remaining apparel and accessories as rapidly as he could. Naked in his arms for the first time, Lupe clung to him and thrilled to hear him tell her that he loved her.

Meanwhile Carl-Adam had escorted Diana to her door.

"Aren't you coming in, Carl-Adam?" she whispered, because it was after three a.m. and most of the dorm was asleep.

"May I?'

"Please."

Diana didn't turn on the light, but pulled back her mauve silk curtains to let the moonlight in through the multi-paned windows. Opening them slightly, a gush of crackling autumn air filled the room. Carl-Adam helped Diana off with her boots first then took off his own as she went behind her screen to peel off the cat suit. When she emerged in a blue cotton wrapper, Diana curled up on Carl-Adam's lap and threw her arms around his neck to kiss him resoundingly. He bounced her on his lap, squeezed her gently though the dressing gown and kissed her ears and throat until she squirmed.

"Oh, Carl-Adam, take me as forcefully as ever you can!" she encouraged him, opening an ebony box filled with condoms and lubricants.

Carl-Adam needed no further prodding to rip off his clothes and attempt to match a rubber to his huge erection.

"My god, Carl-Adam, forget what I just said and do go easy with that thing!" she cried.

Chapter Two

Lupe's Latin Lovers

"That was quite a story you wrote about our party for the paper," Lupe Freeman accused Hector Green, dropping into a chair opposite him at the Vassar canteen.

Like Lupe, Hector was an arresting parfait of Latin and European influences, but this did not dispose her in his favor as much as it might have done before reading his article, which had reported, (with undue sensationalism), on a small, well behaved B&D play party, hosted by her best friend Diana and herself.

"You didn't like it?" he murmured in the accents of Manhattan, not looking up from his laptop.

"Were you even at the party?"

"I came late," he snapped, looking at her for the first time and then regretting his curtness.

"I'll bet."

"So, what didn't you like?" Sudden arousal rendered his whole demeanor soft and conciliatory.

"You invoked the whips and chains cliché, yet there wasn't a whip or a chain in the house. Is it possible that in your stupendous ignorance you actually don't know the difference between a flogger and a crop?"

"Teach me!" Hector flashed her his most persuasive smile.

"Highly unlikely," she replied, getting up, "but I will say this: You write badly enough to work for my father."

"Really? Who's your father?" Hector zipped his laptop into its case and followed her out of the Retreat and into the corridors of Vassar's oldest dorm, Main Hall, erected in 1865, in replication of the Tulleries.

"Ron Freeman," she replied.

"Really! This is an honor."

With Hector adhering to her, Lupe walked one flight up to the Blue parlor.

"I figured you'd admire my father."

"So, you don't like my journalistic style?"

"I do not."

"What's your name?"

"Lupe."

"Where did you get that name?"

"My mother is Mexican. Saturnia X. I'm sure you've heard of her."

"The sexual performance artist from the 80's? You have some lineage. From you I will stand corrected."

"Good."

"You say that on a dismissive note," Hector said, allowing her to precede him into the graceful room.

"Good day, Mr. Green." Lupe sat down on a vine carved loveseat and opened a hardbound volume of Samuel Richardson's Pamela.

"Don't be like that," he urged, sitting beside her. "Meeting you, I want to learn to be kinky."

"You're making me sick."

"Lupe, be nice," he scolded her, "after all, we have so much in common."

"What?" She stared at him.

"Well, I'm half Puerto Rican to your half Mexican."

"That's sexy, but not necessarily the basis for intimacy. And here's my friend, so I hope you'll excuse us," said Lupe, seeing Diana enter the room.

"Please make Lupe tell me what she's into," Hector implored the slender brunette who now joined them.

"Who are you?" the new petite girl asked, perching on a chair opposite them and noticing the devastating contrast between Hector's tawny hazel eyes, golden brown skin and jet-black hair.

"Don't talk to him," advised Lupe, getting to her feet, "he's that tabloid journalist who writes for the Vassarian. Now with a hard-on."

"The muckraker who mocked our party? How dare you address us?" Diana tossed him a censorious glance before following Lupe out.

But Hector didn't give up easily and sensing a tendency in Diana to accommodate, he sat down opposite her in the dining hall the first time he saw her alone.

"Hello. Remember me?" he reached over the table to shake her small hand. She smiled at him briefly then went back to working her Saturday New York Times crossword puzzle. "Won't you help me with our Lupe, kind and beautiful Diana?"

"Help you do what?"

"Get her into bed."

"Why should I do that?"

"Because I'm smitten. She's so Latin, yet so white, just like me. Her father is my publishing idol and her mother is a goddess of porn punk. We're so compatible I'm picking out china."

"She already has quite a serviceable boyfriend, Mr. Clarence Gerard."

"Oh. Him!" Hector received this news gloomily.

"I'm sorry."

"The fact that the odds are against me only makes me more eager to try."

Diana shrugged.

"If you'd tell me what she's into, I'm sure it would help," he urged seductively. As lightning flashed and thunder pealed outside the panoramic windows of the dining hall, Diana nearly succumbed, but the clatter of the chilly Autumn downpour woke her to her first loyalties.

"Even if I told you, you wouldn't understand what it meant or how to use it."

"Why not? Give me some credit for brains. I am here on full scholarship."

"Then shouldn't you be studying?"

"Just tell me what makes Lupe Freeman tick."

"If Clarence Gerard found out for himself so can you."

"You see if I don't!"

Meanwhile, Lupe had dedicated the weekend to Xavier Duarte, the powerfully attractive young male who had slipped his phone number into her hand as she stood penitently in the corner at The Vault the previous week. They had spoken on the phone only once but e-mailed several times since their brief moment of eye contact in that notorious B&D hell mouth. Finally intrigued beyond bearing, she had agreed to go down to the city to meet him, partially in the spirit of adventure, and partially to arouse the jealousy of Clarence Gerard.

Xavier, in the light of day, was closer to thirty than twenty, moodily stern and inclined to take himself too seriously for Lupe's irreverence. He was however, a respectable commercial artist with bold instincts on the use of interior paint and a leather massage table. Lupe learned, as she sipped his thick espresso, that he was half Columbian, half Argentine and a "master".

And as such, Xavier began to express what Lupe considered to be an inordinate degree of disappointment at the fact that she had arrived dressed in preppy woolens rather than fetish skins.

"Why aren't you in leather, as I saw you at the Vault?" he demanded with the slightest of accents.

Rendered momentarily speechless by his toxic reaction to her dove grey sweater set and dark grey wool tweed straight skirt, she simply stared at him and wondered, "Is this a lunatic I see before me?" Eyeing her reflection in a beautifully chased gold and black-rimmed mirror across the room she could find no fault with her appearance, even after two hours on the train.

"I should have known you had the instincts of a tourist when I saw you let a white boy in a ruffled shirt and ponytail top you!"

Lupe gazed at him with wide eyes. Only common courtesy and the fact that he bore a happy resemblance to Jimmy Smits prevented her from telling him exactly what she thought of his Neolithicism.

"If you're displeased with me I'll go," she announced indifferently, rising to her full majestic height of 5'3".

"You'll go when I tell you to."

"Mr. Duarte, I came all the way from Poughkeepsie. You could at least be civil," she retorted, though lighting his cigarette. Their dark eyes met above the flame and a dart pierced her tummy. Xavier was quite the older man and being one hundred per cent Latin wasn't hurting his case.

Astonished at her confidence, Xavier dropped all pretensions to proper B&D protocol and demanded, "Lupe, are you submissive or aren't you? When I saw you at the Vault – "

"I was meek and mild. But I'd just been spanked," she pouted.

"I missed that part. I just saw you standing there."

"Did you think I was some sort of slave?"

"You gave that impression."

"Well, I'm not."

"Well, what are you about?"

"Spanking, just spanking," Lupe explained succinctly.

"So you like to be spanked?"

"I wouldn't say I like it. It's been more like a lifelong obsession and the absolute core of my sexuality."

"Just like a naughty little girl?"

"Yes," she said, blushing.

"But other things besides spanking can happen to bad little girls. Invasive, humiliating things," he suggested, smart enough to soften his tone.

"Well, I'm not a child. I'm eighteen, so if they're safe and not terribly severe, other things can happen," she granted.

Xavier crossed the enormous studio to the quadrant of his bedroom, where the dresser top yielded a solid wooden hairbrush, which he brought straight back to her. As the afternoon waned, sheets of heavy rain darkened the leaf-blown skylights.

Xavier took her across his knee in the proper manner, held her firmly, began with circumspection and followed through with expertise. The spanking lasted almost an hour in its various stages, during which Lupe became predictably inflamed. The consummation lasted only half as long. Then they had more coffee and cigarettes.

They went down to Greenwich Village for Indian food and to purchase a flogger. Although she was enjoying herself, pangs of guilt began to grip her stomach as she remembered that she hadn't told Clarence she would be off campus that night.

She meant to call as soon as they returned to the loft, but Xavier initiated another scene immediately and Lupe, craving the feel of the soft leather whip gave in, allowing him to bend her over the edge of his massage table and flog her, then stretch her out across its length on her tummy for an even longer session with a leather strap. Xavier looked so handsomely masterful in his black jeans and muscle shirt that every time she turned her head to watch him a spasm of excitement gripped her.

A subtle practitioner, Xavier had a mirror set in the wall opposite the principal play space which allowed her to view the entire scene. Watching herself being disciplined for the first time in her life Lupe realized with a shock just how perfectly this position suited her. She looked so cute that she wished Clarence could see her. But this reflection reminded her of her guilt and she suddenly found it impossible to concentrate.

She asked for a break. Xavier made coffee while she checked her e-mail. Immediately she logged on her heart jumped. There was an e-mail from Diana.

"Girlfriend! You were supposed to call me. You also forgot to leave the gentleman's number. Or address. Nor did you let me know when you planned to get back.

Hector and I have been worrying about you all day. And what shall I tell Clarence?"

Lupe logged off and called Diana, who picked up her dorm room phone at once.

"Yes?"

"I'm fine," Lupe said, with an accelerated heartbeat, "but why is Hector in on this?"

"Oh, Hector isn't so bad," Diana reassured her friend while smiling over at Hector, who was curled up in her window seat keeping her company that rainy Saturday evening while Carl-Adam was cramming for a mid-term. "Is Mr. Duarte nice?"

"Quite nice."

"Will you be returning to us this evening?"

"The last train may have left. I'll have to catch the first one in the morning."

"What shall we tell Clarence?"

"We?"

"No doubt Hector will be with me when we encounter that gentleman."

"Just plead ignorance."

"Hector wants to say hi," said Diana, handing the phone to him.

"Hello. I've somehow managed to endear myself to your friend," Hector admitted.

"I've underestimated you."

"Conciliatory, aren't we?"

"Why not?"

"Are you enjoying yourself with that dangerous drug dealer?"

"Every Columbian isn't a drug dealer."

"I'm deeply hurt, Lupe, that you would place yourself in the hands of some South of the Border Sheik when a nice, well-brought up Puerto Rican boy from New York is ready to adore you."

"Hector, what's your point?"

"I guess the last thing in the world you want now is Clarence finding out what a sleazy adventure you've been having."

"Hector, you'd tell Clarence?"

"Of course not."

"Thank you!"

"You're welcome. Now when may I have my way with you?"

"Never."

"Then I'll tell on you."

"I see the tabloid lifestyle is already in your blood."

"Lupe, meet me in the city tomorrow."

Lupe mused to herself, "Can I go from one man's arms straight to another's, and then when I get back to school, to yet another's?" At length she replied, "I'll be waiting for you at the boathouse in Central Park at three tomorrow afternoon."

Except for the guilt, Lupe enjoyed her night of sleeping with a sophisticated adult male in his loft. Lupe liked Xavier without ever needing to see him again.

Additionally, she had no intention of meeting Hector in Central Park. She took the two-fifteen back to Poughkeepsie, eager to return to her room, change her clothes and find her Clarence.

"That will teach you to blackmail girls," she thought to herself, settling into her window seat on the train and pulling Pamela out of her bag.

"So you thought you'd stand me up!" came a voice from above as Hector slipped into the seat opposite her.

"Oh my god," Lupe breathed, extremely impressed. "I have underestimated you!"

"Prudent of you to have called Diana back with Mr. Duarte's address. Happily, I was there when she took the information down and copying it only seemed like good sense to both of us. I've actually been keeping my eye on you all morning. When you got into a cab and told the driver Penn Station I saw my work cut out for me."

"If you're training for your career with the National Enquirer, you're doing well. You already appear to be a practiced stalker."

"I prefer to think of myself as a romantic."

"Hector, I already have a boyfriend."

"You also have a lover. Mr. Duarte."

"Please don't say that. What happened last night was a brief B&D adventure, never to be repeated."

"Oh? And why is that?"

"Hector, why have you fixated on me? Why didn't you move in on Diana while you had the opportunity?"

"What makes you think I didn't?"

"Well, did you or didn't you?"

"Did I or didn't I what?"

"Play with Diana?"

"Diana is so sweet."

"Oh, you barely know her."

"I wish you were more like her."

"Since you two are getting along so well, you don't need me, do you?"

"I need you more than ever."

"Look, I'm not even sure that I like you."

"Did you like Mr. Duarte?"

"At least he knew what he was doing."

"And you don't think I do?"

"I know you don't. How could you? You don't have the slightest idea."

"You go on thinking that."

"Hector, you have to stop. It's not funny any more!"

"Calm down."

"I won't be coerced into intimacy."

"I understand," Hector replied gravely, startled by her sudden anger. "I went too far. I'm sorry."

"You really have to back off."

"I'll do that, Lupe," he assured her, his heart pounding.

"You might grow on me in time," she added with a smile. "I'm not ruling out the possibility."

"Thank you!" Hector beamed.

"Maybe we can study together sometime. Or take a walk to the Cider Mill."

"I'll take you up on both."

When their taxi disgorged Lupe and Hector in front of Cushing several hours later, Clarence Gerard was there to wonder at the sight.

"Lupe!"

"Clarence, hi."

"Don't forget about our study date," said Hector, heading off toward Jocelyn dorm.

"You have a study date with Hector Green?" Lupe's lover demanded, grabbing her overnight duffel and carrying it into their dorm.

"I vaguely committed to one," she explained, following him upstairs.

"What were you doing together?"

"We just happened to take the same train back from the city."

"Oh? You weren't with him this weekend?"

"No, Clarence."

"What were you doing in the city, anyway? You never told me you were going to the city."

"Is that a hint of reproach?" Lupe opened the door to her room and they entered.

"I simply have the sudden and definite feeling that you were up to no good this weekend without me," Clarence declared. When Lupe merely blushed he became more concerned. "Well? Am I going to have to beat it out of you?"

"I guess I had a sort of adventure," she began. Then it all came out, because it was much too exciting a secret for a young girl to keep.

Clarence listened, pacing with folded arms. When she had finished describing her scene with Xavier Duarte in detail Clarence turned on her with blazing eyes.

"So that's what you call being my girlfriend, is it?" Then he slammed out of the room.

Thus began a period of frost that lasted nearly a week as Clarence went about the campus and environs, steadfastly ignoring Lupe, no matter how affectingly she strove to catch his eye and in spite of how charming she looked in a whole new set of woolen skirts and sweaters.

Lupe's pain was unremitting and her despondency grew by the day as she observed Clarence escort Meredith Pels, his leading lady in The Rivals, to local taverns and the dining hall. She was a tall, willowy, deep bosomed, blonde senior who radiated political correctness from every vegetarian pore. Off-stage she wore no makeup, dressed virtually in boy's clothes and barely even seemed to comb her hair, yet she was a goddess and this was known to all, except herself. All of which gave no comfort the petite brunette.

After two days had passed Lupe left a note in Clarence's mail slot. "Can't we talk?" it had pathetically beseeched him. The missive was ignored. Meanwhile, Lupe cried herself sick, stopped eating, dressed in black and for a period of more than 24 hours, did not bathe. Losing interest in everything but her grief (and the novel Pamela) Lupe barely noticed or attempted to discourage the constant presence of Hector by her side. He was happy to be used as a sounding board, to furnish a shoulder to cry on, and revile the name of Clarence Gerard whenever it was spoken. But the afternoon she wore a grey shirt with a black jacket and trousers and forgot to shower, her fascination was too great to resist and he nearly attacked her in her room, begging her to surrender to his need with greater vehemence than it was in her power to repel in her weakened emotional state.

"Do what ever you like, I don't care," she sighed, laying back on her bed and gazing out at the slate grey sky through the mullioned window panes of her lilac dorm room.

Hector rolled her over on her tummy then pulled her up by her hips. Reaching around to loosen her trousers and pull them down he murmured with more honesty than cynicism, "perhaps if you pretend that I'm Clarence, you'll get a thrill."

"Then do it hard," she advised, closing her eyes as she rested her weight evenly on her knees and the palms of her hands.

Hector didn't need a second invitation to comply with her injunction to the letter. He wanted to fuck her hard. He'd been dreaming of doing nothing else since he'd first spoken to her. Nor did this determined young man, one of whose ambitions was to some day edit the National Enquirer, have the slightest qualm about playing surrogate to the girl that he desired above all others.

"You're dry though," he mused. "How do you get wet?" Unconsciously he stroked her bottom as he asked her this.

"Spank me," she replied, though with relative disinterest.

"Really?"

"Go ahead." She slightly rotated her smooth, slim bottom. The gesture added another inch to his already straining erection. He unzipped his jeans to liberate his cock. Out of curiosity she turned to regard the handsome pink specimen of masculine ardor. "Nice cock," she mildly complimented him, dropping her head again with a sigh.

Hector tentatively caressed her bottom.

"That's it," she encouraged him. Her pain and disappointment at losing Clarence had left her too physically exhausted to be either embarrassed or protective about her fetish any longer.

"All right, young lady, you asked for it," he told her, moving to one side and taking her by the waist to give her something like a proper spanking. It was true that she was up on all fours and under his arm rather than over his knee, but Lupe hadn't reckoned with Hector's ethnicity, which included strong spanking influences on both the Latin and European sides. He instinctively knew how to hold a girl for a spanking and how to apply the palm of his hand to her backside.

True to her word, Lupe became moist within moments. Hector ascertained this twenty or so swats into the spanking. Conflicting emotions overwhelmed Lupe as she surrendered to the fantasy that she was once again the beloved of Clarence.

Fifty or sixty smacks later, when Lupe's creamy skin was fully pinkened, Hector found her to be sopping wet and proceeded with the more adult portion of the program, during which safe sex was achieved with characteristic teenage abandon. In spite of her detachment, Lupe succumbed to a climax moments before Hector's. After which she promptly burst into tears.

Hector gathered her into his arms and comforted her, instinctively knowing that he himself was in no way responsible for her sadness.

All of this was duly reported to Diana, who, more shocked by Lupe's taking to dressing in black than her new sexual decadence, seized the first opportunity to reproach Clarence with his dangerous neglect of her friend.

They met in the basement of their dorm while exchanging old sheets for new at the linen lockers.

"Good morning, Miss Stratton," said Clarence, shades cooler than he had ever been with the small, sleek senior before.

"You're very formal today, Clarence. Or are you angry with me too?"

"I'm not angry with anyone," he bristled.

"Not even Lupe?"

Clarence collected his linen.

"Clarence, do me the courtesy of replying to my question."

"I beg your pardon?"

"I would like to know your intentions with regard to my dear friend," demanded Diana imperiously.

"Intentions?"

"Yes. Have you abandoned her?"

Clarence slammed his locker closed.

"No," he shortly replied.

"Then you still care for her?"

"Of course," he reluctantly growled.

"Then why are you being so mean? Have you forgotten that she's a novice in the scene? Ninety percent of why she went to the city was to give you a reason to spank her. Neophytes often behave that way. It's something they grow out of."

"Thanks for telling me that. It's a big relief," Clarence said, unimpressed.

"So I guess you don't care that she's crying herself to sleep every night and starving herself to death in the day?"

This made Clarence pause. He remembered that Lupe had looked utterly drained the previous morning at breakfast, dressed all in black, though with handsome slate grey accents. Her cheeks had looked hollow!

"Where is she now?" he suddenly asked Diana.

"I don't know. Probably walking around in tears. It's what she's been doing all week."

"All right. I'll put a stop to that today. If you see her tell her I'm looking for her."

It was one of those October days that start out golden blue and end up wetly grey. Somewhat revived by the impromptu spanking and rough, satisfying sex from Hector the previous day, Lupe had reacquainted herself with soap and perfume and outfitted in wool knickers, a sweater, thick sox and ankle boots, set out after breakfast to walk the entire day.

First she walked out to Vassar farm to stare at the scarecrows. Then she started down the densely shaded road to the Cider Mill, crunching leaves.

It took some time to reach the strange lodge and halfway there the clouds began to move in. Fortunately, in looking for Lupe, Clarence had run into Carl-Adam, who had just seen her walking on the road and Carl-Adam told Clarence exactly where he might find her. As the drizzle began, Clarence pulled up beside Lupe.

On noticing the handsome, tawny driver of the jeep Lupe's heart contracted.

"Lupe, get in," he stopped the car and severely frowned at her, opening the door. "Where were you going?"

"The Cider Mill." She got in.

Clarence threw the car in gear and they started down the road. "You didn't look well at breakfast yesterday. I was wondering whether you were all right," he began, though without much warmth. They exchanged sidelong glances.

"Were you?"

"As a matter of fact, I was."

"I'm fine," she replied defiantly.

"Yes, I can see that now." Lightning flashed but they barely noticed.

"A lot you care!" A loud clap of thunder startled them both.

"Of course I care."

"Really? It's hard to tell when you get ignored for a week!" Lupe folded her arms.

They debarked at the cafe and went inside. The place was cavernous and weird, filled with taxidermy and awkward antiques. Everywhere one looked there was something to read, examine and recoil at. Clarence bought them hot mulled ciders, which they sipped as they paced the hall.

"Has it been a week?" he asked her casually. This question brought tears to her eyes.

"Yes!" She swallowed the lump in her throat. "And I'm fed up. You don't like me anymore? Fine. I can find another boyfriend."

"I'm sure you can!" he hotly replied.

"There's a mixer at West Point next weekend. For upperclassmen only. They're all but officers, you know."

Clarence put their mugs down on the counter and led her outside. "That's enough about West Point cadets. Get in the car."

"Or I could go with Diana to Yale this weekend. They're a dance there too. You've never seen me on a dance floor."

"Shut up."

"Are we going back?"

"No."

"Where are we going?"

"An inn I discovered in Rhinebeck with cabins in the woods."

"Go to an inn? With me? Now? For what purpose, pray?"

Clarence only gave her a look.

The cabin smelled of cinnamon and apples, the rustic hearth was loaded with firewood and the antique maple bed was swathed in down.

"If you don't forgive me then what are we doing here?" she asked as he locked the door and sealed the windows against the beating rain.

"I do forgive you. But you've been wickedly abandoned." He took her by the hand and made her sit next to him on the bed. Lupe felt embarrassed and couldn't meet his eyes. The next thing she knew she was being pulled across his lap and spanked.

"I should have done this the second you got back from New York," he stated, slapping her bottom hard and repeatedly through the tweed knickers. "Ungrateful girl!" Smack! Smack! "Lift up," he ordered, reaching under her to unbutton her wool knickers and yank them down to mid-thigh. "I bestow my heart on you and this is how you behave!" Clarence squeezed her perfect oval cheeks, snugly wrapped in French cut, white cotton briefs. More stern smacks descended on her pert seat.

"At worst, I was impulsive," she protested, though not seriously trying to resist.

"Really!" Now he swatted her harder.

"Ow! You disagree?" Lupe put one hand back to shield her bottom but he caught her by the wrist and slapped it. "Ow!" She nursed her hand to her face.

"Impulsive nothing. You knew that I would expect fidelity from you, yet you deliberately pursued an affair with another man, not ten days after you started dating me!" Now he pulled her panties down to bare her reddened bottom. "Did you think that you wouldn't get a spanking for that?"

"Are you calling me a slut?" she cried, squirming to avoid his hand, which had begun to descend on her unprotected bottom vehemently.

"No," Clarence replied, staying his punishing hand to examine Lupe's fair skin, now stained dusky rose. "But neither are you a proper young lady!" He kissed each punished cheek just once before setting her on her feet.

"I'm going to the Inn to get us something warm to drink. Get undressed and get in bed," he ordered, leaving her alone.

Lupe went to the window and watched him walk into the woods, her heart aglow at being once more the focus of Clarence's attention.

High tea was being served at the Inn and he was able to return with a basket of sandwiches and tarts. Lupe had not stirred from the window.

"You don't listen very well, do you?" he sighed, drawing a pot of hot chocolate from the basket and filling two mugs.

"It's too early to get in bed," she observed, unwrapping a small sandwich.

"Oh, you think so?"

"Is my punishment over?"

"Don't you wish!"

"I really don't."

"Oh, you admit you've behaved reprehensibly?"

"No."

"Why did you do it, Lupe? I thought you were so happy, so satisfied with our chemistry."

"I just wanted an extra adventure. I was curious. That's all. I began to regret it the second I got there. Although it turned out all right. But nothing like it is with you, Clarence. He wanted to be my master. You only want to be my god. There's a difference."

"Don't be impertinent," Clarence snapped, but the next moment took the sandwich out of her hand and kissed her hard. "There!" he said, letting her go. "That's how I feel about you." Then he set about starting a fire in the hearth.

"Yes, you said you loved me several weeks ago but you haven't gotten around to proving it yet. Just the opposite."

"Haven't you ever heard of tough love?"

"I have something else I need to tell you."

"Oh god, what now?"

"Not that I want to tell you, but inevitably you'll find out and I couldn't stand another week like you just put me through."

"Well?"

"Well, after you abandoned me, another boy quickly moved in."

"What other boy?"

"Remember, I was desolate and therefore detached. It's not as though I was anything but completely indifferent to his overtures. But as day after neglectful day passed, the young man began to realize that he might successfully press his advantage, proximity being nine tenths of possession."

"Lupe, are you saying you let Hector Green have you?" All 6'2" of Clarence bristled as he took her by the slim shoulders and gave her an admonitory shake.

"It's your fault," she pouted up at him.

"My fault!"

"Because you left me alone and unprotected. I mean, what did you think would happen?"

"You are your father's daughter, I'll say that. Your mother's too," he mused, striding towards the door.

"Where are you going?"

"Out to cut a switch!" He fished his Swiss Army knife out of his pocket and exhibited it to her. Then he was out the door.

Lupe paced with indecision for a moment or two, then followed him out into the woods. The rain had abated to a drizzle as the afternoon waned. It was growing chillier by the moment but the woods were glorious in red and gold and Lupe savored the snap in the air. She found Clarence a few seconds later, searching for a dry twig.

"I don't want a switching. They're supposed to really hurt!" she protested.

"We'll soon find out," he promised, moments before seizing upon a perfect specimen, dry beneath a pile of sticks. He began to trim it with his pocketknife.

"I didn't want to do it with Hector, but he virtually forced the issue."

"Are you saying that he raped you?"

"No. Of course not. I was more apathetic than resistant, to be fair to Hector. But I'm sure you'll agree that only a cad in embryo would take advantage of a cruelly abandoned, lovesick girl."

"Sophistry. You could have said no thank you. Hector is a

Philistine, not a Neanderthal. Now come over here!" Clarence found a proper fallen log to thrust her over and let fly with the switch across the back of her wool pants smartly enough to make her shout.

"Ow! No more!" she struggled to break away but he held her fast to the fallen trunk. Swish! Another swat landed painfully. Lupe shrieked and tried to pull away. "Clarence, that really hurts! No!" Again the switch struck with an awful sensation. Tears sprang into her eyes as she attempted to jerk free of his hold. "No more!" Another swat fell and again she wailed aloud. Her sobs soon filled the forest as he delivered the final two of six hard strokes. When he let her go she ran stumbling back to the cabin, her face wet with tears and rain.

He stalked in a moment after her and was surprised to see her curled up in a small ball of tears on the hearth rug.

"Did it really hurt so badly?" he attempted to fold her in his arms.

"Yes!" she protested, thrusting him away. Feeling more sorry for herself by the moment Lupe indulged in a fit of hysterical sobs.

"I'm sorry I was harsh," he vowed, brushing the hair from her damp face to kiss her. "I suppose I didn't realize how severe the switch could feel to a small girl like you."

"Would you like to feel how it felt?" Lupe abruptly stopped sobbing. "Because I'd really like to give you the same six of the best that you just gave me and see how you like it!"

"Oh, Lupe," he hugged her, "you're so cute."

"Don't! That really hurt like hell. I never thought of you as a sadist, Clarence. Until today."

"Lupe dear, I have apologized," he said with a slight trace of impatience. "Now stop being such a baby before I give you another spanking!" This warning elicited such a pretty pout that he seized her by her long, black ponytail, pulled her towards him and kissed her hard. "I'll teach you to let other men have you!" He took her to the bed and pulled her clothes off. When she tried to resist or hold on to various articles of apparel he slapped her hands away or slapped her lightly on all the parts of her body that became exposed.

Bestowing a few light spanks on her small, round, upstanding bosom when he'd removed her lacy brassiere had an unexpectedly stimulating effect on Lupe, who had never thought much about her breasts beyond acknowledging how charmingly they filled out her sweaters and looked in a sweetheart cut gown. Although not a girl to enjoy her nipples pinched, the feel of his admonitory pats on the fleshiest portions of her bosom inflamed her with submissive sensations. She whimpered but deliberately thrusts her breasts towards him, unmistakably asking for more.

"I'm glad you seem to realize how much you need to be beaten," Clarence murmured, while lightly pinkening her creamy, cherry tipped orbs with tender spanks.

The next thing she knew he was pulling off her last remaining garments. Then sitting on the bed he pulled her down across his lap. He made her arch up and present her silken black Venus mound. He told her to hold still. Then curving one hand around her waist, he began to spank her sex quite lightly with the other. The result was immediate intense and panting arousal. She wriggled so violently that he had to press down quite firmly with the other hand to hold her in place.

Pausing in the spanking of her pussy, Clarence began to exquisitely torment her with long periods of examination and probing, consisting of him spreading her labia to glimpse her dewy excitement, then plunging several fingers into this well of darling, young femininity. Lupe writhed and wriggled across his lap.

Finally he turned his attention to her equally fascination second portal of pleasure. The process of examining and probing her from this angle was even more rewarding. She had such a perfect, tiny bottom hole that he got a thrill just looking at it. Utilizing her natural wetness as a lubricant, he inserted his middle finger into her anus. Plunging it deeply inside her, he felt her clamp down on it hard. Pulling it free he spread her and spanked her bottom hole.

"Oh my god!" she cried at the one thing that always sent her over the edge. "You can't!" she protested weakly for form's sake. It was too humiliating. Now he would realize exactly how submissive she was.

"Hold still," he warned her, keeping her cheeks spread with one hand and continuing to spank her anus with the other, less delicately by the moment. "Since this isn't your pussy I don't have to be nearly as gentle with you. Do I?"

"I don't know," she moaned in confusion, shrinking from the increasing though far from unpleasant sting of his punishing palm between her cheeks.

"I'm going to take you there."

"Take my bottom?" she turned to him.

"I'm sure it wouldn't be the first time its been done," he sighed, pulling her up and into his arms.

"There it always feels like the first time."

"Don't worry, I know what I'm doing."

"Yeah, I noticed how expert you were with that switch," Lupe blithely retorted.

"You deserved for it to be real."

"I don't want to be in love with a martinet," Lupe mused, allowing her throat to be nuzzled and her earlobe bitten.

"Oh no? You've been looking sad all week. And I think it's because you missed me," said Clarence, squeezing her small waist.

"So you noticed and still remained a hard, cold thing? Oh Clarence, how could you be so cruel to me?" she lay her head against his chest and murmured.

"Lupe, your behavior has been far worse than mine! Picking up a stranger at the Vault while you were there as my date was bad enough. But then you compound the insult by surrendering yourself to a second and even more insolent male, right here on campus, that I now have to worry about cutting me out every chance he gets."

"So don't give him any chances."

"Unfortunately I can't be with you 24 hours a day," he said, drawing her against him comfortably. "So I'm putting you on your honor to be a good girl from now on."

"Anyway, you've secured a place in my memoirs as the first man to ever beat me for being unfaithful to him."

Chapter Three

Alison's Knight

Alison Albrecht 28, though no fault of her own, was a difficult girl. Fortuitously, her sharp, tense, meticulous personality was suited to her new job as assistant to the bursar of the Braemar Academy. This was her first important position and also her first return to her birthplace in five years.

The death of her father over the summer had transformed Random Point from a dreaded destination into a desirable locale. Her mother, who lived in Paris, did not return for the funeral, but sent Alison an enchanting gown and the deed to the house in which Alison had been raised.

It was a charming cottage in the woods, only five minutes from the cove. Her mother, an obsessively artistic homemaker, had turned it into a showplace.

Alison got a thrill walking through the rooms for the first time without fearing that her father might materialize with a scolding or irrational harangue.

Both her parents had been perfectionists. But at least her mother's concerns: cleanliness, tailoring, grades and comportment, made some degree of sense to Alison. Besides which she had taught Alison many valuable accomplishments, such as skating, drawing and the ability to do her own hair. Appearances were vital to her mother, including that of a happy home, which was of course impossible with her father at the helm.

It was well for Alison that her mother had striven to mold a perfect daughter, because an awkward one might never have survived childhood under Alison's father mentally in tact. Alison was only barely so herself on the happy day she had finally escaped to college in another state. Luckily she had been born pretty and bright. These pleasing attributes – combined with the appearance of filial passivity which she constantly labored to project – had allowed Alison to occasionally tap the extremely modest reserves of tenderness in her father's heart and enjoy the hugs, kisses and prolonged lap sits that her mother never had the time to give her.

She rather imagined that in his own way, her father had loved her. No doubt, he, in his turn had been an abused child. But that didn't counter the fact that she had spent her entire life in cowering fear of him and him alone.

Not that Alison received many spankings as a child. She was too fearful, well behaved and sneaky for that. But the threat was always there.

Once she was of high school age, the threat became that of a strapping, rather than a spanking. Then it became even more vital not to get caught doing whatever it was he didn't want her to do. Which was everything except studying and helping her mother clean.

Not that Alison ever received a strapping from her father as a teenager. She was much too docile to anger him with overt disobedience and much too cautious to get pregnant from the illicit sex she had begun to have with boys from age 15. But the threat was always there.

Alison was sure that the strap was her father's favorite implement for use on girls because she was almost positive that she had once heard him use it on her mother.

Alison questioned the memory whenever it arose, wondering whether she'd merely imagined the entire incident, in view of her fascination.

It seemed that one night, when she was about aged three, her parents went to a dance at a country club. Her mother looked divine in her gown. Alison was put to bed by the babysitter and her parents returned quite late. She awoke to the sounds of a quarrel, not her father's usual vitriolic monologue but two voices raised in anger. Then it was put to a stop by the sounds of – a strapping!

Or had she dreamt the whole thing?

Now that her father had expired, she could write to her mother and ask what had really happened that night. For the first time she wanted the details. If only she could believe that on some level her mother found that thug in a pinstriped suit arousing, she might feel better about their marriage and her childhood.

Quite independently of fearing spankings from her father, Alison was, from toddler age on, completely fascinated by and enraptured with Spanking.

As early as age three, Alison thought about spankings. Then, as a child, she was always the one to initiate spanking games with her playmates. She never wondered why she found it the nicest thing in the world when someone talked about spanking, or she saw a spanking on TV. But she knew instinctively never to discuss this phenomenon with anyone. Because even as a child, Alison observed that other people didn't feel the same way about spanking as she did. Other people thought it was a silly or very bad thing – always to be avoided. Nobody else seemed to feel it was an immensely intriguing subject. Except perhaps the writers who put spankings into TV shows and old movies. And novels. Oh, how she loved to read a book where one might come across a spanking! Perhaps these creative geniuses alone understood about the power of spanking and put the references in, just for the likes of Alison and a handful of others who might also understand.

Alison "came out" at aged seventeen, by answering an ad in The East Village Other when she was a freshman at Sarah Lawrence. It was the first of many correspondence adventures, followed by a collection of somewhat sleazier escapades initiated in pick-up bars around Manhattan. But she never had the fortune to penetrate the actual Spanking Scene, bouncing around instead in the New York BDSM community for years and beginning to hate life.

Then, quite by miraculous chance, during her very first week at Braemar, she happened to discover that two of the other staff members, an English instructor, Mr. Lawrence and a guidance counselor, Miss Rohan, were both into spanking! Not BDSM, alternative lifestyle, or anything like those commitments, but simple, traditional American spanking. She figured it out just hearing them flirting one day during afternoon break and boldly confronted them because she was that sure she was right. Ever since that day they had become an intimate luncheon clique and Mr. Lawrence had lent her a collection of magazines, called The New Rod Quarterly, where she could place ads and find a companion, possibly here on the Cape.

Alison didn't have much faith in personal ads after all these years, but then again, she had never advertised directly in a spanking specific magazine. That concept in itself was mesmerizing and she poured over the ads in the back issues David Lawrence had given her with irrepressible excitement.

Freddie Johanson, 38, also a native of Random Point and the network manager for Braemar, was also into spanking. But Alison did not discover this fact until he answered the coded personal ad that she had placed in The New Rod Quarterly.

If he had known that it was Alison Albrect's ad he was answering, this fact might have discouraged Freddie, because during the past several weeks he'd received the impression that the bursar's smart young assistant didn't care for him. He had felt her frowning at him more than once and this was strange to him – because females, young or old, straight or gay, conservative or wild, generally adored Freddie.

Freddie was as warm and expansive as Alison was cool and controlled, possessing, in her opinion, too much personality. He was a big man of at least 6'4" and rather well set up. Not handsome, but certainly charming. Too charming by half for Alison, who despised on principal anyone who wasted time in idle chatter during a business day.

Freddie did talk, often and on the slightest provocation. But most people enjoyed this about him. He was intelligent, good-humored, sympathetic, helpful, courteous and universally well liked, except by the grumpy and small. He was also highly competent, though Alison could not see how he managed to fit in any work at all in between the vast amount of socializing Freddie did.

In fact he held so many conversations as he went about setting hard discs to rights, that Alison could scarcely find a moment for a private confrontation.

Finally, on Friday afternoon, when everyone was packing up to go home, she knocked on the door of his office, entered and waited as he backed up some work, smiling at her but blessedly taciturn for once. Finally, when he was ready to give her his full attention, she floored him with the statement, "You answered my personal ad in the spanking magazine. Didn't you?"

She held up the envelope she'd received from him the previous day, with his photo and a letter about himself. He gazed at it then her in amazement.

"So, what do you think we should do?" she demanded, adding hurtfully. "I really don't think we should go out. I'm sure we're not suited."

For once at a loss for words, Freddie replied at length, "You never know. They say opposites attract."

"That's nonsense," she declared, fussing with the snaps on her portfolio to avoid meeting his dark eyes.

"Right," he agreed dismissively, beginning to pack his own briefcase. She saw she'd made him angry and this made her heart jump.

"I'm sorry, but I just have a feeling it wouldn't work out," she replied guiltily.

"I understand," he returned indifferently.

"Well, good night," she murmured, scarcely remembering when she had ever felt so uncomfortable with a man.

"Good night, Alison."

She walked towards the door then turned, about to offer him his photo back so that he could send it to someone else. But something made her cram the letter back into her jacket pocket instead.

"Well, good bye," she said once more.

"Well?" His look gave her butterflies.

"Well, what do you think?" she asked timidly.

"I don't know what to think."

"I mean, now that you know that it's me."

"I'd be happy it was you if I thought you didn't hate me."

"I don't hate you. I don't even know you."

"But you feel I'm not you're type."

"Right. And I'm sure I'm not yours."

"What about getting together once, just for fun?"

"Fun?"

"That's what it's all about, isn't it?"

"I guess that would be fine," she agreed.

"Tomorrow afternoon? We could have lunch in the village and go for a walk in the woods."

"All right," she assented.

"Have you been upstairs yet?" Freddie asked Alison as they sipped cappuccinos at the teakwood counter of Marguerite Alexander's bookshop.

"You mean where they used to keep the old Grove Press novels? I used to live up there when I was about fourteen," Alison admitted. "A few of the books were so good I had to actually buy them and smuggle them home."

"Which ones?"

"Frank and I and Sadopaidea."

"Would your parents have minded?"

"My father would. He didn't want me to think about sex."

"When I was in Junior High School a Lionel Albrecht was the principal. Would he be a relation of yours?"

"He was my father."

"Oh my god. You poor child."

"Yes. You know, I went to a Mrs. Johanson's nursery school. Would she be a relation of yours?"

"She's my mother."

"Oh really? Why, she was the nicest teacher I ever had! Is she still alive?"

"Yes. She's living in Florida now."

"Please send her my love," murmured Alison, her eyes filling with tears at the kindness of pretty, blonde Mrs. Johanson.

"What's this?" Freddie caught a tear on his finger, completely revising his opinion of Miss Albrecht.

"It just melts me to think of your mother."

"Why, you darling. She'll be so touched when I tell her."

"But, tell me," she changed the subject to stem the flow of her sentimentality, "what exactly did you think of my father?"

"He was a hard man all right," was all that Freddie would commit to, as he didn't fully understand Alison's feelings for the martinet who had raised her.

"Yes, he was the same way at home."

"Shall I tell you a scandalous secret about your father?"

"A secret about my father? Of course!"

"Well, my mother and I have always been very close and she's confided to me about every major event in her life," he began, holding Alison spellbound.

"How lovely for you," she murmured enviously.

"Well, just before my late father managed to win her, she had a date with your father!"

"Your mother had a date with my father?"

"That's right. Just before your father began to court your mother. They were all employed at the elementary school at the time. Your father was the Vice Principal. Would you like to know what happened on the date?"

"You know?"

"He took her into Boston to see West Side Story. Then, since her parents were out of town, he took her back to their house in Back Bay. Your dad then seized the opportunity to ravish my mother. They didn't have the term date rape in the old days, but Mr. Albrecht's importunities did help my mother to decide in favor of my father's suit."

"So my father was a wolf. I guess there had to be one normal thing about him," Alison chuckled.

When the extremely beautiful blonde girl who worked behind the counter brought them refills Alison asked, "Excuse me, but are you Mrs. Lawrence?"

"Yes, but call me Hope," replied that young bride of less than a year with a smile.

"Your husband told me to come in and say hi. I'm Alison Albrecht." The young ladies shook hands.

"Oh, are you teaching at Braemar?" asked Hope, concealing a hot twinge of jealousy and thinking, 'No sooner do I disengage Miss Rohan from David's toils than a new one emerges to take her place!' And this one was even slim, with a smooth brown ponytail nearly as long as Hope's own, and Hope's was very long.

"No, we're both on the administrative staff. I crunch numbers and I'm not exactly sure what he does," Alison explained, introducing Freddie. "Although he certainly manages to talk a lot while he's doing it," she added in an off-hand manner. Hope noticed the indignant look Freddie threw Alison even if Alison did not and Hope was soothed. If this big, good-looking male was hovering around the brunette fox then her husband would not. David was a wolf, not a dog.

The atmosphere within the bookshop was so enchanting that they decided to stay for sandwiches and princess cake before their walk in the woods. The moment they departed Hope and her boss Sloan Taylor began to speculate about them.

"She was just a bit rude to the large gentleman," Hope reported.

"Perhaps he'll spank her when he gets her in the woods," Sloan suggested with a smile.

"Why? Do you think they were into it?"

"Didn't you hear her talking about reading Grove Press novels?"

"I must have been in the pantry."

"And I've certainly sold him books and magazines."

"Really!"

"Maybe that's why David told her to look you up."

The verbal linking of Alison with David made Hope frown. "I'm beginning to think there are more spanking people in Random Point, Massachusetts than there are in all of Southern California!"

"Don't worry, you're still the fairest of them all," Sloan reassured the resident beauty of the village, smoothing away the worry from her brow.

"Mr. Lawrence's wife is amazingly beautiful," Alison observed as they strolled along the stream that ran through the woods.

"Yes! Making his behavior even more incomprehensible."

"What behavior, Freddie?"

"You've seen the way he flirts with Miss Rohan."

"But that's only because they're both in the scene," Alison explained.

"Really?" cried Freddie in wonder, for he'd never before encountered others in the scene right here in Random Point. Now there was Alison and two others! "Miss Rohan is?"

"I figured it out just by listening to them talk one day. They were comparing the films McClintock and Across the Wide Missouri."

"Aren't you the little spanking detective!"

"Laugh if you want but if I hadn't confronted them I might never have discovered the magazine in which you found my ad."

"Not that it's done me any good so far," he dryly observed.

"You never know."

"Oh? Are you reevaluating me in view of the fact that your father had my mother?"

"No, that your mother was my favorite teacher," she reminded him.

They strolled through the red and gold forest. It was a slightly overcast late September day and quite mild. Alison was pleasantly conscious of how lithe and girlish her figure appeared in her dove grey skirt and vest over a white blouse. Walking shoes and anklets revealed her smooth white legs. At 5' 5" and 120 lbs., she was small waisted and well proportioned. To Freddie she seemed tiny as a toy.

Now and then she stole a look at him. He was looking better by the minute. Although he lacked the personal magnetism of a Mr. Lawrence, Freddie did possess a quantity of robust, classically masculine appeal. He was not the type to ever turn on one, betray one or let one down. One looked at Freddie and saw a rock. Alison had never owned a rock and wondered what it might be like.

"Have you ever played?" she asked him.

"I've tried with every girl I've ever dated. But never with a true devotee."

"That's the way I feel, though I've actually played quite a bit," she admitted.

"Why don't you let me play with you?"

"Maybe I will."

"Tell me what you like."

"It's hard to discuss."

"I realize that."

"Why don't you tell me what you like?"

"Couldn't I just show you?"

"Out here in the woods?"

"Isn't this the best place?" he asked, leading her by the hand to a tree stump. They solemnly regarded it and then each other.

"I don't think I'm ready yet," she protested, even as he sat down and pulled her down across his splendid lap.

"Oh, of course you are," he told her, smoothing down her skirt. "Nice outfit. But you always look so lovely."

Alison thought, 'Cut the smarm." He did have the nicest lap though and she liked the way he held her with one large hand pressed to her waist. This was the perfect positioning she had dreamt about for years and had so seldom found!

Smack! His hand came down on her right cheek. Smack! Then her left. Very firmly! "When a gentleman makes you a compliment, you say thank you," Freddie advised.

"Thank you!"

"You don't have very good manners Miss Albrecht." He spanked her five or six times in a row. He had a very large hand and she could feel it quite well through her skirt.

"I'm sorry," she cried, waiting for his palm to descend again, which it shortly did. Coming down solidly on alternating cheeks, he administered a dozen more swats.

"Think I didn't notice the insult you slipped by Hope Lawrence while you were introducing me?" Smack! Smack! Smack! These three felt more severe because he had pulled up her skirt to deliver them on the seat of her fine mesh sheer white nylon panties.

"Insult?" she gasped as his hand came down hard, bringing the pink up fast under the virtually transparent panties.

"It appears you think I talk too much!" Now he really spanked her hard, though he privately agreed with her assessment. Alison refrained from answering but submitted to her spanking meekly.

Freddie gave a heavenly spanking. By the time he was finished, some thirty minutes later, she was as much in love as she had ever been. He only stopped because her bare skin was becoming, to his eye, dangerously red. The magenta stage had lasted quite a while and looked delightful, but Alison had so seldom been spanked and had such fair and tender skin that Freddie feared to bruise her.

Certainly it was the best half hour of her life. Better a thousand times than actual sex. She got up from his lap under an enchantment, sitting back down upon it directly and wrapping her arms around his neck to hug him in a dreamy state of contentment. Freddie held her tightly, thrilled that she had finally begun to relax.

He tilted back her head and kissed her lightly on the mouth. She yielded to him at once, pressing her lips against his. Freddie kissed her harder. Alison parted her lips and admitted his exploring, aggressive tongue. She wriggled on his lap, feeling his huge erection pressing against his khakis. Suddenly their hands were all over each other, unfastening buttons and caressing bare skin. A sculpted chest emerged, furred with light brown hair. A small, rounded bosom came under his hand, firm and satiny. Panties came off, zipper slid down. Before they knew it he was in her as she sat astride his lap, plunging up into her creamy tightness with his big, athletic cock. Then holding her slim bottom cheeks in his hands he pumped her up and down, doing all the work with pleasure. But it was simply too exciting and his crisis came quickly. With no more warning than a greater heat within her, Alison felt herself pulled free of the pumping ramrod and felt its effusion splash harmlessly against her bottom as it lay between her cheeks.

"We had unsafe sex!" cried Alison, stricken with guilt as she jumped off his lap, her skirt still pulled up as she mopped herself dry with her handkerchief.

"I'm positive I'm safe," he vouched.

"Well, me too," she replied, never in her fanatically cautious life having had sex without a condom.

"And I didn't come in you, so you won't get pregnant."

"Thank you!"

"Thank you," he smiled and kissed her hand.

Having set their clothes to rights, they began to walk back to the village, not holding hands but feeling close.

But Alison had always been a pattern of perversity. So by Monday morning she had put the big man virtually out of her mind. Saturday's mail had disgorged many replies to her personal ad, some from affluent, Boston-based professionals. And then there were two or three intriguing notes and photos from Random Point locals to be considered in the following week. Quite apart from all of this, there was Mr. Lawrence.

Alison hadn't developed an actual crush on a man in years and it gave her a terrible thrill to nurture this new one for the handsomest instructor on the faculty.

Naturally Freddie's first move on Monday was to ask Alison out again. She put him off in characteristic style, explaining hastily that she had received so many responses to her ad that it might take her weeks to sort them out. Also, there was still their inherent incompatibility to be considered. Astonished, he demanded to know what she meant as they drank coffee in the faculty lounge that afternoon.

"I simply feel that you may be too meek and mild to keep me intrigued over time," she disclosed with an apologetic shrug.

Freddie's heart contracted painfully but he stove to conceal his distress while wondering how forceful Alison expected a man to be. It seemed to Freddie that ravishing a girl, in the woods, one hour into their first date, qualified as anything but meek and mild behavior.

"Anyway, we both know you're too good for me," she tactfully softened the brush-off.

"Whereas David Lawrence is just about right?" asked Freddie, having noticed Alison flirting with the married English teacher at lunch. Alison could not but blush. "You should be spanked for even thinking about a married man!" he told her without humor.

"You see, that's what I mean about us, Freddie. I'm a libertine. And you're not."

Freddie now forgot to conceal his emotions and indignantly rose from the table. "You need to be careful who you accuse of being meek and mild or some idiot might get confused and beat the hell out of you!"

"That's more like it," Alison thought to herself as she watched him stride out of the room.

"She is her father's daughter!" Freddie mentally scowled as he endeavored to drink himself blind on Friday night after five hellish days of deprivation. Alison held fast — refusing to accept any of his invitations — and Freddie suffered for it. He felt that he had never come so close to obtaining a compatible partner in the scene. Yet it seemed that – for no good reason – he wasn't to have her! The cold girl had dismissed him before giving him a single chance to prove his worth.

Meek and mild. Her casual words stung him. But what in the world had she meant? Surely not to provoke him. Even three sheets to the wind Freddie knew that. She must sincerely believe that he was no match for the selfish, experienced, thrill-seeker she was. The more Polish vodka that slid down Freddie's throat, the more he blamed Alison's father, the late principal Albrecht, who had mistaken repression for discipline and thus unwittingly nurtured a cynical hedonist in his only child.

A full moon was out and fresh leaves carpeted the ground as Freddie briskly stumbled home along Shadow Lane. The first chilly breezes of autumn sobered him only slightly as he revolved the problem of Alison in his mind. She also lived off the heavily forested road, but two miles past his own modest cottage. So Freddie was not terribly surprised to run into her at the roadside pumpkin stand, where she had stopped to select a large specimen.

It was about eight p.m. and Alison, still in her smart suit, was en route home. The thick, glossy boutique bags that filled the back seat of her car told Freddie exactly what she had been doing while had been swallowing four vodka tonics in a row.

"What a clotheshorse you are," he commented, depositing the pumpkin in her trunk for her.

"It's a compulsion. Like everything else I do. Can I give you a ride home?"

"No thank you. I've been drinking and I might say something I do mean."

"Won't you come home with me and help me carry the pumpkin

in?"

"Why in the world did you get such a big one?" He sounded surly but got in the car. Alison smiled to herself.

"Build a fire for me?" she asked Freddie a few minutes later, after he'd deposited the pumpkin in front of her stone hearth.

"You mean build a fire and then leave?"

"How about you stay for coffee? Maybe sober up a little, huh?"

"Ha! You wouldn't have even known I was drunk if I hadn't told you. That's the kind of self-control I possess Miss Albrecht!"

Alison thought he was adorable but put off kissing him. She'd missed him horribly all week.

When she came back with the coffee service, the fire was fully ablaze and Freddie was leaning on the mantelpiece gazing meditatively into in.

"Tell me more about your self-control, Freddie."

"It's what stopped me from shaking you times without number this past week."

"And what's it stopping you from doing now?"

"Alison, I hope you don't talk to everyone like this."

"I appreciate your concern, Freddie. But I'm not a fucking moron!" she snapped back.

"So you're saying you reserve this attitude for me alone because I'm nice enough not to throttle you?"

"Something like that," she smiled, handing him a cup of coffee.

"Thank you." Freddie gulped the coffee to clear his head, gratified that she had remembered how he liked it. He sat on the piano bench and watched her refill his cup. Their eyes met and he pulled her down on his lap to kiss her. Gently but firmly he grasped her by her long brown ponytail and pulled her head back. She gasped at this and instantly surrendered her lips.

"You know what I think about you?" he said, letting her ponytail go. "I think you're a daddy's girl."

"Go to hell!" she cried, jumping off his lap. "I hated my father."

"Then why are you looking for someone just like him?"

"I'm doing nothing of the sort."

"Nonsense, you'd like nothing better than to be criticized, humiliated, punished and controlled."

"That isn't true."

"What's the opposite of meek and mild? Domineering and harsh, the precise adjectives I would choose to describe your late father."

"That's coincidental."

"No it isn't."

"What do you know about it?"

"I was a psychology major."

"I'm not impressed."

"I didn't expect you to be."

"If you're going to be disagreeable, you might as well go."

"You invited me in so now you can deal with me."

"I don't know if I'm able to deal with you in your present state of crankiness."

"I know why you asked me home, Alison. Since none of your Boston correspondents had enough time to arrange for a Friday night date, you found yourself at loose ends when you stumbled onto me."

"You seem to be the one who was stumbling when we met."

"I'm enough sober now. At least to do the job that I was brought here to do." Freddie stalked her.

"Don't you want to see the rest of the house?" She nimbly evaded his grasp.

After a moment's consideration, Freddie agreed.

"I must say I'm surprised you would choose to dwell amid the memories of all your childhood traumas," Freddie observed as they looked into her erstwhile childhood bedroom. "Is this the room where you got your first spanking from him?"

Alison smiled. "I refuse to give you a hard-on talking about my childhood spankings experiences."

"I'm interested, but not in that way." Freddie demurred, coloring brightly.

"No?" Alison led him through the rooms, which had been her parents'.

"I'd heard your mother was a perfectionist but I didn't quite understand what was meant by that statement until now." Freddie remarked as he minutely examined the four-star inn style decor.

"I know what you're thinking: Mommy Dearest, but it wasn't like that. The only bully in our house was him."

"Damn you, Alison."

"What?"

"Whenever I most want to wring your neck for being the pill that you are, you remind me that it isn't your fault. Who wouldn't grow up screechingly neurotic with Lionel Albrecht for a father?"

"Come on, Freddie, don't go to mush now."

"Affection makes you uncomfortable," he declared.

"Freddie, quit being a psychologist and go back to being drunk and surly."

"Alison, you don't really want a brute. You just think you do."

"I never said I wanted a brute."

"Then exactly what it is you do want?"

"You're smart, figure it out."

"Maybe I should treat you like your father did my mother on their first date?"

"This is beginning to sound like life imitating a Robert A. Heinlein novel."

He took her by the wrist and pulled her back into the master bedroom suite. "Come over here, young lady." He sat on a green leather couch and pulled her down across his lap. "So we can reenact that fateful night in 1958 when your father's caveman tactics allowed him to get over on my mother."

He stroked her bottom through her snug skirt. Wriggling against his monumental thighs and held in place by his very large hand, she began to feel the hot thrills ripple through her.

Freddie patted her bottom, pulled up her skirt and admired the sheer beige briefs, through which her creamy flesh could be glimpsed. Then he lowered her panties to expose her completely and then separated her thighs to examine her charms. The area revealed was too pretty not to softly spank. Alison became instantly wet. He then penetrated her moist recesses with a fingertip.

"I suppose you think I'm easy, because of last time!" Alison shifted away from his hand with some resentment.

"Not so much easy, as accessible." Freddie slapped her hard on either cheek six times in a row.

"Ow!"

"Don't be disobedient, Alison," he warned, deliberately spreading her thighs and continuing to lightly spank her open, dewy sex with his fingertips, then the whole palm of his hand. "If I arrange you in a certain way, stay that way," he instructed, dividing her cheeks and spanking her six more times on the aperture between them. Then keeping her as exposed as possible, he spanked her rosy.

The severity of the onslaught finally elicited a sob. He paused to rub the sting away, managing to keep her well spread. This treatment had begun to titillate her to the point of wringing whimpers from her lips as she squirmed across his thighs.

"Time out, Freddie?" she beseeched him.

"Let me guess. You want a cigarette?"

"I want to ask you a question but I can't do it in this position."

"Oh, very well." He let her up.

"Do you think my father might have actually spanked your mother?"

"According to her diary, which I found, read and jacked off to at age twelve, he spanked her hard enough to make her cry, then took advantage of her sudden, involuntary state of arousal to roughly sodomize her. Which is exactly what I plan to do to you."

"Really!" Alison's eyes widened at him.

"If you have any objections, state them now and I'll take them under serious advisement."

"Of course I object to your sodomizing me with your monstrous cock!"

"I'm sorry but it's the only way my honor will be satisfied."

"What do you mean, your honor?"

"I have been rejected by you due to being excessively mild. My honor demands a retraction."

"Please, Freddie, no, let's talk this over!" Alison cried.

"On the bed. Now," Freddie ordered, unbuckling and slipping his belt off. "Face down." He pulled up her skirt to her waist and separated her legs. "Alison?"

"Yes?"

"Keep your legs apart unless I tell you to close them. Do you understand?" Hard slaps punctuated the query, leaving pink palm prints on either cheek.

"Yes." Alison reluctantly yet throbbingly spread her thighs.

"I want you open," he advised her, spreading her bottom cheeks and spanking her anus, first lightly, then much harder. Alison whimpered and wriggled so extremely at this treatment that he continued with it for some minutes. "You see, in those days, when a girl seemed easy, a man got hard." Freddie explained. "But don't worry, I plan to follow through with a lot more finesse."

"Freddie? Can't I apologize for the meek and mild crack and we'll leave it at that?"

"Don't bother. My heart is set on penetrating you anally."

He covered her with his body, then rolling to one side, pulled her against him, so that her bottom nestled against his crotch. She heard his zipper come down and felt his penis nudge her in between her cheeks.

"Relax," he told her, locking one of his hands on her waist while he slipped the other under her to cradle her flat abdomen and press her hidden g-spot in a way that led her three quarters of the way to a climax in seconds. "We'll do it the usual way first. But just for a while. Remember, my honor is at stake here."

Alison surrendered to him, enthralled by his deft manipulations. Freddie penetrated her creamy canal with his large, throbbing engine to the hilt while continuing to firmly stroke her just above her Venus mound, this treatment causing her to orgasm more resoundingly than any in her life had ever done. After which she looked at him with new respect. The combination of his magnificent cock and educated hands was superior to even double vibrator penetration. Alison felt she'd never been so mistaken in a male.

"Where do you think you're going?" He pulled her back as she tried to break away.

"I came so now I want to stop."

"I'm glad you came but I don't want to stop."

"But you won't do that thing that you mentioned?"

"What? Sodomize you? Yes I will. You're in the perfect position for me to slide it in."

"Please don't, Freddie!"

"If you don't relax it will hurt. And I don't really want to hurt you."

"So, what are you saying? That you will if you have to?" she turned to look at him. Instead of kissing her he took her earlobe between two fingers and pinched it. A hot thrill went through her. She caught her breath and ground back against him.

"Yes. You've been pretty clear about the type of man you can respond to and Mr. Nice Guy is not him. Therefore, meet the new me." Freddie punctuated the introduction by penetrating her anally. She cried out only once as she felt a stabbing pain. But a corresponding hot freshet of pleasure blocked it out.

Still keeping his palm pressed to her tummy, Freddie now thrust his cock into her bottom rapidly, repeatedly and deeply. Alison could only whimper and throb. Waves of sensation rolled through her with every firm thrust.

"You don't like me, Alison, and maybe I don't even like you, but you'll get to like this," he promised. She then experienced a second, even more ticklish climax. Her involuntary contractions wringing his own orgasm from him, Freddie discharged deep inside her. Then he disengaged like a master of the art. This Freddie was a man of parts, she realized. Unfortunately she knew she could never hope to eradicate the effects of her initial disrespect. She almost sobbed when she thought of how she had hurt him with her cavalier assessments of his worth.

She turned to face him and embraced him. "Of course I like you!"

Her sudden softness surprised him. "Oh? Enough to forego meeting all those men you've written to from Boston?"

"Certainly!"

"Really, Alison?" He pulled away to look at her.

"Why should I look any further than you?"

"That's the most sensible thing I've heard you say so far." He drew her back against him and wrapped her in his arms.

"Freddie?"

"Yes, dear?"

"We had unsafe sex again."

"That's okay. I think we're getting married."

Chapter Four

The Diary of Susan Ross

June 15,

Today I started in the design department of Chipper-Knight, wherein everyone seems to know that I got the job through Monte Powell.

Ignorant of the caste system reflected in our corporate attire, I dressed altogether incorrectly in the French blue suit and heels. Everyone else in the studio was in blue or black jeans and white or black shirts. All the boys are pale, pony tailed and look as robust as heroin addicts. The girls are even slighter and in the best art school tradition, liberally pierced and tattooed, with platinum, blue-black or magenta tinted hair.

All the good looking suits work in Accounts, which is also on our floor. Everyone in the studio hates everyone in Accounts, except for Monte, who gives handsome Christmas presents.

The head of digital imaging, Onslow Stiller, is to be my tutor while I learn a new graphics program. He's a faded 35, of some sort of Scandinavian extraction, with straw colored hair and fishy blue eyes. He's about the oldest guy in the studio and the sternest, so of course I'm attracted to him. He disapproved of my short, smart business outfit as much as the rest of the studio, but for different reasons. To them I was conforming, to him I was aspiring. However, his initial contempt dissolved into complete indifference as I interfaced with him throughout the day and he realized how mild I actually am. His demeanor is severe, but his face powerful and arresting. There will be more about him soon.

June 16,

The illustrator, Cornell Page, has a window on Lexington, which he deserves. He has black hair, ivory skin and eyes that pierce me. He's handsome but he never smiles, which naturally inspires me to insert him into my harshest fantasies. I want him to know what I'm about.

Today, in pegged jeans and a cotton shirt, with my hair in a ponytail - everyone warmed up to me. Except the account execs who'd been intrigued by yesterday's heels and upsweep. Like Ralph Blake, the Yalie from Legal with the tawny eyes and burnished hair, who cancelled the luncheon date he begged me for yesterday the second he saw me in jeans. Cornell standing at the water cooler witnessed the brush off and flushed becomingly on my behalf.

I think Onslow might be getting jealous of Cornell, whose illustrative talents fascinate me, because soon after the leathery Swede saw me hanging on Cornell's drawing board, he made a point of scolding me, for "not saving my work" loudly enough to amuse everyone in the studio. My face burned. But I meekly bowed my head. In order to shame him. Which it didn't. He simply returned to his monitor in the most dismissive way.

June 17,

Cornell took me to the park for lunch on the back of his motorcycle. While we ate baguette sandwiches and drank sangria in the outdoor cafe overlooking the Bethesda Fountain, I showed him my fetish sketchbook. After that he looked at me differently. Finally he stammered something about asking them to give me to him as an assistant.

June 18,

Apparently, Cornell has some influence. I'm now his assistant. Instead of working in layout, I'll be rendering comps under his direction.

I couldn't help bragging to Anthony about obtaining a desk overlooking Lexington. But when I admitted to having first displayed my erotic sketchbook to Cornell, Anthony accused me of using sex to further my career.

Ralph was vexed when he strode through the studio and observed my relocation. And even more so when he noted Cornell watching over me like a mommy cat.

The most potentially unmanageable temptation I've encountered so far is Mr. Plastridge Currie, who descended on the studio today like a custom tailored Zeus of industry. The charismatic CEO of the company is a cultivated male of 40-something, with slicked back hair, a pencil moustache and a singularly aristocratic profile.

Obvious genius that he is, Mr. Currie unerringly targeted me for special attention, coming over to inspect my screen, question Cornell about my aptitude, Onslow about my dexterity, and me about how I was settling in. I found myself moving closer to Cornell and unwilling to meet Mr. Currie's penetrating gaze, for I've learned how dangerous it is to look into the eyes of a man who thinks he might want me.

Animal magnetism notwithstanding, this Plastridge Currie is too much of a grown up to be of any personal interest to me. With the weight of the whole company on his Armani-sheathed shoulders, he'd never have time for more than a quick round of presidential-style head, which would only bore me and deprive some other, more deserving young lady of the possible opportunity of rapid advancement. He found my apparent shyness tedious, but seemed to want to linger, probably attempting to discern what Anthony Newton could see in me.

When he walked out of the studio Cornell warned me, "Be careful, that guy is a terrible wolf."

Over dinner I told Anthony, who said, "I know Plastridge Currie. He was one year behind me at Yale. Cornell is right."

June 19,

Everyone goes to the American Cafe for drinks on Friday night, so I went too, escorted by Ralph Blake, who, once he saw me in a short, sleeveless, linen two piece suit this morning, could not refrain from immediately asking me out again.

I asked him if he was going to stand me up at the last minute like before and he looked at me like I was speaking Farsi. As soon as we sat down at the bar Ralph warned me about Plastridge Currie, who had a rep for claiming the rite of the first night with every new girl who started at Chipper Knight. On our second glass of Chardonnay he began a fresh tirade about how I should also keep Cornell Page at arm's length, as he was nothing but a draftsman who would soon be put out of a job by a new illustrator program for the Mac.

Ralph's urgings to caution were as endearing as they were obnoxious, but I couldn't quite decide which attribute took precedence, so I simply asked him to put me in a cab and I went home.

June 22,

I don't think Ralph enjoyed our happy hour Friday night. He barely talked to me today.

Cornell also seemed somewhat withdrawn.

I had a long tutorial with Onslow in the afternoon during which he expected me to remember a prodigious amount of information without allowing me to take any notes. Once when my mind wandered he snapped at me, saying this was what happened when poorly qualified persons were given opportunities they did not deserve only because their bottom happened to look good in jeans!

I was simultaneously delighted and affronted by Onslow's choice of words, thrilled that he'd been looking at my bottom but shocked that he thought me so unworthy of the position which (it is true) my acquaintance with Monte Powell had so easily obtained for me.

I was about to point out that a B.A. from a good college plus a year at the city's top graphic design school should certainly qualified me to occupy the lowest rung in the studio of an ad agency, but I could see by the cold, fishy look in his eyes that he wouldn't be impressed. Instead I (rather insolently) told him to stop looking at my bottom or I'd report him to the Labor Board for sexual harassment. Then I casually strolled off towards the coffee lounge, well aware that he could stare at nothing else.

Glancing back I caught Onslow looking somewhat bemused but almost smiling. He knows I'd never report him to any labor board. He's such a sexy man I may not even report him to Anthony.

June 23,

Valeria Rodriquez, graduate of NYU uptown, 24 and head of the Report department has become my friend at work. She's about my size with almost the same proportions and has the most beautiful long, straight black hair. If I were a man I'd be in crazy love.

We always meet in the smoking lounge and tend to discuss bad girl things. We found we share an interest in pot, pvc and punk. Now I have someone with whom to discuss all the marvelous men at work. (Anthony already knows too much!)

June 24,

Loved going out with Valeria for lunch, especially since it's irritating all those silly men.

V. told me somewhat wistfully that fast track professionals like Ralph generally observe the unwritten nonfraternization rule with regard to pink-collar techies like herself. But she could not help adding that he found a reason to walk into her department at least 5 times today! Apparently beautiful Girlfriend has been daydreaming about pompous Lawboy for some time!

When Valeria asked me which of my critical admirers intrigued me the most I (think I) riveted her by replying, "The one most likely to turn a girl over his knee!" When Valeria recovered her sang froid she asked me which one I thought that might be. I said, "It's too early to tell."

She then said, "I know what you mean. I have to have a man who knows how and when to control me."

I was impressed. But didn't pursue the topic.

As for Cornell, that young man has cast quite a longing/brooding eye on me ever since I showed him my sketchbook. And he has such beautiful eyes. He's asked me out on Saturday for a row on the Central Park lake. I formally asked Anthony's permission to accept the date because this always works better than when he discovers one of my adventures by accident. He said, "I could see that coming," but naturally okayed the mission. The only thing I'm worried about is: what if Cornell is submissive?

June 25,

Thursday is another Happy Hour night. I can't remember the name of the bar Valeria took me to, but it offered pyramids of watercress sandwiches and pate canapés for free with drinks.

Onslow was already lodged in a red leather banquette, with a glass of vodka and a huge plate of (horrible) herring and onions (!) before him. We sat down at his curt invitation. There was no other seating at that moment and this was being gallant for him. I remarked that if that was his daily diet, no wonder he was always so vinegary. He glared at me and drained his glass. Valeria stared at him, her chin on her hand.

I then went to get us champagne cocktails, allowing Onslow yet another view of my bottom as I inched through the press of revelers towards the bar.

While I was waiting for our drinks, standing up on the brass railing and leaning over a bit, Onslow passed behind me on the way to the Men's. And, as though it were the most natural thing in the world, he reached out and smacked me, lustily, on my right back pocket! No one heard or noticed in the general din, but I instantly felt the most telling blush suffice my cheeks and fervently hoped it would subside before the Swede returned. I could feel the imprint of his hand on my bottom for a long time.

Back at the table I couldn't look at him or speak. But he kept steadily looking at me. When Valeria left us to dance with a cute office boy Onslow forced my chin up with his hand and announced, "That's what I do to spoiled brats."

Feeling butterflies, I said, "You're awfully mean to me."

For a few minutes we simply drank in silence. Then his big hand closed tightly over mine. "Come home with me now," he demanded.

"Why?"

"Without preliminaries, I want you."

Admiring his bold approach, I went to tell Valeria I was leaving with Onslow.

We hailed a cab to his loft way downtown. It was located in an industrial warehouse but he had tricked it out smartly. It was altogether utile but not precisely cozy. However, it being a warm summer night, the coolness of the loft was delicious. We hadn't talked on the way over and I knew that as soon as he had locked the door he'd be about his task of taking me, and I was right.

Before I knew it, Onslow was summarily unzipping my jeans, bending me over a sofa arm and yanking down my sheer white panties.

"But wait!" I cried, turning, "we need to be safe."

"Yes, yes," he assured me, pushing me back down, then deftly separating my thighs to drive his large hand in between them and (somewhat) roughly knead the tender flesh there. Needless to say, my tummy had begun contracting like mad the moment he bent me over so decisively. I knew he was probably not the kind to give a formal spanking, but sexually dominant he was, and that in itself is sufficiently arousing, if not overdone.

Next he began to fondle me intimately and probe me with those long, rather harsh fingers. He was moving quickly, but neglecting nothing. One middle finger slipped in, then a second. In and out. I nearly swooned. Then he stopped. He pulled his fingers out of me and actually gave me two hard smacks, one on each bare cheek, before pulling his own zipper down.

I think I heard a condom come out and go on. I might have turned to look, but didn't like to. Hoping he was well endowed and vigorous, I passively prepared for penetration, turning to catch a glimpse of his properly sheathed, large and handsome tool before it began to nudge its way inside me.

Within seconds the Swedish destroyer had me gasping for mercy and begging him to please, slow down!

Onslow hushed me with a couple of firm spanks, which made me lubricate copiously enough to ease a few more inches of his mammoth manhood into my petite girlhood. It all could not fit and we both knew it. But he had to push just a little harder and deeper. Oh, that hurt!

"Please," I nearly sobbed. "I can't take anymore! It's too big!" Apparently these were words to come by, for Onslow disgorged a might effusion forthwith.

After it was all over, Onslow wasn't nearly as surly as before and claimed that he was ready to do whatever it took to make me happy then and there. I didn't tell him I was still rushing from the spontaneous swats and rapid ravishment. Even now when I flash on certain moments of the brief encounter, a tremor of the purest erotic joy pulsates through me.

It's not as though he's suave or well spoken, and given his proclivity for herring and onions, I wouldn't kiss him for money, but what a pure, unadulterated dom!

June 26,

Valeria told me at lunch of her severe crush on Ralph Blake, who disrespects anyone not ivy league. I tried to discourage her but she went on about his amber hair and hazel eyes to such a degree that I knew she was beyond bringing back to her senses.

Whenever they cross paths, she's as contentious as can be, insulting him, baiting him, and twitching her bottom past him with the utmost impertinence. Today she had on black high-heeled sandals, capri pants and a corsety top accented with the greatest amount of clanking gold jewelry I've seen on her so far. All that combined with popping her Bazooka bubble gum whenever she got around Ralph almost triggered an explosion, but at least on that occasion, I saw him exercise his self control.

I said to Ralph as Valeria clicked down the hall, "Doesn't she deserve a really good spanking?" He looked me up and down and said we both did before disappearing back into his department. All day I couldn't help but fantasize about Ralph spanking Valeria. I did some sketches of the visual at break while she and I were up in the roof garden having a smoke. When I told her what Ralph said she tossed her hair and laughed. They're getting to each other all right.

June 27,

An unbelievable day! Cornell and I met in the park at about 11:00. We took a rowboat out on the lake then went into the Met and looked at 18th century portraiture. Cornell made a few quick sketches and encouraged me to do the same. How I envy his technique.

In his basement studio in the upper 60's Cornell has painted the most exquisite Renaissance murals on the walls, and when the afternoon light filters in through the high set windows one receives the illusion of being in a neo-classical garden.

I looked at his art books while he threw together an incredible lunch of some sort of minced chicken and tarragon salad, saffron rice and tangy fruit relish. The chef at Anthony's favorite bistro couldn't have presented a prettier plate. He served me a wine called Blockheadia, with the image of a blockheaded jester on the label. After two glasses I started feeling warm and fuzzy.

I began to grill Cornell about his sexuality. He's 28 so I imagine he's had plenty of experience. When he saw I wasn't coy he asked me if I liked him. I said I liked him fine.

"Enough to let me photograph you in the nude?" He wanted to paint me as Manon Lescaut, reclining on a recamier, with her blonde hair streaming down her back, but he'd have to photograph me in position. I said, sure, if I could also photograph him (not in the nude) as a model for one of my characters. (He's tall and selects his clothes well.) That request seemed to overwhelm him.

I asked him if there was anything he wanted to do with me besides paint me. He said, "All sorts of things!"

I encouraged him to express his desires as I found him very appealing would probably refuse him nothing. Cornell seemed pleased.

"Your sketchbook," he began.

"What about it?"

"It struck a chord."

He suddenly looked so vulnerable that I was sure he was going to tell me he was submissive. I avoided his eyes, strolled around the room, fished out a cigarette and when he jumped up to light it, I was even more convinced. Finally, I asked, "What sort of chord?" all the while wondering what I would do with him now.

"I've always fantasized about dominating girls," he confided in an awesomely hushed tone, as though he were confessing to a priest.

"I see," I replied mildly, deciding to be circumspect for a change.

"What do you think about that?"

"I think I can handle that"

"You can accept that about me?"

"Yes."

"You don't find it offensive, or scary?"

"On the contrary. It makes you more interesting to me."

"I dared to hope, having seen your sketchbook."

"I hoped you'd dare, once you did."

We both drank another glass of Blockheadia. I was starting to like him more and more and he was starting to eye me like a mild mannered predator.

I finally just had to ask him what his idea of domination was, because I'd become too lightheaded to risk getting tied up, even if I quite trusted him, which I didn't. There's something of the Norman Bates about darling Cornell.

He said a naughty minx like me should probably be spanked. I protested. He insisted. I needed to be spanked! My face felt warm as he pulled me from the table, over to the sitting room area and took me across his knee.

I could sense, from the way he held me that he didn't get to do this very often. He seemed to be drinking in the experience on every level. He ran his fingers through my hair with tenderness, smoothed down my skirt delicately in back and reached under me to straighten it in front as well. Charmed, I looked at him over one shoulder, which melted him. The smoldering glance he returned seemed to say, "Thank you for making this easy for me."

Cornell's approach was thoroughly fetishistic. He spanked me over all my layers of clothing first, holding me correctly by the waist through every stage. Even though he had used the word "domination" I sensed he was a spanking person deep inside, who perhaps just felt embarrassed to admit it.

He spanked me sweetly and lingeringly, but so tentatively that at last I felt compelled to provoke him, by means of a lurid confession about what I'd let Onslow do to me after happy hour Thursday night.

After that he became stern, smacking me hard, without saying a word. Now he was truly spanking me. For being "too easy," he said.

Cornell's change of attitude threw the necessary switch. He's normally so gentle that the sudden surge of righteous indignation seemed even more electrifying.

I let myself go to that certain place, wherein I couldn't help but believe he actually had the right to be angry with me for giving myself to Onslow first. The harder his hand stung my bottom, the easier it was to imagine that he was spanking me for the hurt that my workplace promiscuity had inflicted upon him. Thus made deeply sorry for my heartless behavior, I soon began sobbing and shedding real tears!

Stunned at having made me cry, Cornell took me in his arms and comforted me, covering my shoulders and throat with soft kisses while fondly caressing my waist.

We hugged and deeply kissed, which somehow made me feel much more unfaithful to Anthony than the quick sex with Onslow had done.

On the way home I told Cornell about Anthony, to preclude his hoping for a love affair, but promised to introduce him to Diana, whom he could also spank. He said, "Did I dream you?"

July 2,

It being the Thursday before a holiday weekend, Anthony departed for the Cape by plane, leaving Dennis to drive me out tomorrow.

In the interest of stirring things up, I invited both Ralph and Valeria to come to Random Point with me for the 4th.

Climber that he is, Ralph flushed with joy and asked whether "Mr. Newton would be in residence." I said yes, but he had given me leave to invite whomever I liked. As Ralph acquiesced Valeria asked me who this Mr. Newton was and I explained he's the composer and my boyfriend, whom I'd mentioned before. Valeria was awed, having been taken to Anthony's plays for her 12th and 16th birthdays. She knows all his songs by heart and owns all his albums.

Ralph took me aside at the bar that night and asked if I was sure that Valeria was a proper person to bring to Anthony's house. I tossed back, "Don't you want her to come?" He went red and I laughed in his face.

July 3,

Delicious day! Dennis and I took the Bentley first to pick up Ralph, who lives in Tribeca and then to collect Valeria in Morningside Heights. She was waiting outside on the pavement in a sleeveless beige linen dress with a stand up collar, chunky black belt, pencil thin skirt and strappy high heeled sandals, which revealed dark red painted toe nails to match her fingernails and lipstick. Her hair was in a long ponytail and she carried two round, black patent leather band boxes.

She wasn't expecting a chauffeur and couldn't take her eyes off Dennis, while I saw my devoted darling fall instantly in love with Valeria's dainty feet.

The drive passed quickly with Ralph and Valeria bickering all the way. He was critical of her and she creatively told him to fuck himself at least 4 times an hour. It was extremely amusing and I had Dennis keep the slider open the whole way so he could enjoy it too.

When we stopped for lunch at Boston Corners I took my boy aside and promised to arrange for him to serve Valeria in some intimate capacity over the weekend. Making sure that no one could see us, he kissed the palm of my hand. Neither of us will ever forget the night I let him have me, but I am still his mistress and in his well-bred English way, he takes no liberties.

While Ralph went to buy gum before the last leg of the drive I complimented Valeria on her ability to insert herself under his skin. She said she loved getting him mad.

If only she would get him mad enough to spank her, and if only I could be there to watch, oh how happy I would be!

I called Anthony before getting back on the road and sketched the romantic situation developing, explaining my frustration at not knowing how to make the decidedly dominant Ralph Blake and the irreverently flirtatious Valeria Rodriquez stop fighting and start playing.

Anthony suggested I inflame them with appropriate erotica, as I'd done with Cornell. (Of course I told A. about C.)

I put this brilliant plan into effect just before dinner, taking them into the library (sacred sanctum where Anthony first had me) to show them Laura's and my graphic novel, which just came from the presses this week and still smells like (extra expensive) ink. I hastened to admit that Anthony had printed the book for us at his own expense but that we had a distributor and fully expected the first 10,000 to sell out.

I was gratified when they sat down together and went through our Secret Life of an American Girl page by page, their heads all but pressed together. When they were done he looked at her. Then he simply seized her and planted a meaningful kiss on her beautiful mouth.

This momentarily rendered Valeria breathless, but she quickly regained her composure and began to rate Ralph mercilessly for grabbing her and kissing her as though he had the right. Then she exited in a graceful swirl of slim white cotton pleats. (She had on another killer sundress that gave her a waist and cleavage from which it was almost impossible to remove one's gaze.)

But before Ralph could comment, she actually had the nerve to return, march straight back up to him and lightly, carefully, one could almost say lovingly, tap him on the cheek. One tiny slap to impress him with her deepening indignation. Then she ran rather than marched out of the room. I really wanted to laugh but I clamped my hand on my mouth.

Ralph went red and jumped up, muttering, "Where does she get off?" The next thing I knew, he was running upstairs after her. I heard a door open, then slam.

Twenty minutes later they were summoned to dinner. He entered looking as happy, confident and relaxed as any 27-year-old male who has just had sex can do. Valeria followed him with a volatile look and I heard her say under her breath as he passed her the Italian bread, "Rapist!"

Naturally I was concerned, but as soon as I got her alone in her room after dinner she hugged me violently, telling me how devastatingly in love with Ralph Blake she now was. I asked her did he take her. She said yes and added, starry-eyed, against her will! I said, "You're kidding, right?" She shook her head at me and said I didn't understand. She liked a macho man.

I nodded in all innocence. My work is almost done.

July 4,

Going down in history as the best fireworks so far.

It rained all day and the picnic on the beach had to be brought indoors. Friends stopped in from afternoon to evening and Dennis kept pouring a delicious spiked punch that got us drunk faster than beer.

Last night when I filled Anthony in on the progress of the guests he promised to give Valeria ample opportunities of making his fellow Eli jealous throughout the day. He kept his word today by having her sit beside him on the piano bench and sing the lyrics to some of his songs that she had learned by heart in 9th grade glee club. Valeria has a loud, but not mellifluous voice and I could see Ralph being tortured on many levels while we played billiards well in earshot. Anthony was enjoying himself hugely every time he saw Ralph convulse at a particularly strident note.

Finally Anthony and Valeria ceased the musical assault and walked out onto the balcony to watch the summer rain lushly fall on the ocean, leaning over the stone wall and frankly flirting. Even I could see Anthony's arm go around Valeria's slender waist, which is a thing he seldom does in public with a girl who isn't me!

I asked Ralph if he wanted some coffee and made him get up to take it from me, which led him past the open French doors through which Anthony and Valerie, still almost cuddling on the balcony, could be clearly seen. This ploy worked instantaneously. His jaw and fists began to clench.

At first he attempted to control himself by walking into the adjoining room and turning on the TV that he had kept continuously tuned to the stock market channel throughout the previous day. But there was no trading on the 4th! I thought he'd need a Xanex. But no. He had resources! Quickly he switched to ESPN and that calmed him at once. As he subsided in a chair I refilled his punch glass and brought it back to him.

Sitting on the arm of his chair I rallied Ralph. I told him that I too had noticed the balcony business and asked him how he could sit by and let Valeria behave like such a flirt when she had only given herself to him yesterday. He looked up and said, "She told you about that?"

I assured him she had great appreciation for the primeval approach to seduction. He said, "Then why hasn't she spoken to me since it happened?" I told Ralph to ignore her moodiness, as she had told me that she did sincerely love him, but counseled him to aggressively pursue her and force her to behave.

He liked that idea and declared Valeria to be so fresh that he could not look at her without wanting to spank her. Reminding him that women of her culture were susceptible to masterful men, I advised him to follow his heart.

When we returned to the other parlor Anthony was back at the piano and Valeria was having her punch glass refilled by Dennis at the bar. Similarly fortified, Ralph strode up to Valeria, grabbed her arm and conducted her from the room in a style that would brook no interference.

Anthony stopped playing in order to inform me that Ralph's room was situated right above the parlor we were in. Whereupon he and I rushed back out to the balcony to eavesdrop on the scene transpiring above us.

"Did what happened yesterday mean nothing to you? What did you think you were doing with Mr. Newton just now?" we heard Ralph demand.

"Having fun with a gracious gentleman, who unlike you is not a class conscious bore, even though he could buy and sell you 10,000 times over!" she shot back.

"You let him put his hand on your waist!" Ralph rejoined.

"I would let him do much more than that. I adore him!"

"You won't let him do anything more. Do you understand me?"

"I'll do whatever I like!" We heard her stamp her foot for emphasis. If he didn't spank now he was either a fool or a modern male.

"Well see about that!" Ralph growled, obviously seizing her at that moment and turning her over his knee, because the next sound we heard was the unmistakable brisk smacking noise of a spanking being administered to a petitely voluptuous girl on the seat of her skirt.

And yet again life imitates art! Or is there just something about the air in Random Point? When Hope Lawrence dropped in later and I told her the story she reported that she had long been aware of a peculiar aura hovering over the district, which she felt accounted for the high occurrence of erotic corporal punishment activity in the village and environs. But she is a native Californian and they believe whatever they like.

Chapter Five

The Diary of Susan Ross II

Monday, July 6,

Woke up to thunder. Found myself in Anthony's bed and he reached for me... after which I went back to my room to get ready for work. When I looked in to say good-bye he was in the window seat, drinking coffee and looking out at the rain. He'd lost his impetus to work and blamed me for destroying his edge with sex. (I've heard this before.)

While I was putting on lipstick Anthony told me it would help him stay focused if for the next couple of months I would deny myself to him until at least ten p.m. each night. I just looked at him.

Tuesday, July 7,

A. must have gone into withdrawals when he awoke today. I had spent the night at Diana's and went straight to work from there. I called him from the studio and found him cross. When I told him I planned to go out with some friends for dinner he told me he'd send Dennis to pick me up from work so I could stop at home to change my clothes and see him first. I didn't like the tone in his voice, which gave me a pain in my stomach, but agreed.

I got home and put on my heavenly new white sundress with the portrait collar. I found Anthony at the piano.

He stopped notating his sheet music and looked at me in such a way that I got another pain in my stomach.

Then he leapt to his feet in a disturbingly energetic way, exclaiming, "Don't you think you might have called to let me know that you were staying out all night?"

"Uh," I stammered, but he cut me off.

"Didn't you even consider the possibility that I might have missed you, wanted you, needed you with me last night?"

I felt my face go red. Anthony waxing emotional about me staying out all night? I've done it times without number.

Could my beloved be in the grip of the dreaded Mid Life Crisis? As I understand it, even handsome and successful people must endure them.

I apologized for not being there for him and explained that I had only stayed away to help his creative energy to regenerate, just as he had asked me to. To which he replied that he had only asked me to absent myself until 10 p.m. I said, "Oh, I thought last night didn't count because we'd already had sex that morning."

Apparently not the right thing to say. He instantly went from warmly indignant to chillingly detached.

"Well, you don't have to bother coming home tonight either," he told me, sitting down at his keyboard and consulting his notes by way of dismissing me, which instantly brought a lump to my throat.

"You don't want me to come home tonight, Anthony?"

"Suit yourself," he returned with a shrug, not looking at me.

"Oh, you don't know what you want!" I cried before running out the door.

I'm keying this in on my laptop while I wait at the restaurant with Diana for our dinner. She is for us both going home later together, kneeling at Anthony's feet and begging him to punish our impertinence. But I am for staying at her place again. I really think he's going middle aged crazy but Diana says that he is too young. (She knows damn well he's 44!)

Wednesday, July 8,

Last night a disaster. First Diana and I split a bottle of chardonnay and went over and over the question of why Anthony has not yet married me and whether he ever will.

It sometimes hurts my feelings the look he gets on his face whenever I bring up the subject. As a 5-time veteran taker and renouncer of marital vows, Anthony is perfectly indifferent to the "I'm

23 and ought to be married" injunction that currently disturbs and confuses my otherwise reasonable brain.

Afterwards we had the doorman call a cab and we went back to the townhouse to try to jolly Anthony out of his bad mood. But Dennis told us that he had gone out. And there was more. My sweet boy looked troubled, as though he was in some way concerned for our master. Diana and I surrounded him in his own domain.

Diana sat on the kitchen table and sitting Dennis in one of the chairs, she extended her slender, hosed leg and rested her high-heeled pump lightly on his immaculately trousered thigh. She urged Dennis to soothe her tiny feet, which had been confined in the cruelly high heels all night. While he adoringly massaged her stockinged feet, all but overcome by bliss, he was vulnerable to interrogation and we pressed him for details.

Dennis revealed a shocking story of millionaire decadence that made us gasp. First Anthony received a visit from a smartly dressed young man Dennis had never seen before. He only stayed a moment then departed. He'd come over to deliver Anthony cocaine! Which he promptly snorted a portion of right in front of Dennis while he was getting dressed! Then, cool as anything, he called up the newest, most exclusive B&D salon in Manhattan and made an appointment for himself with the most popular submissive in the house, after which he had Dennis call him a cab and breezed out, in his lightest weight black suit, telling Dennis he wouldn't need him any more that night.

Diana and I began to grow curious and worried by degrees. Wasn't he too old to be snorting dangerous drugs? And going to a club to play? That sounded bizarre. His usual style was to engage high quality submissives through correspondences and arrange for elegant rendezvous in 5 star hotels. Visit a tawdry B&D club out of his mind on cocaine? Not to mention the tumbler of Belvedere he'd downed while he was getting dressed. Diana and I quickly convinced ourselves that Anthony was putting himself in grave danger and probably had to be rescued. By us. But we might have only thought this because we ourselves were drunk.

After Dennis helped us find the remaining coke, to which we helped ourselves liberally, it took us at least an hour to get dressed. I had never tried it before. Wow! Diana was super impressed by the quality. She had had some before, but not with such a kick. I really hoped my beloved wouldn't have a heart attack off this stuff at his advanced age.

We wanted to take a cab to the club, but Dennis insisted on driving us. The club occupied a brownstone in the upper 90's. Not the best neighborhood. Dennis, thinking with his dick, never even considered the consequences of having ratted out his boss, which is why he is my boy. Besides, with Diana's perfectly pedicured size 5 foot on his zipper, he couldn't be expected to be anything other than forthcoming with information. Even so, A. would never fire Dennis because he belongs to us now.

We sent Dennis home and went inside the club Surrender. A beautiful young lady in a tight leather dress and collar admitted us to the reception area, which was decidedly more luxe, than any I had seen in California the previous year when Diana and I made our tour of the Hollywood clubs. A stylish matron behind the desk, also clad in black leather, but with long sleeves and no collar, discreetly interviewed us.

I said right away that we were here to meet my master and described him.

"Oh, you mean Anthony!" the hostess declared, as if she'd known him for years. I was awestruck that he had given out his name in a place like this. I said to Diana, "Isn't he full of surprises lately?"

We were told that he was in a session that was due to conclude in 15 minutes and were welcome to wait in the lounge.

The lounge was a cranberry room with a bar out of Twin Peaks. The bartender was a slim, lovely cocoa skinned girl with straight, shiny black hair cut like Louise Brooks, dressed in a white shirt, black vest and black trousers. She looked young and innocent. Considering the neighborhood, I pegged her for a Barnard junior bartending to help with college expenses. With her looks, if she were in the scene, she'd be in a dungeon, not behind the bar. There was only one other person in the small bar and who that person was took my breath away for the second time that night. It's a good thing I was as loaded as I was or I never would have been able to handle the sight of my big boss.

It was too late to run anyway. "It's the CEO of Chipper Knight," I whispered in Diana's ear.

"My god, he looks just like Rod la Rocque," she remarked. (Note: find out who that is.)

"My god, Susan Ross? What the hell are you doing here?" Mr. Currie demanded, jumping off the barstool.

"I'm supposed to meet someone here," I murmured, not knowing whether he knew Anthony was there or not. "This is my friend, Diana." I thrust her forward.

"How do you do?" she dimpled at him.

"You girls shouldn't be in a place like this. Who are you meeting?"

"Why? What are you doing here, Mr. Currie?" I tossed back with a drunken lack of concern. He just looked at me with raised eyebrows and tossed back a shot of hard liquor with equivalent nonchalance. Didn't take him long to size me up.

Diana and I ordered Tattinger splits.

"Card them," Plastridge Currie advised the waitress; just to be a colossal pain in the butt. She took him seriously and asked to see our ID's while he smiled. We sat on stools catty corner from him so we could all see each other. Our wine came and was prettily poured. Diana smiled moonily at the bartender.

"Hey, quit being a bi-slut for 2 seconds," I whispered. "You promised to help me save Anthony from his own excesses tonight. Stay focused."

Why aren't you playing, Mr. Currie?" Diana was bold enough to inquire.

"I'm waiting for someone who's currently tied up," he revealed.

"Literally?" Diana smiled, always ready to pounce on the slightest "B" reference. She's such the little bondager. Yes, she loves spanking. Of course she is an anal slut. But bondage has always been her most secret passion. And it's the one that most seldom gets fulfilled. She's been tied up of course. But never as many times as she would like. When she meets a fabulous bondage man, he's never into spanking. And the spanking doms that she adores just don't get the bondage thing, or won't study it sufficiently to learn its many intricacies. I sympathize with her.

"Uh huh," said Currie.

"Oh, don't tell me you're into bondage?" she flirtatiously queried.

I could almost feel her excitement as he smiled back at her and asked, "Why? Don't tell me you girls are too?"

"Not me," I said.

"Me," Diana confided, going all rosy.

"Really? In that case why don't I just rent a room and we can go play together?"

"You mean just you and I?" Diana asked.

"Would you consider it? I'm very good with rope," Mr. Currie assured her.

Diana looked at me. I said she should do it; I'd take care of the other situation myself. She was practically jumping up and down for joy when he went to make the arrangements for the room.

Within a few minutes they had disappeared into a dungeon. I sat at the bar with the bartender and waited.

Shortly thereafter Anthony emerged into the reception area that was visible from the bar. I rushed out to catch him before he left.

He was stunned to see me there and actually went red in the face.

"What, did you follow me here?"

"I had to talk to you."

"Dennis told you I was coming here?"

"He was concerned."

"Concerned? What the hell are you talking about?"

"I wormed it out of him. It's not his fault."

"Did you come alone?"

"No, Diana is with me."

"I should have known! Where is she?"

"She's doing a session."

"What???"

"With Plastridge Currie."

"Plastridge Currie? How did he get into the picture?"

"He happened to be here when we walked in."

"Huh! It is a small B&D world after all."

"He's a bondager. He's probably got Diana in a hogtie by now."

"Call two cabs," Anthony ordered the reception hostess.

"Two cabs?"

"You're going home. I'm going out," he replied tersely.

I followed him out to the street. I'd heard that people can become exceedingly grouchy on cocaine.

"If you send me off by myself you'll regret it," I threatened without conviction.

"Oh yeah?" He didn't seem to give a damn what I thought or did. I had a good mind to go and see Onslow. I almost told him that, but luckily I wasn't quite that drunk. In fact, I was sobering up.

"You don't want to come home with me?" I asked. "It's after ten."

He ignored this, impatiently awaiting our cabs. So I tried another tactic.

"Diana and I did the rest of your coke," I reported brazenly.

"Is there anything Dennis didn't tell you?" Anthony snapped. Yes, he was plainly going to be furious with Dennis. I experienced a hot flash of guilt.

"It's just because he was so concerned," I tried to soften him up.

"Yeah, sure. Don't think I don't know what's been going on between the two of you for years!"

Wow. It was like someone had socked me in the stomach. He knew?

"Nothing has been going on," I protested.

"Don't insult my intelligence, little girl."

"Maybe I'll just wait until Diana comes out," I suggested.

"I don't want you hanging around in there without an escort," he said curtly.

My cab came and A. put me in it, cool as you please while I was in turmoil! But that is a man for you. I cried myself to sleep, certain that Anthony would not surface until the morning. And of course, he did not.

Was so upset on waking alone that I felt I had to call in sick. Then was about to go downstairs in my dressing gown but remembering A.'s chilling accusation re: me and Dennis, I quickly bathed and dressed in khaki capris that fit glove like and a sleeveless, thin white shirt that revealed my filmy, ruched nylon and point d'esprit lace bra.

I found Dennis in the pantry grinding coffee apprehensively. I begged him not to worry but I'm sure his heart lurched as much as mine did when the front door slammed. Anthony strode into the kitchen as we emerged from the pantry. His tie was gone but he looked showered, shaved and fresh with clear eyes and good color. He'd apparently spent the evening somewhere civilized and hadn't succumbed to any drug misadventures.

Dennis went positively white as Anthony glared steel beams at him.

"Hi," I said faintly. My beloved tossed me an indifferent glance and told me to bring him coffee in 5 minutes. Then he said to Dennis, "Young man, I'll see you in my study!"

Dennis followed him out, throwing me the most stricken look over his shoulder. I waited until they had walked into the study then quietly crept out into the hall and made my way to the study door. There was no way I was going to miss this interview! Luck was with me for Dennis hadn't completely closed the door behind them. I arrived in time to hear Anthony indignantly declaim, "You credit yourself an impeccable manservant, yet you violate every code of that noble breed! Where's your loyalty, your discretion? Have you forgotten who your boss is? Miss Susan Ross does not sign your paychecks. You've been in my employ for 6 years. I've allowed you every liberty. And this is the way you repay me! By betraying me to that little termagant of a girl. And this isn't the first time either!"

I could imagine that by this time Dennis was almost in tears. And it was all my fault. All! I felt utterly wretched.

"I'm very sorry, sir," I heard Dennis murmur with heart rending humility.

Anthony snorted, "Well, you're going to be a lot sorrier, Mr. Cowper. You're not getting off Scott free this time. Oh no!"

I could not imagine what the hell was coming next. I was enormously aroused of course. I know what I wanted to come next. But I knew that would never happen in this lifetime.

"Am I sacked then, Mr. Newton?" I heard Dennis all but whisper.

"Pull yourself together, Dennis. I'm talking about discipline. You need some very badly."

I felt my legs go weak. No, this couldn't be real. No way in hell would Anthony touch a man. But God I would have loved to see him cane Dennis!

"I'm sure you remember where you left the girls last night," Anthony continued; "You're expected there at 3 this afternoon. Ask for Mistress Isabel Bruno. You'll carry a note from me asking her to give you the caning you deserve. And believe me, it will hurt. Now go and see to my breakfast. And it had better be wonderful. You have a lot of atoning to do."

I scrambled down the hall before Dennis emerged; now pink in the face rather than white. We met up again in the pantry where he quickly helped me prepare Anthony's coffee. I told him I'd heard everything. Dennis impulsively hugged me exclaiming, "Thank god he didn't sack me!" I could see that he almost felt faint from the interview.

"I'll come with you," I promised. Dennis looked at me with pure love.

"You will?"

"Of course, my darling. This is all my fault."

Dennis kissed my hands. I took the coffee up to Anthony in his room. He was already changing into khakis and whites, like me. It was the world's balmiest morning and he had that "I'm going to Central Park" look on his face. Which fact led me to believe that he had had sex with someone that morning. Otherwise he'd already be at the piano with his sheet music, full of creative energy.

"Shouldn't you be at work?" he said, taking the coffee.

"I called in sick."

"You don't look sick to me. Go to work."

"Where did you spend the night?" I asked with trembling.

He looked at me with the arrogance of an aristocrat being cross-questioned by his least important mistress. Then glancing at the hairbrush on the dresser he said, "Susan, did I tell you to go to work?"

I ran out of the room.

Spent the early afternoon shopping then met Dennis at Surrender.

He was nervous and excited. Not that caning was even close to his thing, but Isabel Bruno, one of our city's most accomplished dominatrixes was well known to the ardent boy for her magnificent boot collection.

He handed her the note from Anthony and explained to her that I was his employer's mistress. Of course he kept his eyes lowered. How else to study her shoes? I put in that I was accompanying him for moral support.

Isabel Bruno, a graceful, 30 something Puerto Rican goddess in a leather pencil skirt and open collared, exquisitely fitted white tulle blouse with her glossy black hair in an elegant French roll and her size 6 feet in 5" pumps welcomed us graciously into her Edwardian parlor and invited me to sit in a wing chair. Her perfume was an intoxicating mixture of apricots, roses and dark chocolate. She smiled at each of us, then unfolded the note from Anthony and read aloud in a softly mellifluous voice, *"Dearest Isabel, Please give this ungrateful, disrespectful, disloyal, indiscreet and presumptuous boy 12 of the best. Yours truly, A."*

I said, "Mistress Isabel, it's all my fault that Dennis is in trouble. He's not even a corporal punishment enthusiast and I'm sure he's never been caned. He's just an innocent English youth who worships women's feet. My friend and I bewitched him into betraying his master's confidence through the medium of high-heeled pumps. Please don't be severe with him."

Isabel lifted his chin. "He's a pretty young man," she observed, running her lovely, leather gauntleted hand across his smooth cheek. "But Anthony's instructions are clear. I think we'd better carry them out to the letter, don't you?" she asked Dennis softly.

"Yes ma'am," he replied, lost in her black eyes.

"It isn't going to be on the bare, is it?" I demanded.

"Why shouldn't it be?" Isabel smiled.

"If it is I'm going to leave," I declared. For I simply couldn't see Dennis, who is not even a spanking person, so humiliated. I love his sweet devotion to me. I can tolerate him at my feet. But witnessing him submit to a bare bottom punishment like a little boy or an out and out submissive, would decimate all the newfound oomph with which our relationship has somehow been injected since he had found the courage to turn me over his knee that night. If that was Anthony's plan, I would defeat it by simply waiting outside the door! Then I remembered that Anthony didn't even know I was with Dennis now. Though he would surely receive a report on it from Isabel later.

"If it isn't going to be on the bare I'm afraid it will have to be much harder," Isabel warned happily, leading Dennis to an antique desk and deftly bending him over it with the slightest nudge of her gloved hand against the small of his back. He was wearing a pearl grey cotton shirt and darker grey pleated trousers and looked particularly ruddy and appealing in the manner of all healthy young Englishmen. I was proud of his appearance but distressed by the way he flinched when she whistled the cane through the air to warn of the impending first stroke. The fact that he is not in the scene made it ever so much more poignant, but also much more cruel, than if he'd been getting off on this, which I knew he wasn't. At least not on a conscious level. Ever since we've been intimate, he hasn't adored me any less, but I've felt him trying to be more of a man for me. Anthony had certainly thought up a clever way of putting Dennis in his place.

Isabel began to cane Dennis in a brisk, decisive manner that instantly brought tears to his eyes. There was no warm up, no tapping, no stroking and definitely no cooing to the culprit. Isabel aimed properly, followed through powerfully and produced a frightful noise of impact with each stroke, pausing perhaps twenty seconds between them. Dennis made me proud by not crying out, but I could tell he wanted to. I would have been sobbing like a three year old on stroke one. I really was astonished at how hard she was caning my boy. I could hardly believe that Anthony would have wished Dennis treated so harshly.

"But, Mistress," I protested on stroke six, "won't you show a little mercy to a totally inexperienced and not even in the scene young man who was haplessly led astray by his mistress?"

"I thought I was showing mercy," Isabel replied with astonishment.

"Just look at him," I indicated my angel's tear streaked face. Isabel observed and seemed pleased by the effect she was having upon her captive.

"Since Anthony has sent him here for a caning, a proper caning he will receive."

"Believe me, no one is going to be checking for marks," I insisted.

"Not even you, my love?" Isabel looked at me in that bi-girl way that Marguerite and Diana have. I smiled at her to see if I could get around her like this.

"I hadn't thought about it, but perhaps I will. He has such fine, smooth, white skin."

"Now you really make me want to see it. But we'll not prolong his agony too much longer, I promise," Isabel replied, apparently somewhat moved by my plea. At least she paused to rumple his hair. "You're doing very well, young man. Being English I would think you had been quite familiar with caning. Are you sure that this is the first time?"

"Yes, ma'am," Dennis murmured. After all, he's only twenty-six, I thought. They stopped caning kids in the UK before he was even in school.

While watching him stoically endure the final six juicy, thwacking cuts across the seat of his trousers I marveled that men are expected to absorb so much pain without protest. I could never do it! It would simply take all the pleasure out of playing if I were crying my eyes out all the time. Then I remembered that this wasn't Dennis' idea of playing anyway. It was just Anthony's way of making his own acute displeasure felt. I felt extremely aroused contemplating Anthony's power over his household and wanted more than anything to find and be taken by him as soon as possible.

Within a few minutes we were walking out into the hazy warm sunlit afternoon again. We decided to catch a subway uptown and walked down into the dark cavern together. It was the 96th Street station. Not the safest. But Dennis was in a world of his own. His tears had been dried and I expected the pain was beginning to fade. A hot wind blew through the station as we looked down the tracks.

"Are you okay?" I asked him. He assured me he was fine and even smiled.

"Anthony knows something about us," I told him.

"I felt that today as well," Dennis replied, coming out of his dream world. "Though perhaps all he really knows is that I'm desperately in love with you."

"He's smarter than that."

"Well, he's very good not to sack me," Dennis said with heartfelt thanks. "But I can't help the way I feel about you and never will."

"Nevertheless, today should have taught us both a lesson. Right?"

"Right," Dennis agreed, then asked, "that lesson being?"

"That lesson being you are never to allow me to manipulate you into betraying Anthony's confidence again. Do you understand?"

"Yes. I do understand that," he agreed, wincing in retrospect.

When we got home later and found Anthony gone I insisted on going to Dennis' room and examining the damages. Reluctantly he lowered his trousers and boxers to reveal some of the prettiest, neatest red scoring of a pristine bottom I have ever seen. Isabel hadn't raised welts, but rather had ruled his bottom with perfectly even, thin, red marks from lower hip to upper thigh. I was very impressed. Not even Hugo Sands could have done a better job. We also both realized I'd done Dennis a great favor in urging Isabel not to take his pants down.

After tucking his shirt in and zipping back up Dennis was seized by the impulse to take me in his arms and crush my lips with his mouth. I let this go on for a minute or so before pushing him away and lightly slapping his cheek.

"How dare you grab me like that?" I cried. He sighed and timidly lowered his eyes.

"I'm sorry."

"Just because I went with you today that doesn't mean you're my new boyfriend," I told him. He looked so wounded at this that I fell completely apart and threw my arms around him as impulsively as he'd done to me.

"I'm sorry!" I murmured. "But you really can't grab me and kiss me as though you had the right."

"I know, I'm sorry too," he replied, nevertheless squeezing me hard enough to take my breath away.

"What? Did the caning arouse you after all?" I demanded.

"Mistress Isabel is so beautiful. And with you being there. I couldn't help but feeling it was a sacred rite and perhaps a bit more."

"Well, we both need to behave more circumspectly around here.

Don't you agree?"

"Yes."

I ran up to my room before I weakened and let Dennis have me right in his cute little wood paneled room with the nice English boy smell of him in it.

Now I'm going to shower and wait for Anthony to come home, still vibrating to his awesome stroke of assertiveness. Or maybe I'd better just change and go see Diana. Dying to find out how the rest of her night with Plastride Currie went.

Same day, early evening,

Went over to The Dakota, where Diana is apartment sitting fabulously for the summer. But who should I meet in the lobby, strolling in with an extraordinary bouquet of purple orchids and flame colored birds of paradise, but Mr. Currie!

It was just going on 4 and sure enough, in the manner of all bosses, he looked at his watch and said, "Well, Miss Ross, I heard you called in sick today. You don't look sick to me." (This must be some sort of Eli cheer from the 70's.)

I reeled at his ingratitude. As though he'd ever get to meet and tie up Diana Stratton if I hadn't showed up at Surrender with her the previous night!

I mumbled something about needing a personal day as we got into the birdcage together.

"Yes, I can see why," he noted my Bebe and Bisou Bisou shopping bags.

"You're not going to stop being the boss today, huh?"

"Stop being the boss? What an absurd idea."

"I deserve a week off with pay for placing Diana in the palm of your hand," I protested as we exited the elevator and walked down the fifth floor hall.

"You deserve a good spanking for being so impertinent," he returned in a casually avuncular manner. I mentally damned Diana for telling him about me!

"Oh? I thought you were a bondager."

"What's the matter with doing both?"

"Nothing. But you're not doing either to me," I declared.

"Why not?"

"Because Anthony wouldn't like it, I think."

"And you always comply with his wishes?"

"Mostly."

"So, you think he'd wish you to associate with that uncouth Onslow Stiller?"

"How do you know about that?" I recoiled with surprise as he knocked at Diana's door.

"I know about everything that goes on at Chipper Knight."

"That isn't possible."

"I know about you and the boy."

"Me and the boy?"

"Cornell."

"There's nothing to know about us so how could you know anything?"

"You went out with him. Two weeks ago Saturday."

"Are you having me followed?"

Currie laughed and admitted, "I happened to be in the park and I saw you together."

Diana opened the door dressed in a pink gingham playsuit with a halter top and pink, high heeled sandals that displayed her dark red painted toenails and a gold anklet. Her hair was in a small pony tail and she looked more adorable than ever, if that is possible. She practically jumped into Currie's lap while he was standing up. She couldn't kiss his face enough although he had to lift her off the ground to bring her up to his eye level. He is maybe 6'3. He also seemed to go all to pieces as his hands encircled her waist. He even called her his angel as he swept her up into his arms and carried her into the sitting room. I took the flowers to the kitchen to put them in vases.

Diana joined me in a moment.

"Let's make Plastridge some lemonade," she suggested.

"What's he doing now?"

"Just checking the stocks on the business channel."

"So what went on last night?"

"Oh Susan!"

"Yes?"

"He's so divine with rope. And everything else!" She jumped up and down as though on puffs of air, her face alight. She had searched a long time for a bondage master.

"Did you tell him all about me?"

"Dear, he already knew all about you from Monty Powell. In fact, Mr. Currie was at the party where we met Monte, but we never crossed paths that night."

Like Anthony said, it really is a small B&D world! I felt weak in contemplation of my big boss when I joined him with the lemonade. Diana had lingered in the kitchen, fixing her new idol a sandwich and fruit cup. She seemed disposed to fuss over Pastridge Currie as though he were her bridegroom. I was disturbed at the thought of my boss receiving my particulars from Monte, who had spanked me across his knee the very first night we met! Surely this was why he had made the spanking reference.

I realized then that Mr. Currie had only agreed to hire me with no prior experience because I was a cute, young submissive. Which was really no worse than Monte making sure I got hired for the same reason, but somehow it seemed more sinister. It gave me a feeling of unreality, as though being in the scene had suddenly robbed me of all my rights as a working woman. And now, he was apparently threatening to tattle on me, most likely when he ran into Anthony at the Yale club. (Note: find out if Anthony even belongs to Yale Club or ever goes.)

"Oh yes, Miss Ross," said Mr. Currie, hereafter: PC, reading my mind, "I have a lot of information that would interest your master, if you fail to get with the program."

"You think I'd let myself be blackmailed into playing?" I laughed.

"Who said anything about playing? I just think you need to be spanked by me."

"Isn't Diana enough to hold your attention for the moment?"

"I can divide my attention. Can't you?"

Did he mean between bondage and spanking? Or multiple men?

"What are you proposing?" I asked him.

"Office discipline," he said without the slightest hesitation, even rubbing his large hands together in anticipation. "The next time I catch you being naughty I will take you to my office for a good spanking."

My face got red but my abdominals clenched.

"With any luck I'll catch you and small Valeria being naughty together," he added.

"Me and Valeria?"

"Think I don't know about you two smoking weed on the roof?"

"Do you have cameras all over the place?"

PC only smiled, as much as to say, I am the ultimate control freak, that's why I'm your boss.

"Just try breaking another rule and you'll find out," PC promised.

"You're horrible!" I told him. And I will not let him spank me at the office, or anywhere else!

Thursday, July 9,

A. had dinner out and got home around midnight. I'd camped out in his room with Turner Classics. While wandering around in his dressing room I had impulsively lifted the lid of the cedar chest containing A's suits for the cleaners. There I found the light weight brushed silk black one he had worn the previous night. Sure enough, on pressing my nose to the fabric I caught the strong essence of apricot, chocolate and roses, Isabel Bruno's perfume!

Brooding on my rival for hours left me in a state of nervous exhaustion by the time A. arrived home, (looking smooth and fresh, in spite of the hour and his profligate new lifestyle). He smiled mildly to find me waiting there. Then remembering he was angry at me, frowned. But I had faith in the power of my cream silk pajamas to lure him into bed and compel him to take me his arms.

"What am I going to do with you?" he murmured, burying his face in my hair. He pressed his lips to my throat and his hand to my bosom, kissing and squeezing me softly. (Breathed inward sigh of relief. A. still loves me best.)

"You're having an affair with Isabel Bruno. Isn't that enough punishment?"

Anthony couldn't resist smiling smugly, just once. Then he

demurred, "Oh, I am not."

"You spent the night with her, didn't you?"

"Yes."

"I knew you spent the night with her!"

"Figured it out, did you?"

"Naturally!"

"So, I hear you went along with Dennis for his caning. How'd he take it?"

I saw that he wasn't being a wise guy.

"He shed tears," I reported honestly.

"Wow," Anthony seemed impressed. "But was he okay with it?"

"Oh, sure. He's Dennis, after all."

"I almost wondered if I'd carried the joke too far today. I mean, we don't own the boy."

"Yes we do."

"You do."

"He is my slave," I modestly agreed.

"On top of which, he's had you," Anthony shocked me by stating almost mildly.

"No, he hasn't. Of course Diana and I have been letting him take our shoes on and off for years. Other than that, he and I played once."

"Are you telling me that you let my personal assistant turn you over his knee?" Anthony took me by the shoulders and gave me a shake.

"Just once. And I had to practically call his manhood into question to get him to do it."

"When did this happen?"

"Last winter, on a whim. You were out of town and I was bored. And it was too cold to go out. I set him up by letting him massage my feet first. Then I told him he could do something for me. He tried to refuse, but I wouldn't let him. I made him feel so guilty he had to give in. Just like yesterday, it was all my fault."

"Everything is always all your fault. You're the one who should have gotten caned yesterday," Anthony declared. "In fact I'm amazed you didn't volunteer to take Dennis' place. I had a bet with Isabel that you would."

"Gee, that never even occurred to me."

"Selfish brat." Then he pulled me across his lap and spanked me, during which all his various grievances against me came out. I should have come home Monday night. I should not have implied that Anthony was incapable of getting it up for me twice in a 12 hour period. I should not have forced Dennis to rat him out. Having accompanied Dennis to Isabel's, I should have taken his beating for him, seeing as it was all my fault and Anthony had a bet that I would.

"What would you have won if I did in fact offer to take the caning for Dennis?" I lifted my head to ask.

"I might have told you if you'd taken the caning."

"I'll take it from you," I promised.

"Oh really?" He left me and went for the short cane, came back and pulled me back across his lap, but this time pulled up my robe and lay the cane across the seat of my silk pajama pants.

"Twelve of the best. Just like Dennis got," he threatened. Of course he caned me much more lightly than Isabel had caned Dennis. (Initially.) But he also pulled my pants completely down and didn't stop at twelve. He went from tapping to swatting to stroking, transitioning slowly from level to level and putting me completely in heat. In 5 minutes I was arching my bottom and wordlessly begging him to cane me harder, emotionally swept away.

He started to lay on with quick, whippy volleys. I could hear the cane swishing through the air. He struck fast and many times in a row. He'd give me a dozen or eighteen like that, let me catch my breath and stop rushing, then give me another fast round. Every time he did this my tummy fluttered like mad. I was actually getting close to climaxing just from the caning when abruptly he stopped and decided to take me.

That went well.

After we finally put out the lights I curled up against him.

"Did Isabel let you spank her?" I asked, not yet done burning with jealousy over this recent episode.

"Oh sure."

"For how much?"

"She didn't charge me anything. She likes my music."

Anthony then revealed that they had first gone out dancing, after which Isabel taken him home to a cozy brownstone, where she had cooked him both dinner and breakfast, lavishing him with large servings of Latin affection. I felt cold with fear.

"Don't look so stricken," he told me, "it was all done on a whim. Just as with you and Dennis. It will probably never happen again."

I told him that just because I can't cook or dance at present, that doesn't mean I will never be able to. He could not but agree. Or maybe he fell fast asleep.

I think I'll go home right after work today. I also think that Valeria and I need to walk around the block rather than go up to the roof garden to smoke this afternoon. Damned if I'll let that Plastridge Currie spank me at work!

Chapter Six

The Diary of Susan Ross III

Saturday, August 22,

Yesterday was exhausting, though Dennis did most of the work as usual. First he and a few buddies of his loaded up Diana's furniture in a large truck with the Statue of Liberty on the side. Then he, Diana and I got into the cab and drove all the way to Boston, stopping only three times to eat.

On the way Diana beguiled us with anecdotes about (my boss) Plastridge Currie, with whom she has fallen deeply in bondage love. I don't understand why she has chosen to attend grad school in Boston. But she says their relationship may improve even further through deproximity. Anthony rather agreed and allowed us to annex Dennis to get the move accomplished.

Since Diana's parents invested wildly last year, with catastrophic results, she must now economize and share an apartment while attending the first semester of design school. Answering an ad on the board at Vassar for a Boston roommate, she agreed to share expenses on a two bedroom flat in the neighborhood of Coolidge Corner with Horace Maple, whom neither of us remembered ever meeting at school.

The tall, paper thin, bespectacled and rather colorless history scholar (currently enrolled in the graduate school at B.U.), who was in when we arrived, made a satirical comment or two on the excesses of Diana's wardrobe and furnishings, but offered Dennis assistance in unloading the truck. After which we felt it only proper to take him out to a large dinner, which he really looked as though he needed.

Then we went back to the apartment and Diana began to make a list of all the things she had to do and get the next day. Anthony had felt so sorry for her when he heard she had to share a flat to save expenses that he offered to underwrite whatever fittings she needed to feel cozy there.

"I don't understand what more you could possibly need," remarked Horace as the list making continued, looking up from his book while sitting at Diana's carved mahogany table. Horace owned a steamer trunk and a folding chair. The dining room had been empty save for his numerous cartons of books. His bedroom had a futon with a comforter thrown over it, a small desk and chair, a lamp and some cardboard file boxes.

As the refrigerator held nothing more substantial than cereal and milk, we sent Dennis out for morning supplies while Diana and I unpacked her bedroom, dressing her beautiful wooden bed. As soon as some of her things were in place, the apartment began to take on her delicious scent and personality. By the time Dennis returned with several bottles of red wine, along with all the morning provisions a Londoner might think necessary, we had fastened candle sconces to the walls on either side of her bed and had set two fat burnt orange candles aflame. The room was bathed in golden warmth when he brought us our wine in her blue and gold chased Venetian glasses.

We called Horace and he joined us in a glass, but disapprovingly, invoking the indulgences that led to 1789. Diana looked at me and winked but we were all relieved that her new roommate was a tame scholar rather than the usual Boston jock.

The fact that he had nothing thrilled her because it meant she could decorate any way she chose. She planned to make her apartment one of her course projects.

I'm writing this the next morning at The Inn @ Cambridge where Dennis and I rented two rooms but spent the night in mine, where I allowed him to chastely hold me in his arms all night long. Of course, while sitting here on the bed, writing in my laptop, in my cherry red cotton pajamas with the zebras on them, I notice Dennis looking longingly at my bare feet with the toes painted the same cherry red. For all of his hard work, I should allow him to caress them at least. I will send him downstairs for a fresh pot of coffee and when he returns let him find me with my feet bare, and possibly the rest of me too.

Then for a lovely bath in that old copper tub!

Sunday, August 23,

When we went over to Diana's to take her out to breakfast we found her presiding over an impromptu tea party at her own pretty table, around which sat Horace, immersed in the Sunday papers, one jovial, bearded youth constructing a crossword puzzle and another portly young man who was dressed like a 17th century Dutch master. Not sure what that's about.

When we got Diana outside she linked arms with us and murmured, "Well, how do you like me as queen of the geeks?"

"Oh come on, he's not that bad and his friends are darling." I pointed out.

"I can't bear living with someone who isn't pretty," Diana pouted.

"He might have a beautiful soul," I suggested as we got in the rental car and drove off to Kenmore Square for coffee and baklava.

"Oh, that goes without saying. But other than that what have we in common?"

"Did he leave the bathroom neat?"

"Yes, he was up hours before me and left everything pristine. Oh and he was so cute when he tried to pay me for the food."

"You see, it could be worse."

"I miss my daddy," Diana revealed self-indulgently.

"Is that what you call Mr. Currie?"

"Yes," she replied remorselessly.

"God, you're a slut."

"At least you can report to him that baby is safely ensconced with an arch nerd, who would sooner think of burning books than presuming to lust after her."

"Oh, he's lusting after you alright," Dennis sagely put in. I privately agreed. Horace may have been an egghead extraordinaire, but he was still a man, with the fire of classical poetry and epic romance in his intellectual veins. When Diana crossed his threshold he knew a goddess had entered his domain and would for a time rule over it. I was certain he had spent half the night reviewing her various perfections, not the least of which was her tact and charm in the face of his awkwardness, poverty and complete absence of style. Diana was already being kind, and very beautiful, as she flitted around the flat with colorful fabrics and voluptuous scents, transforming everything. I only hoped he'd be able to stand the inevitable rejection from a sexually precious spoiled brat who has a sophisticated older man passionately emailing her all day from his high powered ad agency in New York. To which I must return to work quite shortly.

Monday, August 24,

Wasn't in the studio long enough to drink a cup of coffee before Mr. Currie called me and demanded I come to his office.

Found him at his usual command post, opposite a wall of television monitors, all of which were tuned to different stations. It was no secret that the broadcast division of Chipper Knight was the company's cash cow, causing we in the print ad department to felt suitably slighted and jealous. While PC finished making notes on the various spots he'd been reviewing, I looked out his 20 story corner windows on the tiny specs of cars and buses on Madison below. The skyscraper across the street was even more interesting. I picked up a pair of binoculars I found on the butter soft leather window seat and looked into the office opposite ours, where I saw a beautiful young woman in a business suit being made love to on a desk by a slim man in a glasses, a shirt, loosened tie and trousers hastily unzipped.

"Wow!" I breathed.

"Oh, are they at it again?" PC asked from the computer console where he sat cracking sunflower seeds.

"They do this all the time?" I put the binoculars down.

"They just started day before yesterday. But that was the culmination of a charming week long courtship over legal briefs. From the position of his office, I collect he's a partner. From her taste, confidence and general demeanor, I gather she's an executive too. Isn't it remarkable the way people think that no one can see them just because they're very high up?"

"I'll bet you put on a pretty good show when you've a mind to," I observed, which caused PC to narrow his eyes at me.

"Be happy to show you how good, Miss Ross."

"Aren't you going to ask me about Baby?"

"That's why I asked you to come up," PC replied; content to change the subject to an even more agreeable one. "Irritating girl to leave me flat just when we were getting started."

"When are you buying the engagement ring?" I asked.

"Don't be silly. She's far too young. Anyway, marriage is boring."

"That's what Anthony says."

"He ought to know, he's done it five times. I suppose that's what you're pining for?" PC said without bothering to disguise his contempt.

"Of course it is, I'm a girl," I conceded humbly. And every girl has to get married at least once. Doesn't she? Just to learn not to do it again?

"By the way, I ran into Anthony at The Yale Club," PC disclosed. "Ran the whole office discipline scenario by him. Guess what? He said that I could do whatever I saw fit with you, so long as I taped it for his subsequent enjoyment."

I just gave him a look. Could afford to feel superior as I had asked A. if he ever went to The Yale Club and he'd replied that he'd taken a girl there for tea once about twenty years ago. (Note: When Anthony and Plastridge were first at college together I hadn't even been born yet!)

"Diana isn't charmed with her roommate," I changed the subject.

"Why? What's she like?"

"He's a dear, gawky egghead and something of an embarrassment. But she is being kind to him and he's being unobtrusive in return, so I think it may work out."

"Don't like the sound of any of that! Why did she not mention that her roommate is a man? And how can he already be thought of as dear when you've known him exactly 2 days? Embarrassment indeed. She'll feel some embarrassment when I put her over my knee for lying by omission to me!"

"You punish Baby?" I couldn't help myself. Diana was not one to go into great detail about her playmates, feeling such remarks as, "He is divine!" sufficiently descriptive of any man's style.

"Constantly. In bondage and spread."

"No wonder she had to get out of town. A girl could lose her head over someone like you."

"Actually her departure was brilliantly timed," PC observed generously. "I want her madly so she puts herself out of my reach."

"Fly her back on weekends," I suggested.

"It's very tiresome," he brooded.

"She talked of nothing but you all the way to Boston," I told him soothingly. He smiled.

"What did she say?"

"Take me out to lunch somewhere wonderful and I'll tell you."

So I wound up having lunch at my favorite tea room opposite the big boss. More and more I can see the appeal of this large, suave teddy bear of a male with his hidden cameras and open agendas.

Friday, August 28,

Diana has been emailing me all week about the progress she's been making on the apartment. In one week she transformed his boxlike cell into a page out of the Sunday supplement. She took photos with her digital camera and emailed me them so I could see what she'd done so far. V. impressive!

She had also included a candid shot that she had secretly taken of Horace one afternoon when he'd fallen asleep on her sofa. Without his glasses his face displayed an entirely different aspect. His aquiline features, as refined as those of a youth in a Renaissance portrait, his complexion fair and unflawed and his eyelashes a length any girl would envy, all combined to produce an impression of delicate masculine beauty wrapped around the purest heart and soul. This, I think, is not an image to flash before the eyes of Plastridge Currie.

Sunday, August 30,

Interesting developments @ Boston. Thinking to teach her a good lesson for leaving him, Plastridge Currie decided to pretend to be unavailable for Diana this weekend and neither traveled to see her or asked her to come to him. But because Diana is Diana and doesn't behave like any normal girl I ever met, instead of crying herself to sleep on Friday night, as soon as she discovered it wasn't to be a PC sort of weekend she arranged for her favorite boyfriend from Vassar, the 6'4", switchable Carl-Adam Johanson, who is now a senior there, to meet her in Random Point, where his brother Freddie owns a house. So that when PC finally decided to call Diana on Saturday night to at least give her phone sex, Horace politely told him that she was away for the weekend.

Apparently, PC emailed her this morning and she blithely told him exactly how she was amusing herself and with whom, thinking in all innocence that he would be pleased to find her not a clinging vine and well able to amuse herself without him. But PC was either perfectly furious or pretending to be so, and signed off without even telling her he loved her.

Last night Diana took Carl-Adam to meet Marguerite, who was quite interested to hear of the young Viking's evolution from submissive to switch. A connoisseur of the body beautiful, Marguerite was so taken with Carl-Adam's unassuming charms that she offered to tie him to her whipping post and give him a flogging he would long remember, if not cherish.

But Carl-Adam rather stunningly announced that he no longer cared to be submissive and asked if instead he could whip Marguerite. I only wish I could have seen Marguerite's face at that moment. According to Diana, our favorite redhead first sputtered with indignation then burst out laughing and finally agreed to let the blond god demonstrate his ability with a flogger to her.

Diana watched in fascination as the innocent boy, who had only given his first spanking less than a year before, expertly bound, partially undressed and soundly flogged her elegant friend. Diana must have taught Carl-Adam a great many subtleties because Marguerite does not go submissive to just anyone. If he had been the slightest bit clumsy or inept she would have immediately called the session to a halt. Instead she allowed him to erotically whip her snowy bosom and back as well as her voluptuous bottom, all while Diana watched with rapt attention. She said it was extraordinarily exciting to see Carl-Adam at 21, looking so romantically dominant and being so skillful with the flogger as to melt an experienced player in her 30's. She had actually created a viable dominant out of the soft clay of a submissive. I wonder how I'd react if Dennis suddenly decided he would actually rather dominate me than me him.

Just got a support message from Marguerite confirming the entire story! She calls Carl-Adam adorable and claims she even has a few marks to prove it. I wonder how she plans to explain that to her husband! No doubt he's in Boston instead of out on the Cape at the moment.

I've agreed to meet Diana in Random Point next weekend. We made a bet as to whether PC would show up as well. I said no, not unless he had already planned to do so, as men v. seldom change their plans, even for a lady. But she said that he couldn't keep away from her much longer. And she liked the idea of him chasing after her. The foolish girl was even considering the idea of making fun of him for doing just that. And yet she completely adored him.

Friday, September 4,

First thing this morning, PC sends for me!

"What's she up to?" he demanded, as soon as I got seated opposite him.

"Just keeping busy," I told him.

"Who is this Carl-Adam person?"

"Just a college boy. No one important."

"So I shouldn't be worried?"

"About Carl-Adam? Be yourself Mr. Currie."

"Don't be impertinent, Susan."

PC is still looking for an excuse to turn me over his knee at work and I still don't want him to find one. Just on principal I want to see if I can resist the blandishments of one dominant male.

"And about this Horace fellow," PC continued, "what's the story with him?"

"He's making himself useful."

"Are they sleeping together yet?"

I shrugged. One never knows when Diana will get a whim. "I'll ask her when I see her in Random Point this weekend, though," I promised.

I'm making this entry curled up in the back of the Bentley while

Dennis drives me to Massachusetts. Anthony will be in England for weeks yet, so there's no point in hanging around the townhouse.

Saturday, September 5,
Spent a delightful girly day with Diana until dusk when PC arrived.

This morning Dennis served us coffee, fruit and rolls on the balcony of Anthony's room. It was blue and just a little balmy with the last warm winds of summer blowing in off the sea. We read the papers as Dennis fussed over us. Then we had him drive us down to the village to visit Damaris and Pamela's new dress shop where Anthony says I may spend as much money as I like. Diana didn't want to shop as she's on a budget, but I told her that Damaris could send the bill to PC. Diana shook her head virtuously while I nodded mine forcefully and dresses were purchased.

We then went to visit Hope at the bookshop. Diana was thrilled to meet Hope's husband David, who was drinking coffee at the counter when we arrived. Then Sloan came over too and we held a lively discussion on the state of the scene in New York vs. Massachusetts. Hope saw how interested Diana seemed in David and whispered something in his ear that made him color and murmur, "Don't be silly, dear."

When I demanded to know what had been said Hope naughtily suggested that David take Diana in the back for a few minutes' lesson. Diana glowed at this. It doesn't take her long to make up her mind about playing. "Go on," I encouraged David, putting Diana's hand into his. "She needs it!" David looked as though he couldn't quite believe what was happening. He'll never get used to Hope's accommodating ways. No man ever could. She will always remain the consummate B&D geisha, anticipating the erotic needs of those around her and attempting to satisfy them.

After a short tutorial in Sloan's office, Diana emerged looking very much like a girl who'd just been turned over a gentleman's knee and spanked. But I only knew that because I know her and I know David. In this state I brought her across the street to Hugo's shop, where we found him in and the aisles in their usual state of emptiness. This time he hadn't even Pamela for a chaperone, as she was now assisting Damaris.

Diana and Hugo had met on several previous occasions, but he had never played with her. I saw no reason why this should continue and suggested that Hugo finish the job that David had just begun, only this time I got to watch. Diana was highly in favor of a second spanking. Her color was high all over when Hugo turned her over his knee without even bothering to take us in back or put up the closed sign.

"If someone happens to come in and see Diana being paddled, then they will have something interesting to write in their diaries," Hugo said, carefully turning up her thick, round, 1950's style woolen skirt that she had just bought at Damaris' boutique. This went beautifully with a beige cashmere polo sweater, which I had also urged her to charge to PC's account. With her p-loafers and argyle sox, she gave quite a good imitation of the Lampoon cover that came out before we were born but has always struck such a chord with us both.

Diana gave herself up to this second spanking like a contented child, closing her eyes and grabbing onto the chair legs. I curled up on a velvet love seat to watch. Hugo looked up at me from time to time, with that look he has that always gives me a pain in my tummy. He never has entirely approved of me pulling strings to get other girls spanked. But he had the grace not to complain this time. Diana looked such the perfect little girl across his lap that I became caught up in the illusion and before I knew it I was biting my lip in concern for her pain. When he pulled her panties down she was so pink!

But even with all this attention, she confided to me as we walked along the rocky coast that edges Random Point a little later, that she couldn't seem to shake the feeling of desolation that gripped her at the thought of another weekend without PC. I counseled her to return to Manhattan and attend grad school there so she could have her fill of Plastridge Currie and I wouldn't have to miss my friend. But she's determined to do at least this year in Boston.

Dennis, who had gone marketing, picked us up in the village and we all returned to the Cliff house. Then Dennis and I began to prepare dinner while Diana went into the library to nap. Just as we were simmering a lemon caper sauce for the chicken, there was an insistent ring at the front doorbell. Switching on the kitchen TV and tuning it to the security camera station we were able to glimpse a travel weary but still characteristically robust Plastridge Currie stamping his feet on the door mat while waiting impatiently for admittance.

I told Dennis to stay where he was and ran to let PC in.

"Where is she?" he asked, striding into the hall and handing me his overcoat and handsome fedora.

"In there," I pointed to the appropriate door and he went directly in. The next thing I heard was the distinctive noise of a spanking being administered to the seat of a thick woolen skirt. As usual, Diana made very little protest. I peeked in the open door and observed the end of the spanking but fled when it became obvious that the aftermath would take the form of a passionate reunion. When I saw PC bend Diana over a sofa arm, I left her to him.

A little later, as Diana and I served PC dinner and Dennis poured some of Anthony's nicest wine for us, he regaled us with his adventure at Diana's apartment in Boston, where he ostensibly went in search of his girl, but really to check out his competition with her. There he encountered the helpful Horace, who following Diana's instructions provided her lover with driving directions to Random Point.

"I hope you were nice to Mr. Maple," Diana said, spooning creamy mashed potatoes onto his plate. PC glared at her.

"I want to know why you are living with a man," he said, just as though Dennis wasn't even there.

"Oh PC, it's just to save on expenses," Diana explained. "And of course, Mr. Maple has already proven enormously helpful to me."

"Oh? In what way?" PC extended his empty wine glass to be refilled and I told Dennis to get another bottle just like the first, for PC was a big man and drank like one.

"I've gotten him to hang curtains, run errands, do research for me, there's no end to his usefulness."

"So, you see him as a sort of unpaid servant?" PC demanded.

"He's happy to help all he can," I explained.

"Have you started using him for sex yet?" he asked bluntly.

"Of course not!" Diana cried. "Do you think I'd let that sort of boy touch me?"

"Sure, why not?" PC rejoined as Dennis returned to us with a fresh bottle of wine.

"Because he's not my type," she frostily replied, the little snob. She knows very well that without his specs her roommate's face is perfectly patrician. And we both adore his politeness and restraint, not to mention his highly developed habits of scholarship. I suppose she was only playing down Mr. Maple's merits to deflect PC's jealous accusations, but I found myself growing irritated with her for her lack of gratitude towards a young man who has basically signed on as an unpaid personal assistant to Diana for the rest of the school year.

"I'll bet you've already taught him how to put you in a hogtie," PC said, doing credit to Dennis' cooking.

"Don't be absurd," Diana cried. Perhaps she really still was in an aversion stage with regard to Horace. She does prefer robust males to reedy ones. Look how well she fit with Carl-Adam.

Changing the subject I suggested we repair after dinner to the Dummy Up Club where Pamela, Sloan, David and Hope were meeting for drinks and billiards. PC seemed interested, especially when he heard about the humidor. But then he shocked the hell out of me and Diana, and no doubt Dennis, by turning to Diana and coolly saying, "You're staying here." The way she suddenly colored was a clear indication to me that he meant: in bondage. As Diana's blush deepened I felt I should leave them alone for a while in order to let her protest this decision if she wished. Pretending I wanted some chocolate covered plums I'd seen in the pantry I dragged Dennis back there to help me put them on a dish.

Once I got him alone I clued him in that Plastridge Currie might be leaving Diana alone in her room in a hogtie while we were out. I told him to check on her immediately we left and see if she wanted to be let out, then drive her to the Dummy Up Club if she wished. Dennis seemed to vibrate all over at the concept of rescuing Diana and kissed the back of my hand.

When I returned with the plums PC was staring at her with his chin on his hand while Diana pouted back at him. Diana loves bondage, but she's not a purist and doesn't enjoy being left entirely alone for long stretches.

But PC defeated my plan by claiming he'd drunk too much wine to drive and asking that Dennis drive us.

We didn't leave at once. After all, PC needed time to put Diana in the hogtie. He didn't let me talk to her before we left either. No problem. I planned to send Dennis straight back with the car to check on Diana.

But as soon as we got to the Dummy Up Club, PC insisted on treating Dennis to a drink and immediately challenged him to a game of billiards. Dennis looked at me and I could only shrug.

No problem. I sat down with David, Hope, Sloan and Pamela, ordered an Irish coffee and made a short list of people I could call to go and let Diana out of the hogtie. Hugo came to mind but I was sure he'd approve of Diana being kept in a hogtie so I didn't bother calling him. Marguerite was my next choice. She already knew about the planter in the garden that held the back door key. She adored Diana and would be only too happy to drop everything to affect a rapid rescue. But, did D. even want to be rescued? And how would PC feel about me meddling in his punishment of Diana?

I went to the phone to call Marguerite but as soon as I started to dial a giant hand enclosed mine. I turned to look up at PC, big bullet head and all, in his shirt sleeves, suspenders and pleated trousers, cue stick in hand. He asked me whom I was calling. I said I was asking my friend Marguerite to join us. He said oh good and leaned against the wall to light a cigar while I dialed, smiling pleasantly at me as I left an innocuous message on her answering machine.

I then ducked into the powder room, hoping to find a phone there. But there was none. Anthony keeps urging me to get a cell phone and I keep resisting. Am I a fucking idiot?

Luckily at that instant Hope entered the bathroom and I was able to consult her for advice. Hope said: didn't I think a real bondager would have sense enough to leave a knife nearby in case of an emergency? (I have no reason to suspect PC of possessing any sense other than that of the absurd.) But she did come up with the perfect person to check on Diana, Michael Flagg.

Michael and Hope have been having a semi-affair so she pretty much knows his whereabouts at all times. She said he was likely to be having a night cap with the locals at either the Ball and Feather pub or the Dutch Cabin. She also knew of another phone behind the cigar room and out of sight of the billiards area and promised to go and call him right away. I don't think that Michael and Diana had ever really played before, but she's often expressed her admiration for the former-detective.

When we returned to the Cliff house about two hours later, we did find them playing: chess! They were cozily seated by the fire in the downstairs music room with hot chocolates close by. Michael was introduced to PC, who warmly shook his hand like the hail fellow well met that he is, never giving the slightest indication that he was annoyed by the new male presence around his girl. Diana gave up on the chess game and dragged me off to the kitchen to help her cut some marzipan cake that Dennis had bought in the village.

"Wasn't it delightful, Michael showing up?" she asked.

"You're pretty casual about," I said, surprised. "Did he release you from a hogtie or didn't he?"

Diana laughed and confessed that she'd gotten out of the hogtie in five minutes. She prided herself on being an escape artist and apparently this talent pleased rather than irritated PC, who, she told me, never attempted to stop her from tensing while he tied her, thus permitting her the small amount of wiggle room she would always need to escape. Michael had found her reading when he arrived, letting himself in with the back door key as instructed by Hope. Since they didn't know when to expect us back, they had refrained from playing and instead simply gave themselves up to flirtatious conversation over the chess board.

Michael ate cake and drank coffee with us. He was just about to take his leave when I realized that I myself could utilize him tonight.

I am making this entry, while curled up against the headboard of his vast oaken bedstead, in this lovely little cottage in the woods that my ex-brother in law William designed for Michael when Damaris was Michael's wife. Now she's William's girl, but Michael still has the house in the woods, which I plan to enjoy to the full tonight.

It's going on two a.m. Poor Dennis. It hurts him so when I give myself to anyone other than Anthony in our house. So I thought it best to come over here. Also precludes an awkward situation were Anthony to arrive in Random Point ahead of schedule. He was quite piqued at me the last time he caught me playing with Michael Flagg.

Glorious Michael Flagg. He's in the shower now. I'd better end here.

Monday, September 7,

PC flew back to the city yesterday while Dennis and I drove Diana back to Boston, then continued on to New York.

Today, as soon as I got in, there was a message from PC ordering me to have lunch with him on the later side. Then, I got a big email from Diana, which I copy below.

Susan, my love,

The most unbelievable and vastly confusing discovery since I returned home!

Horace is like no male I've ever met for compulsive putting awayness and I found everything perfectly tidy in the flat when I got there, but him still gone on his climbing weekend.

I was poking around in his room, trying to figure out if I had done absolutely everything I could to make it suitable for my apartment décor project when I noticed for the first time that his black steamer trunk was fastened with a combination lock. Why?

Knowing Horace's mania for writing things down, I thoroughly searched and presently found the combination to the Masters lock neatly inscribed on a piece of paper in a kitchen drawer.

You're wondering how I could think of looking in Horace's private trunk. It's not like me, is it? Something told me it was important for me to do so!

Can you even begin to imagine what I found in there? Let's start with: the last 3 dozen back issues of Bondage Life, hundreds of feet of trimmed, cut, neatly coiled, pristine white and sexy black nylon rope, a variety of hand cuffs, two spreader bars, blindfolds and ball gags, tethers, bridles, even a (dare I say it?) dildo harness! At the bottom of the trunk: a leather straight jacket, leather body bag and selection of lacing and zipping leather hoods. No wonder Horace doesn't possess any smart street clothes! He's invested thousands in the most exquisite bondage equipment I've ever seen.

I locked the trunk back up.

Around dusk, Horace returned to the flat, grimy from the mountains but with a fine, high color. I made some tea and cinnamon toast while he showered off and then we sat together at the table in the dining room to eat this little meal.

He asked me how my weekend had turned out and whether the large gentleman had ever tracked me down. I replied that he had and that as I consequence I had spent the better portion of Saturday night in a hogtie. (As you know, I only spent fifteen minutes in the hogtie, but I had to get his attention.) Horace stared at me, coloring like a cupid.

Then he laughed and said, "Sorry, I thought you said you spent Saturday night in a hogtie."

"I did."

Horace stopped smiling and suddenly looked disconcerted, his brain whirling so fast I could almost hear it. "You opened my trunk, didn't you?" he accused.

"Horace, it's okay. I'm a bondager myself. I practically sensed that stuff in your trunk. Or maybe I just smelled the leather."

Horace was stunned speechless until I opened my leather hat boxes containing my own cuffs and rope. "You???" he could only repeat, as though he were coming out of a trance.

"So tell me, Horace, who you were you playing with to amass such a lot of ravishing equipment?"

"I found two different bondage friendly girlfriends through ads in The New York Press," Horace said, inhaling the scent of the leather items, as we knelt by his open trunk a few minutes later.

"What happened to them?"

"I lost them. To masters!" Horace said with no little amount of rancor.

"Masters?"

"Brutes who thrashed them," he replied indignantly, holding one of the masks against his cheek to appreciate the leather smell once more before returning it neatly to the bottom of the trunk.

Susan, did I mention there wasn't even the suggestion of a paddle, strap or flogger therein?

"So you're a purist, are you?" I asked, unnecessarily. (Q: Should it not be exponentially easier to tutor a bondage person in spanking than a spanker in the use of rope?)

"I am a purist," he admitted, adding, "since age eight."

"What were your earliest influences?" I asked.

"James Bond movies or any crime or spy adventure that involved girls being held captive in bondage."

"Oh yes," I agreed, "all my fetishes came from TV shows in syndication. I got my spanking fetish from I Love Lucy, my bondage fixation from The Man from U.N.C.L.E. and my goddess worship obsession from The Dobie Gillis Show."

"I just can't believe that you, of all people, beautiful, little you, are into bondage," said Horace rather sweetly.

"I expect you'd probably enjoy tying me up," I said to him.

"Diana, don't tease me," he protested.

"As I told you, I'm a bondager, but not a purist. I'm equally a spanking person and can't fully enjoy the one without the other."

"Oh no, please don't say that!" he cried, appalled.

"Horace, bondage without spanking is like a sundae without the hot fudge."

"I could never bring myself to strike a woman," he declared.

"Horace, just as many submissives have been abused by bondage masters as spanking ones. Probably more, given the dynamics of the disciplines. I'm surprised at your narrow mindedness and lack of sophistication in this area. If that's your attitude, perhaps you deserved to lose your playmates!"

This was harsh but I felt he had to be given a shock. I finished him off by telling him that while I was curious to experience his bondage techniques, I would never consent to play with him unless he was prepared to integrate corporal punishment into the scenario. (I must like him more than I realized to give him an ultimatum like that.) Then I flounced into my bedroom leaving Horace to clean up the tea table.

I will give you an update as soon as I have anything interesting to report. Do feel free to share any of this with PC if you think it will torment him.

      Love,

      D.

P.S. Do you think that given how cruel I have just been to poor Horace that I should be alone with him? Ought I to have him put a lock on my bedroom door? Am suddenly afraid he might choose to punish me for my insolence by putting me in one of those diabolical leather hoods and tossing me into that trunk. Am scared!

PC took me to a restaurant so exclusive that we had an entire room to ourselves, just like in the movies of the 20's and 30's. He started to order for the two of us but I stopped him, as how could he possibly know what I wanted to eat?

After the waiter brought our water and wine PC got up and locked the door. Yes, there was an old fashioned key in the door! Then he came over to me, took me by the arm, pulled me out of my seat, reclaimed his own on one of the large, upholstered chairs and turned me directly over his knee!

"What are you doing?" I sputtered, completely amazed. He just positioned me and smoothed down my grey flannel skirt.

"Teaching you a lesson for meddling in Random Point!" His hand came down on the back of my skirt perhaps a dozen times, resoundingly! "That man didn't show up at the Cliff house accidentally," PC shrewdly observed. "You somehow contrived to have someone call him and go to Diana. Didn't you?" PC spanked me over my skirt for several minutes. I think he has the biggest hand I've ever felt. (A nice, comfortable one, to match his huge lap.) I squirmed but was far from unhappy. The flannel of my boss' trousers was finer by far than that of my skirt as I clutched his leg.

"She's my friend," I protested at last, the heat spreading all across my bottom.

"You will not interfere!" he commanded, pushing my skirt up to my waist and dusting off my pantyhose and sheer grey mesh panties with his enormous palm. Again and again his huge hand came down until the sting was palpable. I could sense he intended to continue and attempted to wriggle off his lap, as the waiter's return seemed imminent. No wonder Diana calls him Daddy. Everything about his spanking style made one feel like a v. little girl.

"You hold still!" he warned, hooking his thumbs under my waistband and deftly rolling both my pantyhose and panties down at once. "Unless you want your wrists tied!" I thought of that famous Sassy Bottoms illo of the little chamber maid being spanked with her wrists handkerchief tied.

"You wouldn't dare!" I cried, anxious to experience that piquancy.

"Oh yes, I would," he promised, whipping a snowy napkin off the table, quickly rolling it into a thick cord and ordering me to cross my wrists on the small of my back.

"But shouldn't they be tied in front of me?" I craned my head around to ask. He replied by pinching my earlobe and sternly repeating the command. I obeyed and had my wrists tied with the napkin on the small of my back. Not very comfortable! When he resumed spanking me, PC enclosed my bound wrists under his large hand to hold me firmly in place. More comfortable! To the extent that I felt a series of pre-climactic spasms in my tummy as he held me thus.

The spanking went on until the waiter rapped smartly on the door with our appetizers, at which point, PC put me off his lap in the most unruffled manner imaginable, told me to open the door and gave me a smack on the bottom to encourage this action, without bothering to untie my wrists or help me get my panties and pantyhose back up. That was not sporting. Yanking my wrists free of the napkin and my clothes back into place, I rushed to the door and admitted the waiter, who was young, cute and irrepressibly amused by what he had heard going on. PC welcomed the arrival of his caviar while I settled down to a beautiful pink grapefruit, which PC noted was the exact hue of my bottom at that moment.

PC seemed immensely satisfied to have finally spanked me and commended me for taking my spanking so nicely. Then he patted my hand and said, "You're a good girl after all."

"Does this mean I get a raise?"

"Don't be silly."

Followed Diana's instructions during lunch and revealed the new developments in Boston to PC, which fairly made him blench. I tried to point out that it was safer to have Diana under the protective care of an innocuous and respectful bondager than running around loose for any male with good hunting instincts to light on. Horace as body guard, escort and assistant would preclude the need for Diana to find other male support in the city and preserve her heart intact for PC. Moreover, this meek introvert would be the last person in the world likely to force his attentions on our girl as he was far too deferential to conceive of such brutal treachery. He was, I insisted, probably as trustworthy as Dennis.

But PC would not be consoled and was all for getting on the phone with a realtor as soon as we got back to the office and arranging for a suitable dwelling for Diana to remove to. So then there was nothing for me but to explain why Diana could not accept such a generous gesture at this point in time.

I told PC the whole humiliating story of Diana's downfall with her parents, who when they told her she would have to cut down on her expenses earlier in the year, were shocked to receive her cavalier assurance that what they could not afford to give her, certain older and affluent gentlemen of her acquaintance no doubt could and happily would provide. Her parents had demanded to know what she meant and Diana had blithely revealed that she was currently in a blossoming relationship with the enormously well heeled Plastridge Currie and was also one of Anthony Newton's favorites. Which is perfectly true. And everyone knows he has more money than god.

Diana's parents were deeply scandalized. Her mother, a photo journalist and pioneer feminist of the 70's, who traveled the world and knew her daughter hardly at all, was particularly disgusted, while her dad, an original yuppie and one of the first males to have his consciousness raised without sustaining material harm to his sexual organs, wondered where he had failed his daughter that she should choose to sell her favors to middle aged letches instead of diligently putting her fine education to practical use.

Diana was stunned to tears by her parents' violent disapproval of a lifestyle she had come to take for granted as the due of every charming and well educated beauty. They quarreled for hours. Finally Diana was compelled to promise them she would refrain from taking any more money from her older male friends and would proceed through graduate school with all the dignity and independence that a woman of the 21st century ought to possess.

Just to make the story more interesting for PC I added that Diana's father had very nearly spanked her when he found out what she had been up to for the last several years. This lie caused him to laugh. "Shut up," he said, "you know that's not true." PC is v. smart.

We drank our coffee thoughtfully. PC sensed the bulk of what I had told him about Diana's parents was true and agreed with them in principal but pointed out that they couldn't possibly understand a creature like their daughter, with which I wholly agreed.

Tuesday, September 8,

Got the following from Diana this morning:

Dear Susan,

Yesterday I woke up with a definite sensation of guilt at having been entirely too severe upon Horace. I jumped out of bed, threw on my robe, ran to brush my teeth and hair, then rushed out to the kitchen to see if he had left yet.

Good luck! He was just rinsing out his coffee cup and looked so unhappy! I positively rushed to him and put my arms around him. Then I apologized profusely for my cruelty, begging him to forgive me and promising to let him tie me up the first quiet moment we got. Horace was so surprised he almost fell down.

"You can tie me up," I reiterated. "Later."

And that's how I happened to wind up in my first ever inescapable hogtie last night just before bed.

I knew things were going to be different when he started with the rope because he noticed right away that I was tensing and told me not to.

"Houdini always recommended tensing," I protested.

"Yes, of course, if wiggle room is what you're after, but Diana, getting free is not the object of erotic bondage, just the opposite."

Finally I agreed to let him tie me tightly, just that once, upon his promise that he would release me in not more than twenty minutes and not leave me alone.

He put me face down on my bed to effect the hogtie and had it done in less than five minutes. It was very tight, but not at all uncomfortable. After I was fully secured he didn't seem to know what to do with me. I just looked at him. Did I mention I was dressed in a bias cut lavender satin nightie trimmed with cream lace? Under which I had on matching panties. When he arranged the hogtie he made sure that my arms and legs were bound together in such a way as to expose rather than cover my bottom. Once he had me snugly tied I was shocked to feel him run his hand across my bottom through the gown and panties. Then I felt him flip the skirt of the nightie up to expose my panties Then, most humiliatingly, I felt him tug my panties down to the tops of my thighs, baring my bottom and only my bottom!

He got up, walked about the room and viewed his handiwork from every angle. I quietly pouted and blushed, wriggling a bit on the bed. Then he came and sat down beside me and began to deliriously tease me by stroking my bare bottom and thighs for what seemed a very long time.

I suppose I indicated, through my body language, that I would not find it offensive to be inspected in detail. So the next thing I felt was Horace's long, slender fingers spreading my pussy and bottom hole. Yes, Horace did that! This continued again for some time. Of course, being spread made me wriggle and I quickly became wet! Directly he noticed this change in my response, he began to insert those long and highly skillful fingers into my pussy and bottom hole! He masturbated me for perhaps ten minutes and only stopped because I came, shudderingly, cataclysmically, against his palm which he'd slipped under me and which I had been grinding against.

It was too incredible. We were both trembling when he untied me a few minutes later. Then he put me to sleep like a little girl and left me. I would have let him sleep with me, but perhaps it's best he doesn't.

Better not mention any of this to PC. Woke up this morning feeling horribly guilty, as though I'd done something terribly perverse with someone I barely know and have no reason to trust. Horace has now seen all I have to offer, having turned me into a wriggling bondage slut in less than an hour and forced me to climax with his fingers alone to prove it. I was glad he was gone when I awoke today. I don't know how I'm going to face him again and act normally. How I wish you were here!

Oh, so PC finally gave you a spanking, did he? I think if the day ever came when we didn't share our splendid lovers, I would cry. Isn't he the biggest, warmest, most dangerous teddy bear in the world? And do you not enjoy his abrupt bossiness? Of course (if it amuses you) you must be my surrogate, at least until Anthony returns to the city. PC thinks of you as my counterpart and is mad about you.

I wish you hadn't told him about the scene I had with my parents. We had the most trying telephone conversation last night about it. He is for me disowning them. He simply won't understand that they are idealistic darlings who are hurt and confused by me even considering the notion of being kept or stipended by a man. Please explain that I'm still just a girl and I want my real daddy to love me again and not think that I've become some shallow species of Ivy League call girl as a direct result of his ultra permissive childrearing techniques. As far as my politically correct mother goes, she'll get over it. She at least is not blaming herself, but strangely enough, the subscription to Vogue that I've insisted upon since age 13. My dad is blaming himself, not only for bringing my up to be a spoiled brat, but for no longer being able to afford to keep me honest himself. I really need to have a private conversation with him sometime, to bring him around to my point of view. But I think this needs to settle at least until the holidays.

        Yours always,
        Diana

Today's other most interesting email came from Anthony in London. I paste it in below:

Dear Susan,

I always think it is so cute when you ask my permission to fuck another man. My advice is, accomplish the deed in the next 48 hours then secure PC's permission to take a two week leave from work to join me here. I miss you like crazy (and Dennis even more). I'll expect you both no later than the weekend.

      Yours,

      A.

Thursday, September 10,

Last night was one for the books. Following Anthony's advice, I went into work yesterday disposed to look with kindness upon any proposals my big boss might make, however indecent.

He was in meetings all morning, then he left for a three hour lunch and didn't return to the building until nearly four. Since I hadn't seen him all day I expected him to look into the studio upon his return and this he did. As soon as he caught my eye he nodded his head at me and I took that as a sign to follow him. Cornell was too well bred to notice my departure but Onslow tracked me out with his laser eye beams.

As soon as I joined PC in the hall he took my hand and brought it to his lips. "Have dinner with me tonight," he told me.

"Okay. Where?"

"Just come to my house." He wrote the address down on his business card and handed it to me. 5th Ave. and 56th Street.

It was my first visit to any of the residences within Trump Tower and I was stupefied by the grandeur of PC's 25th floor condominium. It made A.'s cozy little townhouse in the village look like a wee rustic cottage. The view of the park and the lights and the bridges were completely enchanting, especially at rosy sunset. No wonder Diana is so deeply in love.

PC opened a bottle of delicious red wine and gave me a glass which I sipped as I walked around the huge living room. European oils in burnished gold frames, a large marble hearth in which a fire was already ablaze, a glowing, burnished hard wood floor of incomparable beauty and some large, solid pieces of luxuriously upholstered furniture rendered the enormous space warm and welcoming.

"Tell me what you'd like and I'll send the cook an email," said PC, sliding onto a barstool and stroking on a laptop that was open on the bar. I requested a lamb chop and baked macaroni and cheese. He ordered baked salmon. I could have sat staring out at the darkening city without saying a word and been perfectly content but he wanted to discuss his feelings for me.

PC is a joker but he's got a soul and he was searching it to try to discover whether it was quite proper to use me as a surrogate for Diana. I explained that we often shared our boyfriends. He demanded whether that meant that Anthony had had Diana, to which I of course replied honestly that he had done, at least once all the way, while playing with her lightly on a number of other occasions. Plastridge wanted to know what I meant by all the way and I revealed a number of sensational details, which Diana may or may not approve of my disclosing. PC was shocked and intrigued. He then declared that since Anthony had had Diana, it was only right that he, PC, should have me.

I asked him what exactly he had in mind. He replied in the blandest tone imaginable that he wished to put me in bondage and sodomize me. I just stared at him. Then I shook my head. I protested that the thought of that scared me. (I've heard from Diana that PC is no Pee Wee!) I pointed out that being in bondage for even regular sex, no less the anal kind, would make me feel too vulnerable. "Yes!" he agreed with excitement. "But surely you trust me?" PC asked, refilling my wine glass. I was starting to trust him more with every sip.

"I do," I equivocated. "But bondage scares me, PC, honestly it does."

"Don't you like being scared? Just a little?"

"Sure, but I get that from spanking. And then you're adding in the anal sex on top of it. We've never even had regular sex."

"We'll do that on the way to the other," he told me, offering me a cigarette, which I took. He lit it for me. "I noticed the way you responded to my spanking you the other day," PC observed. "Why don't you let me do what I do best?"

"But if I'm in bondage and you jam it in wrong that would just about kill me. Look at you and look at me. You're 6'4"!"

"Diana has no problem accommodating me."

"Sure, but she's in love."

"Susan, Susan, Susan!" PC said theatrically, filling my glass again. "Would I do anything to hurt my angel's best friend? Don't I know you'll report every detail back to her?"

"So, PC, what kind of bondage are we talking about?" I squirmed, though the wine was making me feel somewhat less restrained every second. In fact, I suddenly had the impulse to fling my arms around his neck, which I repressed.

"Well, sweetheart," he took me on his lap to explain, "I thought, a nice spreader bar for your ankles, just to keep your cheeks apart. Then, quite simply, I would bend you over the nearest flat surface and go to work on your pussy and bottom hole for about a half hour with the spanker of a riding crop. Believe me, I wouldn't dream of even nudging my finger into your bottom until you've succumbed to the raptures of severe anal discipline."

Now he was starting to talk my language. When the hot plates arrived from the kitchen we agreed to leave them undisturbed until we could manufacture an even more ravenous appetite for them and proceeded at once to the master bedroom, another Manhattan skyline fantasy.

PC had just the right type of furniture for what he had envisioned, this being a huge carved wooden box sofa, upholstered in plush blue velvet and piled with lavishly trimmed brocaded pillows, looped with gold braid and crimson cords. One of the enormous pillows alone would be enough to bend me over and get my bottom well up in the air. Velvet tasseled curtains framed the box, allowing the inhabitants to gaze out across the vista of the park or turn their faces inward towards the velvet dark. Large candles on columns afforded the only light in the room beside that which came in through the windows and it was perfect.

Diana must have told him not to do anything before giving me a good, long, hard, over the knee spanking first, which is exactly what he did. Have I mentioned that PC's hands are huge and quite well padded? I never really realized that someone could be equally into spanking and bondage before but it seems PC is. Certainly I never felt that he was bored while spanking me. He anything but rushed through the spanking. What killed me was his insistence on inspecting me every few minutes to see just how wet I was getting. And PC's middle finger being bigger than some men's dicks, I almost gave it up across his lap. Finally I had to tell him if he kept on like that what would happen. Smart man that he is he figured out that if I came now I'd never hold still for the sodomy in fifteen minutes. I'd be sated and probably feel like a nap. So PC put me off his lap and went hunting for his favorite leg spreader and what I hoped would be a highly effective lubricant.

I was docile as he put me in position over a cushion with my bottom in the air. PC pushed my new blue heather winter wool dress up to my waist but pulled my panties off entirely. He caressed the calves of my new, chestnut brown walking boots, and then my bare skin above them. Expensive boots, a present from London, that arrived by express delivery this morning and felt perfect the first time I put them on.

I could tell by the delicate way PC was handling me that he was getting a great deal of fun out of having me behave this submissively with him. He was really a v. gentle lover, in spite of his executive bluster. He kept the teasing and the spanking and the foreplay up so relentlessly that I ended up letting him know exactly when I was ready to be taken in the way he desired.

Guys like PC should write a book for the others about patience in seduction being key. My dinner was delicious, even cold. We opened a second bottle of wine and I asked if I could have leave to go visit Anthony for two weeks. PC said that certainly I could. So that's why I'm packing today.

Friday, September 11,
This just in from Diana:

Dearest Susan,
Finally feel quite myself after several days of soul wrenching indecision about Horace and how we are to proceed.

Have decided I can't possibly stay here. It would not be fair to Horace, whom I like, but do not love. And the "incident" the other night still feels like a thing I must confess to PC about and possibly even be punished for. I dangled myself as a bonbon before a starving man. Now I must remove that temptation before I become his addiction. It wasn't that I didn't care for the bondage, but without the spanking it was feeling too much like plain old kinky sex. And I don't want that with Horace. Because our minds will never meet.

So, who do you think has come to my rescue brilliantly and in a way that even my parents will not object to? Hugo Sands! He was in town yesterday and we had lunch. I told him about my problem, being quite frank, as why should I not? Well, he immediately made me an offer. Did you know he has an apartment that he keeps in town? It's a v. pretty two bedroom in a hundred year old building in Back Bay. Hugo says that I may occupy it rent free in exchange for coming out to Random Point on weekends to photograph his stock and put it up on his website. Is that not a perfect solution to my dilemma?

Oh, Susan, the truth is that I made a terrible mistake letting Horace do those things to me. In retrospect it doesn't seem right. Hugo agrees. He says I only let Horace do those things to me because I felt sorry for him and that it is not my job to provide Horace with comfort just because we are both into bondage. He said I ought to have kept Horace at arm's length, as you did Dennis the first few years, until he had proven his merit long term before dispensing special favors. Hugo said that if I remained in the flat I would feel trapped in a very short time. Besides, it isn't fair to Horace. If I'm around he'll dream about tying me up again instead of trying to find a more compatible companion. Therefore, I must go!

Hugo went to transact some business but he's coming back later to take me and my trunk over to his place on Boylston Street, which turns out to be on the same block as the building in which Margaret and her husband have that fabulous rooftop place. This is so excellent because it means I can visit quite easily with Marguerite whenever she is here, which is at least once a week.

I'm expecting Horace back from class shortly, at which time I will tell him a fib about PC giving me an ultimatum that I would have to move out or he would break up with me. Horace need not know that PC is not the ultimatum-giving type. He has seen him once and was suitably awestruck so I think my fabrication will fly. I'm sure he'll get another roommate fast. We're in Boston, after all.

One more thing that you may think is cute. Hugo said that when we go over to his place the first thing he is going to do is give me a good spanking for behaving so outlandishly with Horace. He already gave me quite a scolding for letting Horace put me in an inescapable hogtie the first week of our acquaintance. Then he told me some absolutely gruesome bondage gone wrong stories. Really, you'd think Hugo didn't like bondage at all, if you didn't know about his own unique collection of restraints.

I hate you for going to London without me! I'm flying into New York tonight to spend the weekend with PC, make a complete confession about what a bondage slut I've been and explain about the move. I'll email you with the results.

Sunday, September 13,

So here I am, sitting quite comfortably in business class beside Dennis, while our plane flies over Greenland, as I paste into this journal the following from Diana, which I just received:

Saturday Night
Dearest Susan,

Hugo's place was heaven. Since he has everything I need there, I will wait until a weekend when Horace is away to move my furniture out of his place and into storage.

Giving Horace the news of my imminent departure was not pleasant. He almost cried and I felt dreadful; even worse than on the day my parents both turned Puritan on me. The worst part was attributing PC with such all consuming jealousy as to force me to move out in accordance with his wishes. That was both unfair to PC as a man and me as a woman, but it seemed less hurtful than admitting the truth, that Horace is simply beginning to upset me. I mean just being around him and his bondage intensity.

That inescapable hogtie was what did it. Is there not something just a little bit Norman Batesian about our Horace?

Hugo gave me the most beautiful spanking in my new bedroom! There is a long, upholstered bench at the foot of the grand four poster. It is long enough for a girl to stretch full length across a man's lap. But perhaps you've been there? At any rate, the spanking lasted quite a while! I became entirely enraptured. Then Hugo began to ravish me with his fingers and I wanted to be taken so badly that simply I asked him to. But he told me he preferred not to just then. (Clearly, he had no condoms on hand.)

All of this put me in a marvelously relaxed mood for returning to the city, which I did in the early evening. PC was waiting at the airport for me himself! I was very impressed. (Susan, is it not strange that I felt not the slightest guilt at the liberties I let Hugo enjoy with me, but the gravest self reproach about allowing poor, dear Horace to do almost exactly the same thing? Witness the fact that I felt no urge whatsoever to confess to PC about getting a sexy spanking from Hugo (this is the second time I haven't confessed that to PC) but the most urgent imperative to tell all about my lapse in Coolidge Corners with the bondage boy.

PC transported me to one of his secret hideaway restaurants with the private rooms. You said he took you to one also. May have been the same. Over a few glasses of wine I explained what had happened and about my decision to leave the flat to Horace. PC was naturally displeased to hear about how I'd behaved. In fact before I had half told about the hogtie he had pulled me across his lap and spanked me hard!

"That's for giving yourself to a pencil necked geek and no other reason!" he concluded the spanking and set me back in my chair in time for the fruit compote to arrive.

I waited until the sting had subsided, somewhere around the main course, to introduce the subject of my new patron.

This did not sit well with him (or me, presently) either. In fact he seemed to consider it something of a frying pan into the fire situation with regard to my protectors. He also wanted to know why Hugo would be allowed to patronize me instead of himself. So I had to explain that Hugo had a legitimate job of work for me that applied in great part to my current course of study, i.e. the photographing, cataloging and presenting of (antique) furnishings. So then he was all for creating some sort of fake job title for me with Chipper Knight, to satisfy the parental demand that my gains be lawful. But that seemed absurd in view of the firm offer I already had from Hugo and the charm of the new residence. This logic made him quite cross.

Thanks so much for your last email! It gave me something with which to neutralize PC's pique. As soon as I interrupted his rant about Hugo to ask how his night with you went, he realized that I had the advantage of him and laughed. Susan could you imagine ever going out with a dom who didn't have a sense of humor?

     XXX

     Diana

Chapter Seven

Confusedly Yours

Freddie Johanson wasn't the only man in Random Point looking at Polyxena Guzman, the pretty new owner of the freshly remodeled gym, but he was currently the only one she was looking back at.

Freddie had instantly gained an advantage over all others who entered the lavishly refurbished facility, when he walked through the door at the precise moment Polyxena was berating her partner Dieter Brant, in Dutch, for being hopelessly inept at setting up her new computer system. Freddie, network manager for the prestigious Braemar Academy, naturally offered his sunny assistance at once, garnering 3 months free membership and a surfeit of Polyxena's gratitude. Freddie became her new hero, receiving her special notice on every subsequent visit, which shortly became much more frequent and not just because he needed the exercise.

The really interesting thing about the extremely attractive and well-heeled Western Europeans was that they were in fact a scene couple, with Polyxena apparently being the dominant partner. This intrigued Freddie vastly. For ever since his younger brother Carl-Adam had visited Random Point and been offered a flogging by Marguerite Alexander, Freddie had been fantasizing about what it might feel like to receive, rather than give corporal punishment for a change.

Freddie would admit to no one but himself that he was a secret switch, who had dreamed at various points during his life, though not continuously, of going over a woman's lap! He was particularly interested in keeping this long hidden portion of his libido permanently concealed from his sometimes difficult girlfriend Alison

Albrecht, who could be termed a bedroom submissive but was actually one of the most obsessively controlling people he had ever met. He did adore Alison's intelligent companionship, her willingness to submit to him in all ways erotic and the warm, pleasant atmosphere she created for him in both her home and his own. But he mistrusted her loyalty and with a frank awareness of her long ingrained prejudice against submissive men, Freddie was determined to guard this secret from her of all people.

Then Polyxena came on the local scene with her reputation of being a mistress and Freddie began to think of revealing himself to her. He could tell that she liked him. She always stopped to talk to him on the way to the pool, where she daily engaged in lap swimming, in a one piece suit, with her white blonde hair braided into a coronet around her finely shaped head. She had the form of a classic 40's pinup, slim but lusciously rounded, with a high, firm bosom and a bottom fashioned for adoration.

Polyxena never got involved in any mode of exercise that included undignified sweating or ugly shoes. But come the first frost and snow, she would be seen skating on the frozen duck pond in the prettiest outfits imaginable. She would also have her boyfriend, Dieter, pull her around town on a sled. Therefore it was firmly established that she was a species of goddess, and Freddie took this more seriously than most.

But Polyxena also had a secret of which no one but herself was aware. For she had been struck most agreeably on her former party jaunts to Random Point, by the splendid attributes of the dominant men she had encountered there. They had seemed to her refined, gallant and highly skilled in the subtle administration of the corporal punishment arts. In the European scene, one seemed to encounter either abject slaves or sardonic masters and she was fairly bored with each. Polyxena felt that if ever there were a place to indulge her own suppressed urges to submit, it was Random Point, and if ever there was a time, it was that Autumn she turned 30 and was very much a firm white peach, trembling to be plucked by a powerful male.

Polyxena had heard that Freddie Johanson was a first class player, 100% trustworthy and a true sweetheart. Moreover, she liked the bigness of him. At 5'8" Polyxena felt she needed a tall man to play this game with. She could never realistically submit to her lover Dieter, who was but 5'10"! (Not that he would ever wish her to!) But Freddie was at least 6'2" and substantially set up, a large, strong, solid man. The perfections of the Celtic god Michael Flagg might adorn a future adventure, but for the present Polyxena determined that the modest, gracious and utterly gentle Freddie Johanson should be the one to usher her into the new world of feeling instead of giving sensations of the most exquisite variety.

Polyxena soon began to flirt with Freddie in a manner that even the most unassuming of males could not fail to interpret correctly. Nor could anyone else, as Hope Spencer Lawrence commented to her boss Sloan Taylor, after Freddie and Polyxena had enjoyed a chance encounter at the bookshop coffee bar.

"She likes him," said Hope, polishing the teak counter with a soft cloth. "Did you notice?"

"Freddie is a likable fellow," Sloan observed.

"Indeed," Hope smiled, for she quite liked him herself.

"And Polyxena is quite the seductress," Sloan went on.

"Oh, yes," agreed Hope, for the flaxen hair, rosy cheeks and speaking eyes of her newest rival had certainly not escaped her notice. But on balance to the threat was the new woman's mild and pleasant demeanor and a charming, vague bemusement with which she seemed to view her new domain. The slight accent with its clipped English finish only added allure to the composite of Polyxena.

"I like her boy Dieter too," added Hope, preparing a cup of latte for Sloan just as he liked it.

"I should think so as you're getting free massages from him twice a week!" Sloan snorted. Hope merely grinned.

Not a proponent of any exercise other than shopping, Hope had first heard of the gym renovations from her husband David, who played squash there fairly regularly. Understanding there was a new trainer/masseur who was offering the first lesson or massage for free, Hope had gone to investigate the massage portion of the offer.

Dieter Brant was naturally beside himself with excitement when the blonde Venus of Random Point presented herself for a vigorous pummeling on his leather table. Dieter was a goddess worshipper of German descent, who had met and taken up with Polyxena some 7 years before in Holland, though they had resided in America for the past 5 years and had both recently become citizens. Polyxena was of a monied family and had brought a great deal of it with her to the new world to invest and enjoy. Dieter was her submissive retainer, partner and assistant.

He was a sweet, thoughtful and maternal young man who annoyed no one and generally proved extremely helpful. His method of training fell into the coaxing and praying category rather than the drill sergeant. He grieved when his clients missed their workouts but never nagged. His disposition was cheerful and jolly, slightly opinionated in the way of all educated Europeans but wryly self deprecating in the way of all self conscious submissives. He was aware that in Random Point he had the freedom to be himself around Polyxena, since the village was apparently stuffed with players, but his devotion never surpassed the bounds of good taste. Before a week had passed, he had more clients for training and massages than he ever expected to find. Mostly because Hope Spencer Lawrence passed the word after her first massage.

Dieter Brant was very good with his hands. And luckily for Dieter, those hands were connected to a gymnast's body and a profile off a Greek coin. Dieter was a beautiful boy. It was proper he belonged to Miss Guzman. But that didn't mean he couldn't also serve other deserving local goddesses. And Hope was unmistakably one. The moment she entered his massage cubicle he assured her that she would never have to pay for allowing him the honor of relieving her stress. Hope was not entirely surprised, but none the less extremely charmed, especially when she felt what those strong fingers could do to a pair of shoulders and a lower back.

"Here is where I truly love to be massaged," Hope boldly asserted, placing her hand atop the towel he had draped across her bottom and without which she would have lay nude upon his leather table. Dieter almost swooned with joy.

"May I then remove this?" he asked, lightly grasping the towel. Hope nodded, he pulled it off and beheld one of the most exquisite bottoms he had ever seen. Dieter had of course made his own inquiries. Hope was a famous former-B&D model and submissive, now the wife of an English instructor at the prep school here and herself now a clerk at the extraordinary Marguerite Alexander's bookshop on the next street. She was remarkably beautiful, correspondingly gracious, razor sharp and cosmopolitan to a fault. Dieter loved her violently from their first exchange and studied to be brilliant and lovable for her during every subsequent encounter. This, as Dieter had learned with so many women before, consisted in keeping quiet, giving them pleasure and listening to them talk. And Hope did enjoy talking.

After her first blissful massage Hope felt rather guilty at having no money for him, but promised to send him several beguiling girl friends who could well afford to pay for his services and would not have to be given them for their beauty alone. Dieter was at first well pleased, then quite overwhelmed. Hope's other boss, Marguerite Alexander, writer, co-owner of the bookshop and wife of book chain entrepreneur Malcolm Branwell, that statuesque, bespectacled redhead who lived for boots, was the first girlfriend sent over.

Marguerite was fetish personified, from her high instep to her corseted wasp waist and Dieter nearly floated away on the residuals zephyrs. Marguerite didn't want a massage. She wanted a training session with free weights. And she engaged him for a twice weekly repeat of it after the first satisfactory encounter. The fact that she was a sometimes dominant and he was an always submissive was never discussed but was deeply understood. It would be years before he would lay a hand on her in any way. Massage she deemed too intimate an act to grant a mere practitioner of chiropracty.

Laura Random and her little sister Susan Ross, the girls who had written and drawn that delicious graphic novel that Dieter had found in the bookstore, came in for massages. Laura was well behaved and accepted a standard massage. Her naughty sister Susan, who was barely out of college, like Hope, made Dieter stroke and rub her bottom almost exclusively. He almost dared to spank their indescribably pretty bottoms, but hardly knew what would be made of the noise should it carry to the work out rooms. It was then he conceived the notion of sound proofing his massage room, which plan he carried out before the holidays.

Meanwhile, Freddie's opportunity to transform the tenor of his relationship with Polyxena arrived one rainy Tuesday evening, when she engaged him to assemble her computer system at home.

She and Dieter now occupied the lighthouse at Lilac Cove, which once more testified to the wealth with which the couple was endowed. Freddie arrived at 8:00, finding Polyxena alone in a brown heather wool dress and brown oxfords with a two inch heel and rolled cotton sox, her hair in a long pony tail and her mouth dark red. They chatted as he worked on her computer, she bringing a tray of cocktails and cigarettes. He didn't smoke, but lit hers. She mixed martinis and they had a few drinks while he finished his simple task. Her computer system was new and state of the art so Freddie's expertise was scarcely needed.

After he was finished they took the pitcher of martinis to the large, luxuriously upholstered sofa facing one of the antique wood burning stoves, which helped to heat the lighthouse, and stretched their legs towards it.

"Thank you for making the time to come over," she said, lightly pressing his arm.

"Don't even mention it," he cheerfully rejoined, the alcohol already gone to his head. "I'm happy to be of assistance."

"You're always so kind to me."

"It's my pleasure."

"I hope no one is missing you now," she ventured.

"The evening is entirely my own," he assured her, for Alison was out of town until the weekend.

"Mine too."

"Oh?"

"Quite. Dieter will be at the spa until closing time at 11:00," she explained blithely.

"In that case, would you care to get some dinner with me?"

"Perhaps in a while," Polyxena smiled.

"Suddenly you almost look naughty," Freddie accused merrily. "What's going on?"

"Well, my dear Freddie, perhaps you've noticed that I'm more than fond of you."

"Are you, Polyxena?" Freddie took and stroked her graceful little hand, then placed one kiss on her palm.

"And I think that you are somewhat fond of me, is this not so?" she continued, allowing him to retain her hand between his.

"Extremely fond," he agreed. Then added, frankly but none the less painfully, "However, I should mention Alison."

"That lazy girl of yours who never comes into my gym?" laughed Polyxena.

"Oh, Alison is anything but lazy. She just prefers to run."

"And is that what she's doing at the moment?"

"She's in New York right now."

"Perfect."

"I did want you to understand. Of course, it's not that I don't adore you. But she is my girlfriend."

"I'm happy to hear you adore me but I have no desire to supplant your Alison."

"What is your desire?" Freddie asked, relinquishing her hand to refill both their glasses.

"Merely to play with you," Polyxena explained.

"Tell me more," he urged, his heart racing at once.

"Well, Freddie, as you know, I am the dominant one in my relationship with Dieter. In fact, I have always been the dominant one within my relationships."

"Yes, I can understand that!"

"In Europe most men who play are submissive," she declared.

"I think over here it's more like a 50-50 split."

"Oh? Is that so? Then why have all the ladies told Dieter that he's the only male submissive in the village?"

"Really? I'd have thought there would be at least a couple of switches around," Freddie replied.

"Oh? Does that frequently occur? The combination of both orientations in the same person?"

"Oh, it happens more often than you might think," Freddie assured her.

"Do you know that I've never even played with a dominant male?"

"No reason you should ever have to," Freddie patted her hand reassuringly. "And no one around here would ever expect you to either."

"No?" Polyxena looked disappointed.

"I mean, of course they'd all covet your glorious bottom," he hastened to explain. "But respect for your position as an avowed dominant woman would naturally prevent them from expressing this."

"Is this true?" Polyxena sipped her drink with acute dissatisfaction.

"Of course. A man can be a dominant and still be a gentleman, you know."

"I'm not interested in gentlemen," she rather growled. "I'm interested in players."

"Well, sometimes a dominant can be persuaded to play in a way that is untypical," he said mildly, his heart pounding once more.

"Yes, yes, that's exactly what I mean!" she cried. "Sometimes a dominant, with the right person, may wish to behave like a submissive!"

"Oh, my dear, I understand what you're saying completely," he agreed, clasping both her hands between his and ready to go down on his knees to her.

"You do, Freddie? Really?"

"Yes, of course. That is, I think I do," he replied, teetering on the verge of a confession that would change everything between them and perhaps between Freddie and all women for the rest of his life.

"Sometimes a dominant wishes to relinquish control," she went on. "And that's a fine thing, is it not?"

"That's a beautiful thing," he agreed, once more tenderly kissing the palm of her hand, which was pink.

"What does it feel like to do that?" she wondered aloud.

"I honestly don't know," he admitted, on the very brink of adding, "but I'd love to find out," when she threw herself into his arms, hid her white blonde head against his chest and murmured, "You are the one, my dear Freddie, to whom I wish to relinquish control!"

Momentarily speechless, Freddie locked his arms around her and felt the entire illusion of Polyxena's forceful dominance dissolve into a feminine entity as soft as duck down. The dear weight of her rounded form against him, the petal scents wafting from her skin, even the sound of her satisfied sigh as he tightly embraced her inspired an enormously masculine reaction that even she could not fail to notice as she lay in his lap.

"Tell me what you want," he murmured against her ear, hugging her closer still, so she could whisper it to him. She replied not with words, but by taking one of his very large hands, and placing it upon her curvaceous bottom. Then she rather gracefully turned face down on his lap.

"Just a nice, good, firm spanking, like you give your Alison," said Polyxena, wriggling her agreeable weight across his lap until she had settled herself comfortably. Freddie curved his hand around her waist to hold her in place and smoothed down her skirt.

"Very brave of you to ask like that," he complimented her. "You must trust me."

"Mmmm," she agreed, grinding against his lap, already lost in the different world.

"But, why me?" he wondered to himself as he gave her a dozen firm smacks through her skirt. She responded with a purr and settled in deeper, looking back at him over one shoulder, with a very pretty smile.

"Good!" she encouraged him, then turned her head the other way, to hide her face. So Freddie continued spanking her over her skirt, somewhat harder, for she was amply formed for it and seemed already to enjoy his big hand coming down on her bottom. And yet it was hard, so hard to pull his mind away from the previous image he had held of Polyxena, as the woman to dominate him! Was this nature's way of telling him that it was absurd to imagine that any woman would ever want to take control of him? Here was a hitherto dominant woman, and observe what she wanted from him!

But by and by Polyxena's warm, girlish response to his spanking technique blocked out every imperative but the urge to bare her bottom and see how the palm of his hand might affect it. She made no protest when he pulled up her skirt and renewed the spanking on the seat of her finely figured white silk panties. Full panties for a full, round, creamy bisque and deeply pink tinged bottom. She allowed him every liberty. And one quickly led to another.

It would have been a crime against Aphrodite to merely spank her. The spanking was rather the incendiary device, which sparked the subsequent sexual combustion. Freddie had entered the lighthouse a system installer and exited the lover of the second most beautiful blonde in Random Point.

Alison Albrecht arrived back on Saturday afternoon. She had driven all the way from New York and wanted only coffee, a bath and to see her Freddie after the long week's absence. She was leafing through her large accumulation of mail when a hand delivered, hand lettered envelope came to her hand with a character she recognized as Freddie's. She had not received a letter from him in the mail since he had first answered her personal ad several months before and wondered why it had to be delivered before her return, not postmarked, but by hand. Freddie was sweet, but not particularly romantic about love notes.

Alison ripped the blue envelope open as she ran her bath and sat on the edge of the tub in her new raw silk dressing gown to read it. Her heart contracted painfully as she scanned the letter quickly, then read it over once more.

Alison lit a cigarette and burned the letter in the ashtray. She took a quick rather than a luxurious bath and then got dressed in autumn tweeds, dashing tears from her eyes on the way.

Fatigued as she was from her long day on the road, she also felt compelled to drive into the village and visit the gym.

Dieter was seated at the front desk when Alison walked in, but behind him Polyxena sat within her inner office, speaking on the phone while twisting a long blonde tendril of hair around one dark red painted fingernail. Alison took a good look, told Dieter never mind the membership now; she'd come back later, and walked out into the overcast gloom of a chilly Autumn afternoon. As she was deciding what to do next she was hailed by Freddie, who came running across the cobbled street towards her from the direction of the bookstore.

"Alison!"

"Oh, hi Freddie," she said shakily. "Interesting letter."

"It wasn't easy to write," he tried to take her hand but she avoided this.

"Believe me, it was harder to read," she replied, unlocking her car.

"Alison, come have coffee with me and we'll talk."

"No, thank you."

"You hate me?"

"I have to think this over. I just saw her."

"Alison, it's you I love. I love you more than ever," Freddie had the good sense to murmur, while crushing her to his chest. But Alison could not erase the impression that just a glimpse of her radiant rival had given her. Polyxena seemed exponentially stronger, more confident, graceful and feminine than she, Alison, could ever dream of being. An extreme sense of insecurity and inferiority caused her to sob briefly, but as much as she wanted to hide in Freddie's arms and pretend that it had never happened, that she had no rival, some vestige of pride compelled her to gently push him away.

"You made me give you my word I wouldn't answer any more ads or see any new men in the scene," she reminded him indignantly.

"I know," he agreed. "Oh, Alison, I'm so sorry this happened. But as I tried to explain in my letter, I didn't really visit Miss Guzman planning to be unfaithful to you."

"Oh yes, your other bombshell. You're a switch! I could have lived without knowing that too." Alison got into her car, slammed the door shut hard and pulled out into the narrow street as a light rain began to fall.

Freddie now felt only slightly less wretched than the day he had written the letter. At least she had let him embrace her, if but for a moment. She hadn't cursed him to his face or even told him not to call her again. On the other hand, she hadn't disagreed when he suggested that she hated him. And she had driven away without saying goodbye.

As he walked home to his small frame house in the village Freddie wondered if he had been foolish to admit that he'd gone to Polyxena looking only for a good licking. Instead of mitigating his error, it only seemed to put him in worse with his girl. "If she comes back to me now," Freddie finally concluded, "that will mean she really loves me, in spite of everything. And isn't that the only love worth having?"

Instead of going straight home, Alison went around the block and parked at the other entrance of Marguerite Alexander's Bookshop, where she made straight for the coffee bar. That day Hope was behind the counter and her husband David, an English instructor at the Braemar Academy where she, Alison, was assistant comptroller and Freddie was network manager, was sitting on one of the stools, wiling away the chilly afternoon reading The Brothers Karamazov aloud to Hope.

David was happy to see Alison and stopped reading in order to deliver the gossip that she had missed on her week away from school. Hope wandered away to serve coffee and cakes to one of the tables, uneasy at leaving her handsome husband with Alison, whom Hope deemed altogether too coolly seductive.

It was a busy day at the bookshop and both Marguerite and her partner Sloan were rapidly ringing up sales behind the counters. Under the general din of conversation, David's and Alison's went unheard.

"Alison? What's wrong? You look terribly unhappy," observed her perceptive co-worker.

"Can we go outside where I can smoke?" she asked.

"There's a patio," he helpfully suggested, calling to Hope to bring Alison's coffee out as they left. The afternoon was turning cold and drizzly but Sloan had installed heaters outside and David and Alison were cozily surrounded by dripping stones and autumn dappled shrubs.

"Didn't you have a good time with your mother in New York?" David asked.

"New York was fine. But as soon as I got home I got a written confession from Freddie that he'd cheated on me!"

"You don't say!" David had been eyeing Alison since the beginning of the school year. But her relationship with Freddie still being so fresh, he had hardly dared hope to play with the slim brunette submissive any time soon. Suddenly, however, he dared hope. (He also dared Hope to try and stop him, he thought with amusement.)

"Yes, and with that stupefyingly glamorous blonde who's just bought the gym."

"With Polyxena Guzman?"

"My god, is that really her name?"

"Freddie scored with her?" David didn't bother to conceal his admiration and Alison quite understood his wonder. Freddie was comfortable rather than flashy, not the type anyone would have expected the Dutch millionairess to notice, no less grant extreme favors to. She shrugged and said, "Somehow it happened. And this after he asked me to stop playing with other men!"

"That's not fair."

"Although I think I must believe him when he says this happened somewhat unexpectedly."

"That's what you get for going out of town," David suggested.

Hope brought out Alison's coffee and roll, giving David such a saucy look as she exited that he couldn't resist smacking her blue jeaned bottom.

Alison sighed, "This Polyxena is a powerhouse of pulchritude."

"I doubt any mortal male, either straight or kinky, could resist an invitation from that divine force of nature," mused David.

"So Random Point now has its own Lorelei?"

"Precisely. She even swims in the pool frequently. We all steal surreptitious peeks as we pass by the spectator window. Alison, never forget that Freddie is a man and all men are dogs."

"Dogs are supposed to be loyal."

"Yes, but place them anywhere near a skirt and their noses will go up it."

"Well, what should I do?"

"Even the score. At once! By the way, I am available."

Alison felt her face grow warm and her tummy jump.

"You, David?"

"Me, Alison." David took her gloved hand and briefly squeezed it.

"You who are lord and master of Hope Spencer Lawrence? Would offer your services to me?"

"You know, Alison, you're not the only member of the My-Partner-Is-A-Slut Club. Hope's been carrying on with Michael Flagg for months. I've done everything I can think of to stop her. I've beaten her. Beaten her some more. She still sees him at least once a week. And I think she's begun to like the beatings. But let's not talk about that tiresome girl. Let's talk about getting even with old Freddie. Think about it, Alison. The sooner you behave as reprehensibly as he has, the sooner you can forgive him and go back to being sweethearts."

"What you say makes sense. And it is cheering me up," Alison smiled for the first time. Mr. Lawrence was so charming, so good looking and well spoken. She had often fantasized about being scolded and paddled by him!

"You must have gone shopping in New York," David ventured, "why don't you take me home with you and try on your new outfits for me?"

"I did buy a perfect little pleated, fringed, safety-pinned wrap skirt and cardigan set. I was planning to wear it the next time I cooked dinner for Freddie, adding stockings, garters, well behaved pumps and pearls, for a late 50's effect."

"Will you wear them for me?"

"When?"

"Now. Before you lose your resolve," David urged her.

"Are you serious?"

"About wanting to go home with you? Perfectly. I've always wanted to turn you over my knee. Especially when you wear those glove tight pencil skirts to work."

Alison colored prettily. "You noticed?"

"Noticed! You should be spanked just for wearing those. I'm surprised Freddie lets you. Your slim, jutting bottom swishing down the halls provides prime viewing enjoyment for all at Braemar."

David accompanied Alison back to her house in the woods with great pleasure. He needed an experience like this to put Hope's on-going infatuation with Michael Flagg into its proper perspective. And dear Alison needed his attention to blot out the pain of her lover's perceived disloyalty. David knew when a lady was taken with him and he had felt Alison's quiet affection for some time. Therefore this seemed very right.

"Damn you, Alison, you're tempting me to smoke all over the place!" David snapped, finding clever art deco cigarette boxes in her living room, kitchen, bedroom and study. "For that alone you should get a good spanking!"

Alison blushed but led him by the hand into the pantry where she let him pick out a bottle of wine and decant it.

"Good girl," he commended her, "distract me from a vice I oughtn't to indulge in with an acceptable one."

Alison beamed at the praise. "I should quit," she agreed, snuffing out her cigarette.

"I'm surprised Freddie allows it!" David said.

"He's not a tyrant, after all," Alison smiled. Then she remembered that her lover was instead a disloyal, unfaithful switch, apparently at the disposal of any pretty woman in the scene.

"Never the less, you do need a good paddling for smoking so much. Especially in front of someone who's so recently quit!" Alison felt a spasm pulse through her very core at his casual threat. "A really hard one," he added in his creamy, dulcet toned voice. Mr. Lawrence had one of the most beautiful voices she had ever heard and his lecturing was bringing her exquisite joy. "Why don't you go and put on the pleated skirt and sweater set?"

David awaited her, sipping his wine and building a cheerful fire in her master bedroom hearth. He had already placed an upholstered bench on the hearth rug and as an insolent touch, had turned down the rich green figured brocade comforter to expose an edge of under linen the color and smoothness of Devonshire cream.

The room was large beneath a pitched roof with exposed beams. Everything was polished and perfect, thanks to Alison's compulsiveness and that of her mother, who had recently deeded her the house. He had also found a solid wooden hairbrush, large, of oval shape and stout handled, which he placed on the bench.

Alison emerged as the image of a pampered sorority girl, circa 1958, which greatly aroused him.

"Come over here, young lady," he said at once, reaching out and grasping her by the wrist then sitting down and pulling her over his lap. "No use putting this off!" David began to spank her in a way and for a length of time, which he judged proper to distract her from brooding about Freddie. "You see," he scolded, "you're a very bad girl. Not only do you smoke, but you're vindictive. Here you are being naughty just so you can brag to Freddie about it later."

"But that was your idea!" Alison protested.

"That may be so, but a nice girl wouldn't have agreed to it so readily. Would she?"

"What have I gotten out of being nice so far?" Alison turned her head to ask.

"Eyes forward, young lady!" David smacked her, pinching her velvety earlobe for emphasis. "And stop wriggling. This skirt is so thick. I'm going to raise it."

"So long as you've sufficiently admired it," said Alison complacently. David rewarded her impertinence with a series of very hard smacks. Then he pulled her skirt up smartly to reveal her sheer beige panties, seamed stockings and beige garter belt. Alison had a slim bottom, oval cheeked and pink on white, which glowed through the sheer nylon mesh of her snug, French cut briefs. David bestowed many compliments upon her luscious backside and toned thighs, while stroking them mildly. Then he began the spanking afresh, this time taking up the paddle-like hairbrush.

"A good, hard, hairbrush spanking should take your mind off that worthless boyfriend of yours," David said, unconsciously reading her thoughts as he steadied her across his lap and began to paddle her with the back of the brush. She whimpered and twitched but stayed in place as best she could. David saw she wanted to take a good spanking from him and paced the swats and their progressive severity accordingly.

Having been an obsessive and adoring spanking enthusiast since early childhood, spanking ladies was David's favorite form of entertainment and he therefore drew Alison's chastisement out for a considerable length of time. She reacted as one who had also been enthralled by spanking since toddlerhood and found no position more enjoyable to assume than the over the knee posture. To be held and spanked by a man like David was an activity that could never do other than enchant her. The encounter lasted nearly two hours, during which they moved in due course from the bench to the bed, though not before

David ascertained that Freddie did not have a key to the front door.

"You turned down the bed," said Alison, rubbing her pinkened bottom in the cheval glass opposite the bed while David finally lost his jacket and loosened his tie. The wine bottle was only half empty and now they paused to drink a glass.

"There's no turning back now Alison," David advised. "We won't have made a good job of this adventure until we've gone all the way." He sat on the edge of the bed and made her stand between his legs while he unbuttoned her outer garments and began to pull them off. Once she had been divested of her skirt, sweater and shell, he gently turned her back over his knee and patted her through the panties that she had pulled back up. She was grateful for the opportunity to hide her face while he told her his plans for the conclusion of the afternoon.

"Can we do it safely?" Alison asked, turning towards him.

"Safety first, my dear," said David, flourishing a modest but mighty brown wrapped Rough Rider condom for her approval.

"Do you always carry those?" she giggled. Whereupon he slapped her sternly.

"And why should I not be prepared, at all times, for an unexpected adventure?"

"But, you're married!" Alison protested, wriggling away from the hard whacks he was delivering with the hairbrush he'd just seized again.

"Yes, I'm married, not dead!" A firm six with the hair brush, evenly spaced and properly severe, caused her to take notice. "Now let that be the last discussion of our respective partners," David ordered, holding her and stroking her in a way that produced intense flutters in the pit of her stomach. "For the rest of the afternoon, you must think only of me." David unhooked her bra and slipped it off. Then he lifted her to the bed and arranged her on all fours, facing the mirror. She had a small, firm bosom saucily tipped with cherry nipples that were fully erect. He freed her long, straight brown hair from its velvet bow and caused it to stream down her back. "I want you to look in the mirror while I take you from behind so as to remember it in every detail the next time we meet, which will no doubt be on Monday at school."

"Oh David, won't you do one thing for me first?" Alison suddenly asked, sitting back on her heels.

"Of course," he agreed, in the process of discarding his tie and unbuttoning his shirt.

"Smoke a cigarette with me?"

"You're a little brat," he snapped, but none the less lit a cigarette and took one drag before handing it to her. "And you're getting a good strapping for that!"

He took off his belt and doubled it. Then he strapped her face down on the bed a hundred strokes, rather sternly throughout. Since David had long ago developed a flawless strapping technique from practicing so often on Hope's tender alabaster bottom while seldom if ever marking it, he quickly had Alison wriggling in submissive heat under the unremitting lashes that fell upon her exposed cheeks. David had pulled off her panties and Alison's excitement was becoming tangible.

"Have I mentioned that I plan to take you from behind?" said David. At which Alison could only whimper in abandon. Miniature climaxes rippled through her entire lower torso when he pressed his hand to the small of her back to deliver the last twenty strokes with his belt. Then she felt herself being pulled up into the all-fours position again and penetrated slowly, firmly and at last, very deeply, from behind.

David directed her gaze towards the mirror and she saw him with his hands pressed to her waist, himself stripped nude and lean, behind her and in her, holding and driving into her, pumping hard and deep, with masterful control. Feeling pre-orgasmic flutters ripple through her, she devoured the handsome angle on the action he'd arranged for her to see. And what she couldn't see, she felt deeply, for David had a sizable cock.

It was a visual memory she would retain forever, and one of the most compelling erotic images to ever be imprinted on her mind. That she looked so sleek and lovely being taken (by her new boyfriend on the side) was balm to her wounded female ego. Voyeuring themselves served as a powerful stimulant. Alison had never climaxed more than once or twice during a sex act. That afternoon she came more times than that.

"Cigarettes," she thought, "is there anything they can't do?"

But for David, Alison might have cried herself to sleep that night. As it was, she awoke on Sunday morning feeling beautiful, beloved, well rested and content. Forgiveness for Freddie's weakness flowed into her heart. She even imagined that he might be suffering in uncertainty. Just as these thoughts caused a frown to crease her brow the phone rang. She monitored it, found it to be Freddie and picked up.

"Hello, Freddie," she said unsteadily but differently nervous than yesterday. "How are you?"

"Terrible!" her lover cried, greatly cheered by the kind tone of her voice. "You don't completely hate me, do you Alison?"

"No. I don't hate you. But I'm very angry with you. You'd better come over and—take your medicine. At once!" Alison hung up before he could reply, thinking, "Now I've done it. There's no going back. But he's such a dear man. If this is what he wants, he should have it."

Alison had showered and dressed in a smoky blue polo sweater, black wool skirt and stack heeled pumps with a high vamp by the time he arrived some thirty minutes later. She had tea, buttered toast and his favorite cherry preserves ready and served him in the sitting room looking out on the rain drenched garden as though nothing whatever had happened the previous day.

Freddie, who was still trying to figure out her exact attitude, was wholly enjoying the swift reprieve, though he was too upset to eat his toast and mistakenly gulped his tea when it was far too hot. Alison looked so charming and seemed so calm. It was as though some fairy godmother had intervened on his behalf overnight to somehow lessen his offence.

"It seems I can't leave you alone for even a week," said Alison at length and with a steeliness that he had never before noticed in her. "You were supposed to be the dominant, the grown up, the one who could be relied upon to set a good example. And this is how you conduct yourself?"

"It was very wrong of me," he admitted, picking up his toast and putting it down again, then sighing and staring quite helplessly at

Alison, who was still on her feet and looking down at him with folded arms.

"I think you should be punished."

"Just don't exile me," he beseeched her. "I do love you so."

"Talk is cheap, Freddie. Do you agree that you ought to be punished, or not?"

"As long as it doesn't involve me not seeing you for any length of time."

Alison permitted herself one smile. He still didn't understand what she was talking about. Her modest, adorable Freddie didn't even understand that he was about to receive a gift.

"In that case, go up to my room, get my hairbrush and bring it down to me," said Alison coolly. Freddie, turning very red, nearly tumbled off the chair he'd been teetering on the edge of. "Freddie, what are you waiting for? You know damn well it's exactly what you'd do to me if our positions were reversed!"

"Alison, that would be silly," he protested. "It isn't like that between us, and it shouldn't be."

"No? Why shouldn't it?"

"Because I'm big and you're small."

Alison laughed with derision. "You're wasting my time. Get the hairbrush or get the hell out of my house! The only terms upon which I will have you back is if I am the dominant one in our relationship from now on!"

"What's this you're saying?" Freddie now sprang to his feet.

"I'm saying that everything has changed. And I'm saying get the hairbrush. And I'm not saying it again."

Freddie felt a horrible thrill as he met her flinty gaze.

"Alison, you can't possibly be serious about this," he protested, still unable to completely absorb what was happening. "It doesn't make sense. It's too radical a change," he further mused. "It could wreck our entire relationship."

"Fine, if you won't bring the hairbrush to me, I'll just have to bring you to it," said Alison, taking Freddie by the hand and leading him upstairs. He followed like a sleepwalker, his logical, analytical brain quarreling with his dormantly submissive heart all the way. "If I let her do this, she'll hate and despise me. We'll never be able to go back," he thought, desperately trying to make himself take back control but hopelessly enthralled by the sudden prospect of real discipline.

They entered her bedroom and she picked the hairbrush up off the dresser without relinquishing her hold on him, then drew him with her to the large, armless chair, upholstered in dark green nap, that generally served as the throne of her ginger cat. Alison sat down and putting Freddie on her right side pointed to his belt. "Undo that," she said and folded her arms to wait.

Instead of obeying her, Freddie knelt to her and took her hand. "Darling, I don't feel that this would be the proper thing for us to do," he said, kissing the back of her hand and rubbing it against his cheek. At this, Alison almost melted, almost believed him sincere. Indeed, at that moment, Freddie almost believed himself sincere. He only knew that he was a man and that men were supposed to make sacrifices to win fair ladies. To sacrifice the momentary pleasure of a spanking to ultimately preserve her respect seemed the very least he could attempt. For in Freddie's mind, the issue was no longer the infidelity, it was the exposure of his sexuality dichotomy and how that might adversely affect his first beautiful spanking relationship.

"I know exactly what's going on in your head," she told him. "You're afraid I'll think you less a man if you submit to me. Is that not so?"

"I know your opinion of men who submit," he replied, still holding her hand to his cheek.

"If you'd behaved properly when I was away we'd never have come to this pass," she said, finally pulling her hand away. "Therefore, you're going to have to live with each and every one of the repercussions. Including submitting to one who holds a poor opinion of men who do! And forfeiting the right to dominate her."

"Alison, I beg you not to keep saying that," Freddie said, torn once more between the urge to abandon himself to the most rapturous of sensations and the imperative to retain his masculine control over his girlfriend.

"Freddie, please stop arguing. I've told you how it has to be. If you find my terms for keeping you as my boyfriend unsatisfactory, you can leave right now. Personally, I think I'm being extremely kind. After all, you ran to that Aryan slut for discipline. If you'd only bothered to ask, you might have discovered that it's always been available to you right here. And then you wouldn't have had to break my heart like you did yesterday!"

"Oh Alison!" he sighed in defeat.

'That's right, Freddie, I'm determined to have my way in this. Now undo your belt and lower your trousers," said Alison, taking up the hairbrush. Freddie obeyed now as in a dream, doing as she said and then going over her lap.

"Right down across my lap, Freddie," she said, pushing him down.

"But I'll crush you," he protested.

"Never mind that," she advised, pushing his boxers and trousers down to his knees and pulling his blue chambray shirt tail up to reveal his athletic buttocks, softly downed with light hair and creamy white in hue. Alison rested the back of the hairbrush on his right cheek as she considered how she should start. She raised the hairbrush high, then paused and stopped with it against his bare skin again, remembered that Freddie had never spanked her harshly or hurtfully, but always kindly and well. She also wondered whether Freddie had ever been spanked in his life.

"Hold this," she told him, handing him the hairbrush and instead starting the spanking with her bare hand. It wasn't the first spanking she had given a male. One of her main disappointments in the New York scene, where she had first begun to play, was that so many of the men who answered her ad wished to be spanked much more than they wished to spank her! In the spirit of scene camaraderie, she had spanked at least a dozen different men. She knew how to give a warm up and when to become more serious. And she had also learned that what was sufficiently severe to satisfy her own most submissive needs, was often the starting point for a male. But she had also met more than one boy with no greater tolerance for pain than she, so she took nothing for granted with a new man. This case was of course quite different. This was the first time she was in love with the man she was spanking. And this was the first time she was actually punishing a man for an offence against herself, so that tenderness battled with cruelty in her heart. In the end she yielded to her greater affection for Freddie and only gave him a very sound, but not a severe first spanking.

His fair skin became pink so quickly! And merely from her hand. She very much wanted to ask him how he was, but forced herself to show not the slightest concern and instead finally asked for the hairbrush.

She had decided to give him one hundred strokes in sets of two on alternate cheeks. The brush stained his pink flesh magenta instantly and Freddie gasped as the blows rained down on his backside in a steady, measured rhythm.

After the hundred swats had been duly delivered and passively received Alison decided to drive the lesson home somewhat more harshly. Taking up the brush again, she administered an additional hard, fast two dozen swats on alternate cheeks in a way that had him wriggling and squirming by stroke three.

"Hold still!" she told him, tightening her grip on his trim waist, paying no attention to his gasps of shock and pain and adding another dozen smacks, even harder and faster for a rousing finish.

"There," she said, allowing him to slide off her lap. Before she had a chance to blink he had his clothes back up and was zipping and buckling himself into them. "Just a minute," she said, "Get back here. On your knees, just as you were before."

Freddie knelt to her and she forced him to look at her. He was still flushed, confused and undone. She grabbed a handful of his thick brown hair and forced him to look into her eyes. "Do you feel humiliated?" she asked sardonically, already the mistress in every way.

"Yes," he said, somewhat unhappily.

"You aren't going to resent me for those last three dozen are you? You know you had them coming for being such a cad."

"No," he replied, too dazed by his own emotions to respond to her sudden gentleness.

"In that case, I think you should probably go now. Spend the rest of the day thinking about our discussion and we'll see each other later tonight."

Freddie spent the rest of the day in an unknown land between euphoria and despair. The spanking had been splendid, exceeding all expectations. Every time he thought about the sternest portions of it, his cock throbbed violently. But when he remembered her codicil edict of his never being able to dominate her again, the entire situation made him dreadfully uneasy.

Alison had proven a wonderful dominant. And he was fairly sure that the novelty of today's situation had amused her on a certain level. But she was fundamentally submissive and Freddie felt she had painted herself into a corner with her threats of dominating him from now on. How long would it be before she got bored of the strain of being dominant over him? And how would they ever get back again to where they were supposed to be? For that matter, how long would he be able to adhere to her whims without rebelling? True, she had been divine today. Her dignified authority had never flagged for a moment. But how long could she pleasantly maintain an attitude so contrary to her nature? And how addicted might he become to this new side of Alison before she wearied of it?

He had always imagined it might be delightful to receive a moderate spanking, but he had never anticipated thrills so acute as those she had given him, just through the vigorous application of the hairbrush! Intensely stimulating was the only way to describe the sensations. Somewhat painful towards the end, but when she held him so firmly to her lap and placed her swats so carefully, even the sharpness of the sting was translated into a kind of caress.

Freddie would never know just how much her arm and shoulder ached from her exertions the following day. To give such a sustained and lusty spanking would have been nothing to him. Alison, on the other hand, realized that it behooved her to join the gym if only to strengthen her arms for the coming challenge of turning Freddie from a romping dominant into a tame submissive.

By dinner time, drained from giving in to the rapturous memories of his first real spanking, twice, Freddie was resolved to do everything in his power to change Alison's mind about him. Being spanked was all well and good. It had aroused him greatly. But he could get a spanking now and then from a professional dominant. They advertised in Hugo Sands' magazine. A spanking every 3 or 4 months, or maybe every other month, would be more than enough to satisfy his mild craving for such attentions. And Alison need never be bothered with that side of spanking again.

Freddie hopefully outlined this plan to her over pre-dinner cocktails at The Golden Owl Inn in Woodbridge. Alison was looking particularly handsome in a cranberry red wool dress with a chunky black leather belt and thigh boots. She listened to his idea without smiling and after he was finished simply sighed.

"No," she said. "I've told you how it's going to be. You can take it or leave it."

"But why, Alison, why? You know it's not like you to be like this with a man."

"I think it suits me to be like this with a man. I think I've always had it in me and it took you to bring it out. Perhaps you should just relax and enjoy it."

"Alison, you don't mean any of that."

"Tell me, Freddie. Can you feel it still? The spanking I gave you, I mean."

"No, of course not," he replied impatiently, feeling worse than ever about the turn of the conversation. He had been so convinced that Alison would like the idea of him seeing a pro dom now and then that he could scarcely believe she was continuing on with her outlandish plan.

"But you did feel it for an hour or so, right?"

"Yes," he replied, breaking breadsticks violently.

"You took it very well, by the way. I was impressed."

"Alison, why are you torturing me like this? You've gotten back at me, humiliated me. Isn't it time to forgive, forget and put it behind us?"

"Freddie, I really don't understand why you're fighting this. I'm only offering to give you what you've always wanted and never had. You're acting like I'm being mean to you."

"Damn it, Alison, you are being mean. Very mean!" he folded his arms on his chest for emphasis.

"You can still make love to me, just as you did before," she said, caressing his hand.

"Tonight?" he asked, clasping both of hers in his.

"Of course, tonight," she replied, vicariously aroused from the afternoon's unusual activity. She expected he'd be apt to take her forcefully that night and looked forward to yielding to him in at least this one small way.

"Thank god!" he said, clasping her to him like a parent who had just found a lost child. "I've never wanted you so badly!"

Alison smiled up at him and said no more.

Chapter Eight

Hope for Freddie

Several weeks later, it was Hope Spencer Lawrence, who rescued Freddie Johanson from the velvet hell of being Alison Albrecht's whipping boy, for almost purely selfish reasons.

After Alison learned of Freddie's intimacy with Polyxena, it was Hope's husband David who had repaired Alison's damaged ego, by being every bit as intimate with Alison himself! What Alison could not anticipate was David Lawrence electing to confide every detail of his altruistic strategy to Hope almost immediately thereafter.

Hope and David Lawrence had wed, just before departing Hollywood, while sharing the misapprehension that Random Point was the living stereotype of a puritanical New England village circa 1950, and that the Braemar Academy where David was to teach, was a bastion of rigid moral strictures. They discovered instead a rich vein of spanking enthusiasts concentrated in the tiny coastal village. The Braemar Academy they found to be a most progressive prep school, with students more sophisticated than their teachers. David and Hope realized that they had rushed to legitimize their union for no actual reason.

It wasn't that they didn't enjoy living together. If anything, their love had grown deeper while sheltered in the cottage on the cove. Hope worked in the enchanted bookstore where she held court daily at the coffee bar. They had friends in the scene who were charming to them and each had played separately with some of these new friends, without causing material damage to their relationship.

Neither of them wished to own the other, but this did not prevent them from becoming violently jealous of new rivals as they appeared.

And they did appear regularly. So they had made an agreement that to conserve their peace of mind and preclude any number of nasty surprises, which might be communicated to them through idle gossip, to share all relevant information about each other's adventures. Mostly they observed this agreement.

Therefore, the night of the first Alison encounter, while Hope stirred spaghetti sauce in the kitchen and David uncorked a bottle of wine, he exclaimed, "Poor Alison," in a most regretful tone.

"Why so?" Hope asked.

"Freddie Johanson made love to Polyxena Guzman."

"I knew something was up with those two!" Hope replied.

"She was so upset!" said David, handing Hope a glass of burgundy. "Alison."

"I thought Polyxena was a dominant. Isn't Freddie a dominant?"

"She went submissive to him," David explained.

"Polyxena's going submissive now, is she?" Hope said, chilled.

"I really felt I had to comfort Alison," said David, "and distract her from the pain of Freddie's betrayal."

"That's a strong word, isn't it?"

"According to Alison, Freddie made her promise not to date other men in the scene. And she had complied."

"Until today, I take it?" Hope asked, carelessly, in spite of the fact that her heart was thumping with jealousy.

"She needed something, Hope," said David selflessly.

"I expect she got it," Hope replied dryly.

"Polyxena loomed as a powerful threat in Alison's mind."

"I can fully understand that!" Hope cried sincerely.

"I didn't want Alison crying herself to sleep tonight," David explained.

"Which she undoubtedly would have done if not for your strictly humanitarian intervention," Hope agreed, gulping her wine and holding her glass out for a refill.

"I expect she'll forgive him no later than tomorrow."

"Will she tell him, do you think?" wondered Hope. "I mean about you?"

"No," David guessed with conviction.

Hope did not like any of this. Alison was assistant comptroller at Braemar and came into contact with her husband every day. There were thick woods behind the school that a pair of lovers could easily conceal themselves within during a long lunch hour. They might be sharing every break. They might even start leaving love notes on each other's desks if something was not done to bring this affair to an immediate halt.

It was becoming Hope's manner to tolerate the first transgression, then subtly manipulate to obviate the need for a second. So at once Hope set her busy brain to work on a plan for returning Alison fully to the keeping of Freddie Johanson. But it was not until a fortnight later that she had a chance to act upon it. For this was the first time she saw Freddie after the incident. It was late one Sunday afternoon when he walked into the bookshop shedding drops of rain from his old, cracked leather bomber jacket which Hope decided suited him well.

"Freddie, it's been weeks since you've been in," said Hope reproachfully.

"I know," he said with a sigh, sitting at the counter. "A lot has been going on."

"Really?" Hope started preparing a hazelnut coffee for him. "Anything you can discuss in mixed company?"

"Probably not," he replied with only the ghost of a smile.

"Why are you sad, Freddie? Is Alison giving you a hard time?" Hope placed his coffee before him.

"Why do you say that?" he looked at her with surprise.

"Well, if you must know, I heard about you and Der Lorelei," said Hope in a conspiratorial whisper.

"What's this you're saying now?"

"I know that you played with Polyxena," Hope replied.

"How do you know that?" Freddie looked perfectly astonished.

"David told me."

"David?"

"Yes, David, the one who comforted Alison the same day she found out about you and Polyxena."

"David comforted Alison?" Freddie repeated. "You mean he let her cry on his shoulder? Or something else?"

"Freddie, be yourself. Everything else, if I know David."

"You mean Alison has been with David?"

"I can't believe she's been keeping it to herself," Hope marveled. "I could never keep such a thrilling secret from someone who'd just cheated on me."

"Oh, I can believe it," said Freddie, more irritated with Alison than he had ever felt.

"So you see Freddie, she has no reason to continue to persecute you for what you did with Polyxena," Hope helpfully hammered home, refilling his cup. "Has she been just dreadful to you lately?"

"You have no idea!" Freddie replied.

"So, how was it with Polyxena?"

"I'm not exactly sure why she's been so nice to me," he replied with a characteristically modest smile.

"Maybe she likes that jacket," Hope said flirtatiously before rushing off to wait on another customer.

Freddie walked home in a spin, feeling sick with apprehension about David and Alison, but giddy with joy at finally having a valid reason for throwing off the yoke of female dominant oppression that had ruled him for the past two weeks.

It was anxious making to recall David and Alison together at break, sitting outside in the cold watching the kids play Lacrosse, she smoking, he sipping coffee from a silver bullet mug. Freddie felt a thrill of resentment, that Alison should prefer a man who wore a tailored tweed top coat, short brimmed hat and gloves when it was no cooler than 50 degrees! To Freddie, David was almost effete, a cynical, thin, sophisticate, of that long gone cocktail set you saw in films of the early 60's, a character who might have been portrayed by Mel Ferrer. Freddie felt he could blow David Lawrence over with one good breath. But Alison was obviously intensely charmed!

Freddie walked the two miles to Alison's house in the rain. She lived on the edge of the woods, just off Shadow Lane. He found her engaged in a typical Alison occupation, distressing a refectory table on her broad back porch facing the tawny woods. She was dressed in jeans rolled to midcalf and a tucked out oxford cloth shirt, with tassel loafers and thick woolen sox. Her long straight brown hair was arranged in a ponytail bound with a blue grosgrain ribbon and her face was rosy with her exertions in the chilly air.

"Oh, hi Freddie. Did you come to visit?" she asked pleasantly, while vigorously pounding divots into the new table with a mallet and awl.

"No, to talk about something important," he said in a tone that stopped her hammer in mid-air. She put it down on the table, took off her work gloves and quietly looked at him.

"Yes, Freddie?"

Unconsciously folding his arms and tapping his foot, he stared at her until she felt quite unnerved, and he remembered exactly what he'd decided to say.

"Alison, do you remember when I wrote you that letter, the one where I confessed to being with Polyxena?"

"Of course," Alison replied, her own chin going up and her arms folding defensively across her chest.

"Apart from the shock and annoyance you suffered, I think you appreciated the fact that I told you about it myself, rather than letting you hear it from someone else. Right?"

"Yes, I suppose so," Alison slowly replied.

"After all, knowledge is power," Freddie told her, walking off the porch and into Alison's woods to pick up the first slim, dry switch he found amidst the pine cones. Then he remounted the steps, leaned his back against the porch railing, took out his Swiss army knife and began to trim it.

"Freddie, what are you getting at?" Alison demanded.

"Alison, why didn't you tell me about you and David Lawrence?"

Alison blushed violently and stammered, "What about me and David?"

"Yes, what about you and David? Tell me your side of the story and I'll let you know if it matches the version I got straight from his wife!"

"David told his Hope that we..."

"Yes, they're honest with each other! Not sanctimonious

hypocrites, like someone I know!" Freddie vigorously pared his switch.

"And Hope told you?"

"Of course she told me. Can you blame her? In fact, I think she's depending on me to put a stop to this right now."

"There's nothing whatever to stop, Freddie. It was just something we did that once. And it was only because David felt sorry for me."

"That isn't true. It was because you two are crazy about each other."

"Anyway, it was only that once. And now we're even. Right?"

"You think so?" Freddie snapped.

"Sure. You cheated on me once, I cheated on you once. Even."

"Aren't you forgetting the emotional roller coaster you've put me on for the last two weeks? The humiliations? Your utter refusal to listen to reason? Do you think that's been fun?"

"Wasn't some of it fun? Aren't you glad you experienced one caning, one strapping, one birching, from someone who cared?"

"You should have been a lawyer," Freddie admitted, taken aback by the strength of her argument. "Some of it was too much fun and you know it."

"I meant no harm," she protested.

"What I object to was the element of force. You didn't give me a choice. Yes, you are an artist with a hair brush, but I absolutely hate being bossed around by you, Alison! And you know damn well I would never have let you get away with the insanity you've been inflicting on me if I'd known about your fling with David two weeks ago!"

Freddie had finished trimming the switch. Alison knew there was nothing more to be said. For the first time in weeks she felt butterflies in her stomach.

Freddie crossed the porch to Alison, who leaned back against her wooden table and looked up at him with a mute appeal for mercy in her doe eyes.

Pretending coolness but inwardly pulsating with excitement at her obvious fear, Freddie took her by her velvet earlobe and bent her face down over the table. Then placing his hand in the small of her back he laid the switch against her slim, blue jeaned bottom. He whistled it through the air several times, but didn't strike. She flinched and tried to bolt but he held her firmly against the table and began the switching forthwith, bringing it down across the centermost portion of her bottom, then once a little higher, and once a little lower, then back to the center, and so fourth, at least a dozen times, vigorously enough to cause Alison to cry out at every swat.

Then he ordered her to stand up, tucking the switch under his arm.

"Oh please, Freddie, you aren't going to use that dreadful switch on my bare bottom?" she asked, tears already forming in her eyes, which both melted and hardened him, but in different ways.

"Come over here, young lady," he said, ignoring her question but taking her by the arm and dragging her over to the porch steps, whereupon he sat down, dragging her across his knee. Then he broke the switch in half, tossed one half away, and pinned one of her slender wrists to her waist before continuing to use the shortened switch on her denim clad bottom some two dozen more times.

He became so caught up in the thrill of switching Alison's blue jeaned bottom hard and fast that he never noticed that she was sobbing until the end of the twenty four swats. Then he noticed her distress and turned her around on his lap to cradle her in his arms.

Getting out a handkerchief he mopped her face dry and kissed her several times on her soft, full, mouth. Then he said, "I wish I hadn't made you cry - so soon!"

Chapter Nine

The Diary of Susan Ross IV

October 24,

    Never would I have expected Anthony, the best of men, to be mean spirited about anything -- no less the upcoming nuptials of my best friend!

    Yet that was exactly his reaction when we disclosed our witty plan for her to wed dear P.C. in full bridal regalia on the night of Hugo's Halloween party next week in Random Point.

    Anthony was hidden behind the The Times when we made the announcement, and didn't throw the paper down to glare at us until we added our hope that we'd be permitted to hold the actual ceremony at the Cliff house, which Anthony habitually opens to Hugo's party guests during the later half of the party.

    "Oh god, Oh god, Oh god!" he cried, lunging at the sideboard, grabbing a decanter of whiskey and sloshing a few ounces into his coffee. After gulping and shuddering deeply he narrowly eyed us and demanded, "Why? Why? Why?"

    "Because I want to wear a glorious bridal gown," Diana explained guilelessly, "but not solemnly. If we engage a Justice of the Peace to casually perform the ceremony during the party, we can play bride and groom to the hilt as part of the masquerade without bringing the rest of the world to a measured halt."

    "I mean why must you marry at all?" Anthony burst out impatiently, startling Diana into speechlessness.

    "Well, I am 22 after all!" she finally said. As if Anthony would ever begin to understand how important it seems for girls of our age to be married! I've tried to explain it to him several times.

"People like us shouldn't marry," he warned her. "I've been married five times, so I know."

"What do you mean, people like us?" she cried, taken aback by his vehemence.

"Easy ones," he replied. Diana could but blush, remembering that Anthony knew her whole history and had himself augmented it.

"Just because P.C. and I happen to be polyamorous, that doesn't mean we can't be happily married," Diana pointed out.

"Do you know how old he is?"

"Just about your age," she replied; "But if it doesn't bother me, why should it bother you?" she wondered.

"It bothers your parents, I'll warrant!" Anthony cried triumphantly.

"They're being prigs about the whole thing," she fretted.

"I'm glad that they don't want to come!" I said cheerfully. "How else could we have managed a scene wedding?"

"It's absurd," snapped Anthony, making himself another Irish coffee.

"P.C. loves the unconventionality of our idea," protested Diana.

"Oh god!" Anthony groaned again.

"But that doesn't mean he wouldn't stand up in church with me or anywhere else if I asked him to." Diana was beginning to get angry!

"That's because he's an idiot!" Anthony rejoined.

Diana opened her mouth to reply but seemed on the verge of either sobbing or screaming and looked at me for support.

"Does this mean you don't want to give Diana away?" I asked.

"Don't you understand? P.C. isn't doing this to placate me. He thought this up entirely on his own!" Diana insisted before turning her back on us.

"It's true," I explained to my irritable master. "Ever since Diana moved into that apartment of Hugo's in Back Bay, P.C.'s been asking her to marry him five times a day." (It's been more like once every five days.) "They are bondagers, you know. Part of their fantasy involves her being under his control. Doesn't making her his wife fit in with that?"

Anthony is starting to depress my spirits with his cynical attitudes towards marriage. He never denigrates love. But the concept of marriage drives him nearly to despair. He keeps forgetting that he himself was intrigued enough to try the adventure 5 times. Though he's told me time and again that marriage is the death of love, I still long to experience that change of situation.

"All right," he said brusquely, "you can do it at my house. But I'll be damned if I'll give her away or play Lohengrin!"

I couldn't believe Anthony was being so unkind! Diana did start sobbing then. I took her to a love seat and glared at him while I caressed and soothed her. Finally he relented and gave her the congratulatory embrace she had been waiting for. Still he couldn't resist passing a few additional remarks about anyone who could actually fetish the state of wedlock.

"I shouldn't be given away anyway," Diana told me during lunch when we met at Bonwit Teller's to view bridal gowns. "It would annoy P.C. to be handed me by another man."

"I agree. You give yourself freely as an adult," I told her, spotting the gown of our dreams, tailored according to the daintily feminine lines of the mid-1950's, with a fitted bodice and bell shaped skirt.

I couldn't bear to try on any wedding gowns but assisted Diana. We had the perfect one fitted and charged it to the Chipper Knight account. I almost fell down when I saw how much of P.C.'s money Diana was presuming to spend, but according to Diana, he has pots of it.

I brought Diana up to the studio to construct our guest list for Halloween, thinking: why shouldn't we work on Diana's wedding invitation in the studio? She was marrying our big boss after all.

"Who's your friend?" Onslow Stiller had the nerve to demand, eyeing Diana with typical insolence. "Lunch is over, you know." He was leaning over my monitor and soaking in every delicious Diana detail with those ice chips he uses for eyes.

"It's okay, Onslow. This young lady is soon to be Mrs. Currie," I explained to my surly, sometimes playmate.

"Oh?"

Diana ingenuously purred up at him, "Oh, aren't you the one who's pony-hung?" Onslow went red in the face and quickly returned to his station, not knowing what to think. "He is so cute!" she whispered to me, gazing at him long and hard. Onslow sat behind his hooded screen, unable to tear his eyes away from us.

"You'd better not do that," I whispered, to stop her from peeking, winking and waving at Onslow during our guest list construction. "It's my belief that P.C. has cameras all over the place."

Before we'd finished the list Onslow was back at my desk, demanding to know whether where we were going for lunch. Diana gave me a look that I have come to interpret as: I want him!

I told Onslow that we'd already had lunch but would join him for an early dinner, which made the Swedish ice floes in his head dilate into pools of chilled chartreuse. Yes, that uncivilized man was being favored again. There's something about that iron hard face of his that melts girls like Diana and me.

We picked up a little light dinner, a few bottles of wine and went straight to Onslow's loft after work. I'd like to say I didn't watch, but it was an intense little bachelorette party. I told Onslow Stiller what would be required. He had everything necessary. She went limp in his arms the moment he touched her.

Luckily Onslow isn't sensitive enough to resent being used by us. Give him a girl he can sodomize and he questions not. And I did. That stuff about a male code of honor, men not fucking their buddies' girlfriends, wives, etc., is the bunk, I've found. Onslow has been friends with P.C. for longer than Diana and I have been born, but did it even occur to him not to accept the gift of Diana? Even if he hadn't had two or three vodkas first, it wouldn't have made the slightest difference.

I instructed Onslow to tie her down over a hassock with a cord around her waist and one at the knees, and her wrists together behind her back, then spank her with his open hand for at least twenty minutes. But I had him untie her before penetrating her from behind. She is my best friend and he's huge. I didn't want her pinned like a helpless butterfly. She told me later I ought to have left her tied.

After Onslow had her from behind he wanted to sodomize her too. Diana whimpered no, she couldn't. No, it was too big. No, no, no. I gave him the nod and he proceeded. She wriggled and sobbed to get away. I told him to slap her until she stopped doing that. Onslow knew me well enough to follow my instructions and slapped her bottom with his big, hard hand many times, until she agreed to let him spread her cheeks and penetrate her anally.

She cried and squirmed! I urged him to spank her until she became completely docile. He slapped her bottom and forced it apart, nudging his large cock ever so deftly into her extremely tiny bottom hole. I trusted Onslow because I'd been in Diana's position. This man has learned the art of sodomy the way some learn to play piano. He'd mastered it. Diana sobbed and sighed at once. He was in -- smoothly and painlessly in. It must have been the helpful spanking. I sipped my wine and watched in a delightful state of vicarious arousal.

I returned Diana to P.C.'s before he was due home from a business dinner, leaving her ample time to luxuriously bathe and await her fiancé's arrival.

I was restless and still painfully aroused by what I had witnessed between Onslow and Diana when I walked into the house through Dennis' pantry found Anthony sitting in the kitchen eating a sandwich and reading the paper. Dennis was out that night and the food had been delivered. He was half way through a bottle of wine, from which I poured myself a glass.

He smiled, then remembered to be grouchy instead.

"I know why you're being so horrid about Diana's wedding," I announced. "It's because you're afraid I'm going to start whining about how I want to get married too!"

Anthony just looked at me.

"Well, you don't have to worry about that," I assured him. "If you say marriage is a bore, I will take your word for it, as you're more experienced in these matters."

Anthony was pleased and took me into the sitting room, where a fire had been lit, and sat me on his lap. He said gallantly, that although he'd had many wives, he'd only ever had one mistress, and I'd lasted longer than any of the wives as well as making him happier. Since he was being so civil I, in turn, humbly apologized for forcing him to get involved in a marriage ceremony of which he disapproved.

He read the invitation in my statement and emphatically joined in my condemnation of myself, telling me that I should have known better and adding that it had thrown him off his work all day. Then I knew I was getting spanked.

As Anthony began to spank me vigorously over my wool flannel knickers, I revealed where I'd been earlier in the evening, and what I had seen.

"You are bad!" Anthony told, me with a connoisseur's appreciation. "But who is this Onslow Stiller? You've barely mentioned him before," he said, pushing me off his lap. I jumped up and retreated across the room, really feeling the heat of his hand even through my trousers. "And how do you know him so well to trust him doing those things to Diana? Huh?"

I admitted that I knew Onslow Stiller only from one or two insignificant, post-happy hour adventures that we'd had, stressing that he was crude, gruff and bore only the most passing resemblance to Lars Hansen in Flesh and The Devil.

Anthony shrewdly observed that I must have let Onslow have me in every possible way before deciding to give him Diana like that.

"Not recently!" I replied.

"You see! This is exactly what I mean about you girls. Neither of you have any business whatever thinking of marriage!"

"I'm not!" I replied, still feeling the sting of his hand.

"I ought to enlighten P.C.," Anthony threatened.

"Oh, please don't!" I cried. "After all, he's a terrible slut himself."

"It's all so wrong. So unnecessary."

"Well, I think P.C. is a darling to marry our girl," I ventured, with space between us. "I love him for allowing her to add his initial to her monogram. It shows he has a very big heart!"

"And a very vacant brain," Anthony retorted, unmoved by my eloquence and irritable again with the marriage talk. Feeling a lump in my throat, I ran off to my room. As he didn't follow, I ended up soaking my pillow with tears. He'd upset me so that I forgot how much I wanted to be made love to. Finally I fell asleep.

I awoke in the middle of the night feeling terribly disconcerted. I thought I'd die if Anthony had gone out. Found him sitting up in bed watching Flesh and the Devil. Got into bed with him and let him pull me across his lap and spank me again. I felt that he was jealous of Onslow and this gave me joy. After he made love to me, he held me in his arms and praised me for being so mature for my age.

I must now force myself to be as mature as he thinks I am, and not torment myself as to why I cannot also enjoy bridal status. I'll just have to enjoy the state vicariously, through Diana. She will be happy to allow this and P.C. will have no objection to my hearing of their little intimacies. He is v. fond of me, himself.

In all, it was rather an overly full day!

October 30,

Anthony finally came to his senses today and began behaving as he ought to have done re: Diana from the start. As soon as we arrived in Random Point, we had tea at the bookstore, served by Hope, too flirtatiously - her husband should spank her more, or harder, then proceeded to Damaris' dress shop to select an exquisite trousseau. I knew Diana would be touched by a brocaded corselet, a diaphanous negligee and gown set, wool dresses, skirts, vests, sweaters, and cocktail dresses in velvet, silk and satin, plus matching jackets and gloves. When Anthony started adding numerous pairs of shoes I knew she would also be deeply aroused. But he had a lot to make up for. And he knew it.

Then we went around the village buying her all sorts of other wedding presents from the tiny shops, lingering until they all closed. When we got to the house, Diana was already in her bedroom, trying on the wedding gown. We went up with the presents, Dennis helping us get most of them out of the car. She was overwhelmed and went pink in the face, clung to Anthony and pretty much sobbed for joy. He looked at me over her dark head with an expression I interpreted to mean: Bachelorette Party Part 2 commencing in ten and counting.

Then PC called from the Ball and Feather. I told him I would meet there and entertain him for a while, thinking that maybe A. would feel even more relaxed about expressing his sincere affection for Diana if I were from the house.

PC was arranging his outfits for the weekend when I was admitted to The Magistrate's Suite. He had chosen a tux for tomorrow night and was delighted to hear an inventory of the lingerie we had equipped Diana with for their honeymoon in Italy. PC opened a bottle of wine and we drank to the bride and talked about how much fun we would all have together in the coming years. PC waxed eloquent upon the notion of Diana becoming officially his. Then he couldn't help remembering that he never would have met Diana if I hadn't had the temerity to go looking for my own master at Surrender that night, bringing Diana with me. P.C. became sentimental.

Then I suddenly seemed to find myself in his arms. He wished to relive the night before I left for Europe. I let him bend me over a sofa arm. He wouldn't let me go until I'd yielded to him in every way and made sure I did so by pinning my wrist to my waist and slapping my bottom repeatedly. Finally I gave in and let him penetrate me anally. (I guess I must really like him.) After which I again asked him for a raise and he again refused, reminding me of how much I had let her spend on the wedding dress.

On the way home, I stopped at Hugo's. He and Laura gave me dinner. I told them I didn't know what to wear tomorrow night and Hugo showed me a charming black velvet Little Lord Fauntleroy suit he'd bought for Laura, but which was too small for her. I tried it on and it fit me perfectly. Anthony will love it.

I wanted to stop at Michael Flagg's on the way home but realized that would be too decadent on top of letting PC have me again. I did stop at Hope's cottage just to find out what she was wearing tomorrow. But she was at belly dancing class. David was at home, however and we had a long chat. We had just begun seriously flirting when Hope walked in. While she was in the bedroom trying putting on her belly dancers' skirt and midriff for me to see, David looked at me meaningfully.

We agreed to try to get away together during tomorrow's various festivities. I have never been caned by a real school teacher and would like to experience that. Hope came out in the dancing girl outfit and looked enchanting. I left her to seduce her husband and proceeded to William's house. William was at the gym but Damaris was at home and showed me her outfit for tomorrow, a stunning Cleopatra costume.

We talked about the shop and Pamela Crane. Damaris told me Pamela was not a good girl. Even though she has that nice Sloan Taylor in love with her, she is running after Hugo Sands! Pamela, enamored of my sister's boyfriend? That is scary, considering how pretty and elegant Pamela is. I have complete faith in Laura's ability to continue fascinating Hugo, but here is certainly a dangerous rival. I was eager for all the details but Damaris didn't know any. I must quiz Sloan on this!

When I finally got home everyone had gone to bed!

November 1,

It was everything a Halloween ball should be, including surprises. For example, Polyxena Guzman's submissive boyfriend Dieter Brant practically flipped when he walked into a room where his mistress had decided to descend her pedestal for 20 minutes in order to allow Michael Flagg to tie her to a whipping post and flog her.

First Dieter marched to down to the bar, demanded and tossed back a double peppermint schnapps! Then, (and I actually saw this!) when Polyxena emerged from the library in which she had been sequestered with M. Flagg, Dieter summoned the raw nerve to grab his dominant by her shell-like earlobe and drag her over to a hall settee where he flung her down and began to lecture her in either Dutch or German rapid fire. I was agog and moved closer to hear and see what would happen next, casually pretending to study the portrait gallery.

I was soon amazed and gratified to see the wiry physical trainer sit right down beside the beautiful European goddess and administer a sharp little cuff to her right cheek. Polyxena's hand flew to her face and she blushed magenta at her slave's effrontery. She tried to rise but he pulled her back down and then straight across his lap! Dieter spanked her right there in front of me and several other passing guests on the second floor landing, and vigorously!

Polyxena struggled to get free. She kicked and yipped. He just kept spanking her through her black velvet gown and scolding her in his guttural tongue. I suspect this was the first time he ever turned her over knee but I bet it won't be the last. He had caught her going submissive to someone and I suppose felt cheated. When Dieter released her she was red as a rose and sparks shot from her blue eyes. She then ran down the stairs. He looked after her then saw me staring at him. He gave me a stern glance, as much as to say, say one thing and you'll get the same! I scampered down the stairs after Polyxena.

Hope Lawrence introduced me to a man named Ambrose Bartlett whom she said owned a department store. He took me into the library and spanked me over his knee. I liked him! Especially when he said I could come to his store tomorrow and choose a present for being so obliging as to let him spank me bare bottom on such short acquaintance. Hope told me later he lets her go on shopping sprees at his store in return for spanking sessions. Later on I met his fiancée, Paula Rohan, a delectable blond guidance counselor at Braemar. Hope told me that she and David had had a spanking affair, but that Ambrose Bartlett had put a stop to it. Hugo Sands had brokered that relationship too, on Hope's instigation. Still later in the evening, Hope introduced me to Carl-Adam's brother Freddie Johanson and his girlfriend Alison Albrecht. Alison is yet another submissive with whom David has had a brief affair. Looking at Hope I wondered why David was finding it so hard to remember he was married. Hope told me he was just living up to being her husband.

Next I had a significant encounter with Malcolm Branwell. We went down to the wine cellar to bring up a few more bottles and got bogged down for at least a half hour there. He is very new to spanking girls at parties and still takes a gee whiz delight in the privilege. He loved my ruffled panties under the black velvet knickers. Yummy interlude but really perfectly well behaved. He is Marguerite's husband and she doesn't quite share Hope's attitudes on the annexing of spouses.

Then I ran into Lupe and Carl-Adam on the first floor. They had been dancing, (handsomely tricked out like a G.I. and WAC from the 40's or 50's in beautifully tailored khakis), but happily came up to my room to smoke. This Carl-Adam is an interesting boy. 6'4" or 5" I should think, with lovely, huge hands and thighs. In the retro uniform and crisp crew cut he portrayed a slice of smartly masculine Americana that would have girls lining up for spankings from him all night. The fascinating thing is that his brother, Freddie, who works at

Braemar, where Lupe went to prep school, is also in the scene! Just as it runs in my family, it runs in the Johanson bloodline! We discussed that with great interest. I could see Carl-Adam looking at me with even greater. As Diana's best friend I was somewhat sacred to him, which I liked. But I also wanted him to give me just a little spanking over his knee. What a big hand he has! Just charming.

Randy Price tried to pull me into the billiards room, which was empty, but I ran away, bumping into Polyxena. We looked at each other and remembered that I had recently witnessed her shame. Then William (dressed as Ramses) passed, and noting our complimentary costumes, (her Victorian black velvet gown and my black velvet knicker suit), persuaded us to pose for some photos for his album. (Naturally some shots of her spanking me!) I agreed with the stipulation that I could choose some of the images to make drawings from. Of course, Polyxena very much wanted to be photographed as dominant in that devastatingly beautiful gown that clung to her waist and cleavage so dramatically.

We went up to the solarium to take the stills, posing on a marble bench. Then PC and Diana passed by and William snagged them for photos also. Polyxena and I stood by arm in arm and watched the tiny bride pose across the groom's massive lap. Polyxena, of course, didn't know that these were true wedding photos. But William did.

I could tell that Diana was thrilled to pose in this position in her fairy wedding gown while PC delicately raised layer after layer of petticoat to arrive at her pristine white bottom, wrapped in pearly white silk satin. PC also seemed taken with the spectacle. The whole evening seemed to amuse the hell out of him. After all, they've only known each other a couple of months. They're at the beginning of their love and scarcely ever spend time together. I'm certain those moments were exquisite for both of them. How they will enjoy perusing those adorable photos of themselves later on.

After that, I went down to the music room, where Anthony was at the piano surrounded by guests, and Sloan Taylor had just walked in, in sunglasses, with his hair slicked back and a summer suit straight out of La Dolce Vita. He was very tall, very sexy and suddenly looked very much more Italian than ever before.

I went up to him, linked arms and brought him over to the bar to request a Cosmopolitan from Dennis. Across the room, Pamela, in a breathtaking Renaissance gown of midnight blue satin brocade set off by magnificent costume jewelry, looked at us before giving her full attention to a tall, striking Clark Kent, whom I recognized later in the evening as Michael Flagg in glasses with his hair dyed blue-black and slicked back.

Soon Hope joined us, in her exotic outfit. Anthony had bribed her into dancing for us while he played Little Egypt type hooch piano. She had performance anxiety and protested repeatedly that she had only had three lessons so far and was the worst student in the class. But no one knows how to bribe like Anthony, for he planned to enjoy the best view of Hope undulating her perfect bottom in the pearl and velvet trimmed sheer blue chiffon skirt. Her cap sleeved midriff top was closely fitted in the Indian style, and her wavy blonde hair floated to her waist. Enchanting. Her husband David was nowhere to be seen at that moment, but I ran into him later, as a rather dashing buccaneer. However, I never did get my caning!

I discovered that for a greater portion of the evening David was kept busy tracking a couple of teenagers from his senior lit class who had been cruising around, spotted he and Hope on the way to the party, followed them, and got in, dressed in their prep school uniforms as though they were costumes. David didn't even run into them until they'd been soaking up interior color for an hour! Luckily, both are eighteen, but was he mad! Apparently Hugo told them they could stay if they would each submit to a spanking, which made the kids hoot with laughter. They willingly agreed, enchanted to be at a sophisticated masquerade ball with their favorite instructor and his ravishing wife. Marguerite dragged the good looking blond boy in the shorts, blazer and knee sox off to a private room for his initiation.

The girl, a tiny slip of a brunette, more imp than female, was already half lit on champagne when Hugo laid hold of her and turned her over his knee to give her a very mild spanking over her black and yellow plaid skirt. Then she leaned up and whispered something to him, which I later discovered was something to the effect of, "My boyfriend spanks me much harder than that!" Hugo then flipped up the skirt to reveal her tiny bottom in pure white cotton Calvin Klein panties, which he presently paddled smartly. In a couple of seconds she was squirming and begging to be released. But as soon she was, she went back to giggling and jumping up and down with excitement at being there with us. David was shocked beyond words at what he was witnessing but a few drinks took the edge off that.

As a sidebar I'd like to add that this surprising ingénue, whose name is Gigi, wasn't satisfied until she'd been over the knee of every man in the house, including that of her initially reluctant teacher, David Lawrence. Except for myself, I have never seen someone so young plunge into the scene with such unabashed gusto. I must know this newcomer better!

While I was complimenting Sloan on his Marcello look Marguerite made a spectacular entrance as Barbarella. Malcolm seemed to wish to melt into the wall whenever anyone made a fuss about her costume. He was simply clad in a monochromatic grey on grey shirt and suit. I then saw him checking Sloan out and heard him pass a remark about Sloan's sunglasses being pretentious since it was night. He just didn't get it that Sloan was paying homage to Fellini's decadent period here. (He's still burning over Sloan having Marguerite that once, which was really neither of their faults, just a chemical reaction.) But Malcolm has a lot of nerve being so edgy about Marguerite after the way he let Hope give him a b.j. in the shop that day!

Clark Kent's head certainly turned when Marguerite entered, which similarly irritated Malcolm. Unfortunately, whenever Malcolm goes to any sort of scene party he runs into men who have had his wife at every sofa cushion. Same thing happens with Anthony and me, but Anthony doesn't care.

I saw Pamela bristle when her companion gazed lingeringly at Marguerite; then Pamela abruptly strolled away from Michael to hold a conversation with Pascal Robbins, that photographer who took her to Europe last year. Diana and I teased the hell out of him last party trying to get him to play with us, though I'm not really sure he is one of us. His wife, Phoebe is though. They came dressed for a 50's prom, he in a dinner jacket, and she in a luscious chiffon gown with a poufy skirt and form sculpting surplice bodice. Her full creamy bosom and tiny girlish waist, counter pointed by those seductively womanly hips scored her a perfect ten for ultra femininity. I know Anthony agreed, for the moment Phoebe appeared, he seemed to forget all about dear Hope. Luckily, our inexperienced dancer was rapidly exhausted by her gyrations, though the audience could have watched her sway and shimmy for an hour, and was relieved to yield the spotlight to Phoebe, whose classically trained voice had delighted Anthony at the previous party when he had accompanied her.

As much as I wanted to keep my eye on Anthony and Phoebe, who looked even prettier than I remembered her, tonight with her shiny brown hair in a tight, elegant upsweep, I was also intrigued by the Sloan-Pamela dumb show. Pamela couldn't keep her eyes off us and Sloan persisted in pretending not to notice. As soon as Marguerite drifted away I asked Sloan why he hadn't escorted Pamela to the party and why she was keeping so strangely aloof.

"Oh, that's down to me," said Sloan, finishing his first drink quickly and politely requesting a second. "But I shouldn't discuss such things."

"Sure you should. Make that a double for Sloan, Dennis," I said soothingly, stroking the raw silk of his jacket sleeve.

"Anyway, you can confide details of an intimate nature to me, because we have been intimate."

"I don't see where that follows," Sloan protested.

"Have you two broken up? I hope not, because I recall she goes into a decline."

"She's in one right now, but not over me," the second martini induced Sloan to declare.

"So the rumor about her and Hugo is true?"

"You know about it?" Sloan snapped.

"Well, my sister is his girlfriend," I explained.

Sloan then told me that a few weeks ago, Pamela confessed that she and Hugo had made love once in the back of the shop. (Random Point shops seem to double as motels these days!) Sloan said he had temporarily suspended relations with Pamela but was not opposed to resuming them at some future date.

"Hugo takes all his submissives sooner or later," I pointed out.

"You oughtn't to let such a little thing keep you apart this winter. See how she's looking at you!"

"I don't feel the least resentment towards Hugo or Pamela for expressing their animal spirits. But I need to distance myself from her until she's over him."

"Fine, but tonight she's a Florentine princess. Couldn't you at least let her know how stunning she looks?"

"It's not that simple!" Sloan insisted, putting out his glass for another round.

'Wouldn't you adore to see what's under that skirt?" I tempted him.

"It's a pannier. I doubt I could even gain access to her bottom under that device."

"Then take her up to my bedroom, strip her dress and cage off and enjoy."

"No!"

I told him he was becoming a true dom, arrogant and indifferent, and left him to rush across the room and greet Portia and Monty, who had just arrived, dressed in replicas of costumes from Forbidden Planet, a great visual success! They had brought a Justice of the Peace, dressed, (at our expense) as an old fashioned parson, in keeping with the Halloween spirit. This person was not in the scene and we had determined to hustle him up to the solarium, have him perform the ceremony as rapidly as possible and then eject him with a handsome tip at the same speed, hoping he didn't gawk too much on the way in and out at the various players who were disporting themselves all over the house by that time. Dressed as he was and looking about himself in amazement as we dragged him up the stairs, he gave the impression of a fairly good Christian of several centuries past being led through the gates of purgatory.

"Someone's marrying here?" he gasped as Marguerite bounded up the stairs ahead of us to clear the solarium of all but the selected ceremony guests. Meanwhile, I dispatched Dennis to collect everyone. When we finally assembled upstairs we were: PC and Diana, Portia and Monty, Marguerite and Malcolm, Lupe and Carl-Adam, Hope and David, Hugo and Laura, Anthony, Dennis and me. The room was moonlit from above and candles glowed on sconces all around the circular perimeter. Champagne, glasses and a sinful dark chocolate and raspberry wedding cake with a tiny Sir Distic D'Arcy and Sweet Gwendolyn on top, were already in place on a marble table.

Diana, who had been practically pulled off someone's lap and summoned upstairs with the arrival of the Justice of the Peace, appeared intoxicated with excitement. Her face was flushed and she couldn't stop laughing at whatever was said. I think she'd already had three or four glasses of champagne.

The ceremony was over in 3 minutes and then the little parson was lavishly tipped and escorted out of the house by Monty, who returned in time to be the last to kiss the bride, which privilege he drew out to such a degree that PC offered to sock him if he didn't let Diana go.

Other guests began to pass through the room, unaware that anything usual had just taken place. One of them was the daintily voluptuous Phoebe Casper, Pascal Robbins' wife, that little thespian songbird that Anthony's patronage has already helped land a couple of plum engagements in Manhattan. When Phoebe said she had to speak to me in private, I led her out to the hall where we then met Pamela, whom Phoebe then decided to include in our conspiratorial circle. I led them into the peacock blue sitting room to conduct our meeting.

Phoebe was blunt as she begged Pamela and I to distract her jealous husband Pascal so that she could play with a few people at the party. Pamela agreed to take the first shift and went off in search of Pascal while I asked Phoebe who she meant to play with. Phoebe blushed (!) and murmured, Anthony, if I didn't mind. (Saw that coming!) I assured her (with a thumping heart) that she could not have picked a better partner and redoubled Pamela's promise to keep her husband engaged for at least the next 45 minutes. Phoebe embraced me and rushed off to make good use of her time.

Pamela wisely grabbed a bottle of Chivas and a glass and dragged Pascal into the billiards room. They were still shooting pool and mildly flirting when I tracked them down a half hour later. All was going well. When Pascal asked me if I'd seen Phoebe I reported that she was still accompanying Anthony. It wasn't exactly a lie. I made sure to remain with them until Phoebe actually appeared in the room, her face glowing seraphically. Whether Pascal later discovered what happened to Phoebe in the intervening hour, I won't know until I see her next.

A few moments later, Anthony joined us, apparently also in an excellent mood. He pulled me aside and said he wanted to give me a present but we had to go out to get it. I put on my black velvet cloak and a tiny, jaunty hat and we went out together in the car. We drove down into the village until we reached the end, just past Marguerite's house, then up a gentle two block hill, at one side of which sat the village graveyard. Surmounting the hill on either side of the road were just a couple of old Victorian painted ladies, slim, three story structures of the 1890's, each of which commanded a handsome view of the narrow, rocky coast line at the very tip of town. We parked across from the cemetery and I waited for him to pull out a jewelry case.

Anthony said he knew I was disappointed that I couldn't have a wedding but was delighted at how good I was being about it, so he'd decided to give me something really nice for a change. I protested out loud that the jeep had been really nice, not to mention the Biedermeier desk. He pulled out a set of keys and handed them to me.

They were the keys to the grey painted lady, the one with cream and pink trim on the graveyard side of Shadow Lane. He explained it isn't very large, just four bedrooms. And needs a good deal of work, which he will see to. Diana can help me decorate my own personal playhouse in any girly way that we choose. It's just a few minutes walking distance from Marguerite's, the bookstore, Hugo's, the inn, everywhere in the village.

We got the flashlight out of the trunk and went inside. It smelt very musty but I saw its potential at once, given Anthony's deep pockets. In addition to the four bedrooms, each floor also has a few little half rooms, which perhaps served as maid's quarters or sewing rooms in the house's original usage. Anthony suggested that each one of these could be transformed into perfect little disciplinaria, for example, a caning room, a strapping closet, a flogging chamber, etc. He said William would be happy to plan them perfectly for me, just as he had done for Michael and Damaris when they were married and first lived in the cottage in the woods. Anthony said William had just hired a new carpenter who he suspected was one of us and would send this boy over to do the work on the house for us.

I didn't have much time to contemplate my beautiful present because Anthony thought we should be returning to our guests. Indeed, the party had begun to simmer a little warmer in our absence.

I discovered Marguerite sequestered with Dennis in my dressing room, him at her feet, stroking her suede boots as they rested against him. She had been feeding them both sips of Anthony's best champagne almost since we'd been gone and attempting to reconcile herself to Malcolm being closeted with Polyxena in one of the upstairs bedrooms for almost the last hour. Naturally, she didn't dare disturb them. This was the first party where Malcolm was really starting to seem comfortable about playing. But an hour was a long time and Polyxena was a capricious white blonde goddess just suddenly turned submissive, radiating pheromones from every cultured pore. Both Marguerite and Dennis had become somewhat tipsy but only I could tell this. Dennis sat with his cheek against the lacings of her boots and inhaled their leather scent contentedly. But when I entered, he sprung up. Marguerite was surprised at this but waited until he went to get me the drink I asked for until commenting.

I explained that ever since I had allowed Dennis certain liberties with me, given him a taste of the other side, he hadn't liked to be so submissive around me anymore. Marguerite was shocked that I had allowed Dennis to lay hands on me and thought it the height of folly to turn a sub into a dom. Especially a servant, she added. Dennis returned with my miniature bottle of coke and opened it for me. He was perfectly polite but his eyes burned into mine.

When Marguerite strolled out to discover whether the new Lorelei of Random Point had yet released her husband, Dennis stunned me with a kiss on the lips, then apologized by kissing my hand and fled the room mumbling that he would see if he was needed. He is getting so bold and so bad!

I followed him down to the kitchen where I watched him give the catering staff succinct orders. He seemed quite composed. I stared at him until he noticed me, which made him blush. I told him that he was becoming impertinent and that I had a good mind to turn him over to one of the female dominants at the party for a good thrashing while I watched. Dennis' chin went up and his arms crossed rebelliously across his ever deepening chest. "I won't submit in front of you again," he insisted.

"No? Why not?"

"I don't wish to."

"So you're saying you're no longer my slave?"

Dennis merely looked at me. I said, "Fine, don't be my slave," and began to exit, resolving never to let him drink champagne while on duty again. The cellar door opened and a guest emerged made up as the pathetic clown portrayed by Lon Chaney in He Who Gets Slapped. He was tall, slim and cradled some expensive vintages in the crook of his arm.

"I'll be your slave if I can spank you through those velvet knickers," the clown addressed me boldly in such a recognizable voice that I looked at him.

It was Marcus Gower! Back from grad school in England and now with the Boston Shakespeare company. We had parted on such a disturbing note that we hardly knew how to greet each other. He'd have kissed me, but for his greasepaint and mimed kisses at me instead.

Dennis looked less happy than ever as I led my college boyfriend from the room.

Young and undiplomatic as he is, Marcus couldn't help passing a few remarks on the richness of my lifestyle, what a spoiled brat I still am, etc., as I led him through the house up to my room. He looked so unappealing in his makeup that it was well we were at a spanking party, because at least being turned over his knee didn't require my looking at him. But while he was spanking me, and I could hear his delicious voice, the old feelings of attraction returned full force!

I now know who the first guest at my new house will be.

The party wound down around three thirty. Anthony retired and I saw out the last guest who wasn't spending the night. I found Dennis in my room, collecting half filled wine glasses and ashtrays. He'd cracked my windows, lit a pretty little fire in my hearth and even a candle or two. He must have been exhausted after helping all night and yet his last thought was that I shouldn't sleep in a cold or stuffy room. He slid back a panel in the wall, placed the tray on the dumb waiter, tugged the pulley to send it down to the kitchen and replaced the wall panel.

I told him my feet hurt from being on the 3" Victorian boots all night. He sank to his knees and began to unhook my boots, then removed each one and began to gently massage my sore feet. While he ministered to his favorite part of my body, I mildly reminded him that it was not proper for him to grab and kiss me. He mumbled a faint apology and kissed each instep.

"You need a girl of your own," I told him. He shook his head as though I'd suggested the most impossible notion in the world. I reminded him that I had only allowed him certain intimacies over the years because I believed him to be submissive. If he was no longer submissive I would have to ask him to keep a more respectful distance. (Great knife twisting, if I do say so myself.) Dennis promised on his knees never to offend me again, sealing his words with a kiss upon each instep.

Bet he doesn't keep his word. I'm told slaves never do.

Chapter Ten

The Honeymoon is Over

Ambrose Bartlett, luxe entrepreneur, connoisseur of all things beautiful and stuffily dominant male, had waited forty-two years to take a wife, during which time he had formed some pretty definite opinions as to the type of girl he wished her to be.

He thought he'd found all the traits of perfection in Paula Rohan, the flaxen haired, sexually submissive, thirty year old guidance counselor at Braemar Prep. After just a few weeks of dating, the managing and uncompromising Bartlett had decided that the Ivy League bred beauty was ideally suited to host his parties, spend his money and share his bed.

Accordingly, he brought all the usual pressures to bear, wooing Paula with small presents and large, intimate dinners and weekends away, and finally presenting her with a handsome engagement ring. Meanwhile, he had also brought her infatuation with the married English teacher, Mr. Lawrence, to a swift conclusion.

Paula had never sought an affair with a married man. But (always on the make) David Lawrence had figured out that she was the type of woman who actually enjoyed being turned over a man's knee and pressed his advantage to give her a spanking or two. Which had led to perhaps a bit more. Then Ambrose had entered the picture and Paula had relinquished the illicit thrills of yielding to someone else's husband, for the more conventional and ultimately rewarding prospect of a real relationship with the erudite department store owner.

But they were not perfectly suited. Ambrose was domineering while Paula was accustomed to exerting her independence. Among the specific issues upon which they vehemently disagreed was that of

Paula keeping her job at Braemar after they were wed. Sensible Paula was far too uncertain of her mercurial new lover to risk giving up such an excellent position before his devotion proved constant and reliable. Of course, it wasn't Paula continuing to earn her own living but the continued presence of David Lawrence on the Braemar faculty that irritated Bartlett.

The meticulous, perfectionist husband began to criticize his bride just one week after returning from their honeymoon in Italy, where the sensual Paula had politely shown her appreciation of the exquisite cuisine presented to her at the five star hotels where they stayed, to the extent of returning home a size eight instead of a size six. Being detail oriented to a degree of compulsion, Ambrose noticed. But he withheld comment until the following week, when the eight became a ten.

Paula was not in the habit of watching her weight or having anyone else watch it for her. Her figure had been more or less that of a Renoir nude since high school, with a complexion of marbled peach and rose to compliment her classic proportions. She'd had her slender moments, but more often then not, tended to fall into the slightly voluptuous category, well proportioned, well rounded and firm but seldom lean. Sometimes this troubled her, since she lived in the modern world, but more often than not, she thanked the gods that she was lovable and lovely and seldom complained, even to her girl friends, that her sizes mainly ran in double digits.

The nervous energy with which Paula had plunged into her brief spanking affair with David Lawrence, which was the first real spanking relationship of her life, had caused the weight to drop off at a remarkable rate. By the time Hope Spencer Lawrence urged the influential Hugo Sands to set up a meeting between the dangerously intelligent vamp who was stealing her husband and the wealthy sophisticate Bartlett, Paula had achieved her smallest waist ever, about twenty-five inches.

Paula was wed in a size four Valentino wedding gown, the picture of elegance and chic. But after the luxurious honeymoon in Italy and the return to Random Point while that village was still in the holiday season, with its many delicious temptations, Paula's relapse into comfortable plumpness was almost guaranteed. And Ambrose was far from pleased.

Paula really was still remarkably pretty, with a soft femininity that most males found themselves intensely drawn to. She radiated pheromones in every direction. The boys at school were all in love with her. Also, some of the girls. And every man on the faculty that deserved the name had had dreams about her. The cashmere sweaters, pearls and straight skirts out of the 50's added immensely to her appeal. But she was also a delightful person, calm but merry, with a winning personality.

Possessing the power to universally charm, Paula was wholly unused to the sort of severe criticism, which her husband routinely dispensed. She received her rude awakening that Saturday morning.

Paula had just had her bath and gone into her dressing room where she'd left her new, smoky blue DKNY trouser, shirt and cardigan set on wooden hangers with a pale blue lace lingerie combination ready to don on her vanity table and her neat little walking boots under the chair. The only thing that didn't belong in the cedar paneled chamber was a husband examining inner garment tags.

In retail, Saturday is the most important day of the week, and it being the second weekend in November, this was also one of the busiest shopping days of the year. Bartlett was about to leave for the store and was not in the best mood. To him, Christmas shoppers were amateur shoppers. They just annoyed him. They knew they couldn't afford to shop at Bartlett's, but to impress their friends at Christmas, they would scramble for the least expensive gift items carried there. Then, on the twenty-sixth, the unsentimental recipients seeking cash credits would return half of the presents. Perhaps he was thinking of this holiday unpleasantness when he caught sight of the size 8 labels, which then piqued the suave tyrant into making the sort of tart observations which he might reduce any bride to tears.

"What are you up to?" he asked Paula, without his usual warmth.

"I thought I'd go to the video store and rent some foreign films for the weekend," Paula replied, grabbing up the lingerie and outer garments and going behind a painted screen to change from her silk dressing gown into the street clothes.

"When was the last time you went to the gym?" Ambrose asked, adjusting his tie in a mirror. There was a long silence.

At last Paula murmured, "I don't remember."

Ambrose rejoined, "Well, don't you think it's time?" Again came a long silence accompanied by the sound of straps and zippers as Paula dressed.

"I'll have to renew my membership," she finally replied.

"You know a membership won't do you much good if you never use it," he declared unnecessarily.

"Is there something you're trying to say, Ambrose?" asked Paula, emerging from behind the screen fully dressed.

"A DKNY size eight is pretty much a ten or a twelve. What's going on, dear?" he demanded, none too compassionately.

Paula flushed deeply, suddenly seeing her husband's true harshness for the first time. She replied reproachfully, "So Mrs. Bartlett is not allowed to be a size ten?"

"Of course she isn't," Ambrose shot back.

"I see," Paula murmured, her mind racing for solutions to her overly hasty marriage. Was it too late for an annulment? Suppose she just packed and left? They might not even have rented her old apartment yet. "Well, I guess I'd better lose some weight," she said brightly, so as not to betray how hurt she felt.

"Do you want to come to the store with me and get some nice, new work out clothes, dear?" said Ambrose, more gently, feeling he had made his point and could now afford to be kindly supportive.

"No, that's okay. I have some."

"So, you'll go to the gym today?"

"Yes," she replied, managing a smile.

"Good girl," he approved. "I don't mean to be critical," he added, with a smile. "You've been blessed with a degree of beauty that most women would sell their souls for, but it's up to you to maintain it. Right, darling?"

"Of course," she replied, eager to end the hateful conversation. Yes, she would go to the gym all right. Because David Lawrence played racquet ball there every Saturday afternoon and at least he loved her exactly as she was!

At the gym she decided to swim while she waited for David to appear. Then she was tempted to indulge in a massage from the new personal trainer.

Face down on the leather table, under the German boy's capable hands, Paula began to feel pampered again. But suddenly remembering her husband's criticism, she stiffened.

"Did I hurt you, Mrs. Bartlett?"

"No."

"You're all in knots," he observed, unnecessarily. "Do try to relax."

Paula realized that her tension sprang as much from inner guilt as from resentment against Ambrose for putting what were essentially her own thoughts into words. Of course she had noticed that she was putting on weight and of course it distressed her greatly. In spite of her great attraction for the opposite sex and the confidence it was bound to inspire, her feelings about her own form were often ambivalent. Her last chubby funk had in fact been terminated by her brief affair with David Lawrence, who hungered for her then, and even now, in spite of constant access to a slim, young, blonde wife of his own.

But her recent satisfaction in achieving a size 6 for the first time since college had proven illusory. Her body obviously wanted to be rounded and only the most stringent attention to diet and exercise on a daily basis would ever counteract this natural tendency. Paula sighed as she realized that Ambrose was right. She owed it to him to look smart and svelte.

After the massage Paula pulled a twenty out of the pocket of her terry robe and pressed it into Dieter's hand. "Thanks, I'll come back again," she promised.

"Good! You need me, I think," he observed. Then, just as she went out the door he added impulsively, "You're a beautiful woman."

"Thanks! My husband told me today that I must lose weight."

"American men are so stupid," Dieter thought, but said aloud, "I think you're lovely just as you are. But if you like, next time you're in, I can show you a few simple exercises to keep your waist nipped and your thighs smooth."

"Thank you," said Paula, glowing with his gentle encouragement.

"Perhaps you should be my trainer."

"I would be honored," he bowed his head, then smiled softly at her. "And don't worry, I would never shout at you."

They agreed to begin the following day and Dieter was thrilled. Ever since the altercation with his mistress, Polyxena Guzman, on Halloween, they had barely spoken to each other, no less made love, and he was aching for an alternate blonde goddess upon whom to lavish his attentions. Paula had a form, complexion and demeanor remarkably similar to that of his ex-lover and this enraptured the sophisticated immigrant, who was also a player.

Of course at that moment, Dieter didn't even suspect that Paula was in the scene, no less a spanking submissive.

He himself he had considered, up until Halloween, an amiable body slave, the pleasure facilitator of any cosmopolitan woman with a dominant flare. But something awful had happened on that supernatural night to turn his sexuality on end. He had witnessed his lover and mistress, whom he had faultlessly served for seven years, followed to America, partnered tirelessly and intensely adored, go abjectly and rapturously submissive to another man, while tied to a whipping post at a decadent B&D ball. Glimpsing this outrageous spectacle, Dieter had short circuited. The careful training of the best European mistresses over the last ten years fell away in seconds, instinctively supplanted by the heavy handed, paternalistic dominance which was his Germanic heritage. The next thing he knew, he was turning his mistress over his knee and spanking her hard enough to hurt his own hand. After that, things would never be the same between them.

Paula ran into David in the lobby. They stepped into the juice bar and purchased drinks. When she admitted that she'd been sent to the gym to exercise, David demanded that she play racquetball with him.

"But aren't you playing with Michael?" Paula asked.

"You think he cares to be disturbed?" David replied, jerking his thumb towards the inner office of Polyxena, owner of the gym and spa, who was sitting on her desk, while Michael sat in a chair by her side, with the lovely one's foot in his hand, flirting up at her. "I like how he's sniffing around that one," David said; "Maybe if he's gets somewhere with her he'll leave Hope alone."

Paula enjoyed two games of racquetball with David, becoming pink and damp with her exertions. It was after four when she finally left the gym, planning to drink a cappuccino with David at the bookshop. A thick fog had blown in off tiny Random Point's coastline just a few blocks away, rendering the atmosphere so dense with grey mist that she never noticed her husband until he was at her shoulder.

"A.B.!" she cried, his initials being her most common nickname for her new spouse. "What are you doing here? I was just going for coffee with David. You two have met before, right?"

"No. How do you do?" Bartlett said coldly, shaking David's bare hand with his expensively gloved one.

"Fine, thanks," murmured David, with a sunny smile.

"We've just been playing racquetball," Paula admitted gaily. "Two games."

"Listen, Paula, I'll let you go," said David, sensing Bartlett's impatience to speak to his wife. "Nice meeting you." He had an impulse to add, "Shall I give my wife your regards?" for he remembered that Hope had once done a paid caning session with Bartlett that had marked her for a week. But David didn't think that Paula knew about that and decided to reserve the information for her if and when it might be necessary to supply it.

After David disappeared into the mist Paula regarded her husband with a pounding heart. The first sight of him had given her a pain in her stomach that made her rethink the annulment idea. "What are you doing here, A.B.?" she asked, as he led her to his car and put her in it.

"I missed you," he said, squeezing her knee and rumpling her hair before starting the car.

"What about my car?"

"You can pick it up tomorrow."

"Okay. I have an appointment with my new personal trainer, anyway," she announced, still glowing from her recent exertions and the positive attention she had received from both Dieter and David. "You see how I listen to you?" she added.

"That's good, dear," said Bartlett, still distracted by the image of David and his wife exiting the gym together so merrily.

"And I'm going to play racquetball with David on Saturdays as well. In fact, I expect to become a real gym rat from now on," she added, still in high spirits. They drove for the next several minutes in silence, with Ambrose striving mightily to control his temper while Paula, still flooded with endorphins, gazed out the window peacefully.

"Now, see here, Paula," said Bartlett as he parked in the circular driveway outside his large, fieldstone house, just off the Cliff Road, overlooking the sea.

"Yes, A.B.?"

"I don't want you seeing David Lawrence outside of school."

"I'm not seeing him!" she cried as she followed him into the house. "Just meeting to play racquetball isn't seeing someone."

"Being that he's your ex-lover and you're my new wife, I don't like the concept of you locked in a tiny room with him getting sweaty together every Saturday afternoon. Do you understand me, young lady?"

"But Dieter says that regular racquetball would be the perfect aerobic counterbalance to the toning we'll be working on."

"Who's Dieter?"

"My trainer. He's also a masseur. I had the most wonderful massage earlier."

"You did, did you?"

"Yes!" said Paula and leaving her gym bag in the closet, marched out to the vast, gleaming kitchen to start dinner. Bartlett followed her, entirely dissatisfied with her attitude and the way his day was going. The store had been hell on earth that afternoon.

"Paula, you didn't give me an answer about the racquetball. And what are you doing? We're going out for dinner."

"It will be easier for me to eat more sensibly if we eat in," she rejoined, ignoring his first question.

"Paula," he said, taking her by the hand and leading her out of the kitchen, "we need to have a talk."

"But I want to start dinner. Let's talk in the kitchen."

"It's not going to be that kind of talk," he said, pulling her upstairs behind him and into his master bedroom suite. Now her heart began racing again.

"No, don't!" she cried as he sat down on his favorite armless chair, a particularly handsome carved one, upholstered in dark green with tigers and elephants embroidered in gold, and turned her over his knee. "How dare you spank me?" she demanded as his palm descended on her wool trousered bottom rapidly and hard. "I didn't do a thing today but follow your explicit command to go to the gym!"

"Do you honestly believe you're going to be allowed to date your ex-lover?" Bartlett asked, spanking her firmly on alternate cheeks while gripping her securely about the waist.

"Allowed?" she sputtered, trying to squirm off his lap. "I'll do as I please!"

"Is that so?" Bartlett wasted no time in yanking down the thick woolen leggings and exposing her blue lace high cut French briefs. Her skin was already pinkened through the lace, now he deepened it with his hard palm to magenta. "You'll do as you please, will you?" Smack, smack, smack! He only paused to pull her panties smartly down to her upper thighs. She tried to pull them back up and ended with her wrist locked to the small of her back. "Insolent brat!"

"Ow! That hurts! It really hurts!!!" she cried, pulling her hand free and trying to cover her bottom again.

He paused and held her in place.

"Are you going to cancel the dates with David Lawrence?" he demanded.

"I'll think it over," she replied carelessly. Her husband promptly renewed the spanking, slapping her cheeks dark rose. Paula kicked and whimpered but stubbornly refused to yield.

"You do that," he said, pushing her off his lap, "while I get my hairbrush."

But once she was off his lap, her pants were back up in an instant and she was out of the room in the next. Running to the second floor landing Paula did something she'd been waiting her whole life to do, she slid down the banister to evade her pursuing husband. Unfortunately the momentum tumbled her off at the bottom and she had to scramble back up to her feet to flee the hall just a few yards ahead of Bartlett, who had barreled down the stairs after her.

Now Paula took off running through the ground floor rooms, going in one sitting room and out the connecting one and from there out into the side garden. The day was quickly waning and between the fog and deepening shadows it was cool and strange outside. The garden and then the back yard disappeared under Paula's little boots as she scrambled up the landscaped terraces that climbed the hill behind the house. Stone steps led from one to the other and each terrace was planted with shrubs and verdant ground cover and furnished with a bench, a table and chairs or a telescope. Up and up Paula ran, the chill air exhilarating after all the various forms of heat her body had been subjected to that afternoon. Bartlett scrambled after her, becoming extremely annoyed by these hoydenish antics, which he never would have expected from his calm, deliberate, ladylike bride.

Golden lights were already gleaming in all the terraces, but there was still a chance of slipping on the moist stone stairs and they both consciously slowed the chase to a safer speed, and one at which Paula was inevitably caught.

"You think this is funny?" he said, grabbing her by the shoulders and giving her a light shake when she laughed up at him.

"Yes, I do," she asserted. "Because you're winded and I'm not."

"Oh, you'll be winded by the time I'm through with you!" he declared, sitting down on the bench in the terrace alcove and pulling her back over his knee. Paula had never been spanked on a cliffside before and wondered if many woman had. This time when he pulled her pants down she could feel an extremely chill breeze cool her punished skin. But this sensation did not last, as his hand came down to renew the heat in her bottom.

He spanked her for several minutes, hard enough to make her begin to feel sorry for herself. Finally she exclaimed vehemently, "At least they don't think I'm too fat!"

"What's this you're saying, now?"

"David and Dieter. They think I'm just right as I am."

"Is that what all this is about?" he helped her pull her clothes up and turned her around to sit on his lap. "Were you brooding about what I said to you this morning?"

"Not so much brooding as thinking about divorce," she admitted, while allowing him to gather her in his arms and bury his face in her hair.

"I wondered if I might have upset you. That's why I came to find you at the gym. I'm sorry if I hurt your feelings this morning, Paula."

"That's all right. I want to get back to a size 6 as much as you want me to. I just didn't like hearing it put into words."

"I'll try not to be so critical in future," he pledged, though certainly not for the first time in his life.

"I'll try not merit your criticism in the future," she promised, confident that with Dieter's help, she could please him.

"It would also make me happy if you promised not to see David outside of school," Ambrose pressed his advantage gently.

"All right," she agreed, too soundly spanked to risk any other reply.

Meanwhile, Polyxena and Dieter were squaring away the spa for the night. Dressed in a white cotton wrap dress and white clogs, the Dutch beauty was picking up pool weights and putting them back in the rack. Dieter was slatting the blinds and dimming the lights, virtually ignoring his ex-mistress in the same style he had done since the party. But the image of Paula's enchanting face and form still with him, the young man realized how much he had been missing Polyxena each night.

The night after the Halloween party Dieter had packed one bag and left the lighthouse where he had been living with Polyxena since moving to district several months before. He now had a room at the inn, which he had obtained at a special rate, based on innkeeper Connie's adoration of his massages. Now he intended to repair to this hostelry, eat a quiet meal in the Ball and Feather pub and take his frustration to bed.

He had stubbornly ruled out the possibility of reuniting with Polyxena, as the fabric of their intimate relationship seemed to him rent beyond repair. He had been her humble and hard working submissive, content to serve and adulate his mistress and partner. In all that time he had never so much as lightly pinched her bottom, so respectful had he been of her status not only as a dominant woman, but as his own revered mistress.

But on the night of Halloween, when he had actually witnessed Polyxena going submissive to a man for the first time, an American and a relative stranger at that, the flimsy house of cards upon which Dieter had structured his rather esoteric sexuality instantly collapsed.

Two revolutionary ideas then crowded his mind at once, first, that Polyxena was no dominant at all, but merely a vulnerable, sensual girl goddess, who could behave with determination when the situation called for a strong, aggressive woman, but who might be more submissive than even he himself was, when presented with the opportunity.

For all his instep nuzzling, bottom worshipping obsequiousness, Dieter was not himself a corporal punishment enthusiast. His submissiveness lay in the desire and capability to serve the daintily feminine object of his admiration. Polyxena had now and then flogged him, beautifully, while he stood tied to a whipping post, but mostly their play consisted in him doing for and to her, with his fingers, lips, tongue, and when she felt like it, his cock. His function was to provide pleasure, in every possible way. And he did.

But when he saw her being whipped by another man, a terrible jealousy consumed him. In a brilliant moment of clarity he saw what Michael was doing to Polyxena not as an outrage to her dominance but as the ultimate act of seduction. For he noted how his pampered girl was reacting to her whipping, with what sublime abandon she was giving herself up to the former detective's lash. Still he faulted her for giving in. For the change was so sudden, so shocking and so opposite to everything that seemed proper to him in a mistress and a goddess.

As soon as Polyxena emerged from her session with Michael Flagg, Dieter had grabbed her by the arm and turned her over his knee. Sitting on an antique Sheraton-style sofa on the third floor landing of Anthony Newton's mansion, the exceedingly strong young masseur had spanked his own dominant, vigorously, relentlessly, until she kicked and sobbed with indignation, while guests streamed up and down the staircase or paused to watch with interest. He didn't know exactly why he did it, but he did know that it felt exactly right.

They returned to the lighthouse that night, each in their own white fury. Dieter slept in the pantry on a plank shelf and repaired to the inn on the following day. Polyxena would have allowed him into her bed in the middle of the night, but the fact that he didn't seem to wish to join her there and made no attempt to apologize or even explain his boorish behavior hardened her against him and kept her anger fresh throughout the following day.

She was of course astonished when he left her to live at the inn, tersely informing her that their professional partnership would continue as before, since he had bothered to cultivate no other profession over the last seven years and indeed had thrown in with her so completely as to immigrate to America with her from Holland. They had reopened the Random Point gym as a European health spa with her funds exclusively. Everything had been done with her money since the first day they met. Since he had no money, he labored long and hard to maintain her business and look after her. But he acknowledged that she owed him nothing beyond his salary, which was always augmented by handsome tips from the ladies he massaged.

Polyxena was shocked at Dieter's decision to leave her. She was also puzzled, as she hadn't thrown him out. In fact, she was quite prepared to forgive him his impertinence and continue on as before. He was the one to take the radical step of removing himself from her domain and she couldn't think why.

Twenty four hours after the quarrel, she was eager to forgive him, make up and have him back in her home and her bed. But Dieter seemed to have no intention of ever returning to her. Every day he'd stop by the lighthouse to pick up some more things of his. At work he barely spoke to her. The friendly, smiling Dieter was no longer for Polyxena. He spoke to her about the business and nothing more, reserving all his friendliness for the women who came into the gym to work out or lie on his massage table.

This attitude of Dieter's provoked Polyxena beyond measure, as she was fully ready to forgive him. It seemed nearly incomprehensible to the Dutch heiress that her charming Dieter should no longer be her slave. And yet she suddenly felt more attracted to him than ever and deeply missed his presence at night and in the early morning hours. Because she had a great deal of pride, the situation made her very angry with her ex-lover. She expressed her pique by flirting with every good looking male who walked into the gym forty times more provocatively than she had ever done before. This disgusted Dieter and he didn't hesitate to show his contempt of her antics with the worst looks he could manage.

Capricious and perverse, as most goddesses are, Polyxena responded to Dieter's hardening and withdrawal with a new and passionate desire for him. Night after night she lay alone in the lighthouse, wondering why her boy was not with her.

So she had offended him by going submissive in public to another man. Fine. She understood that. But had he not taken more than ample revenge by administering a public spanking to her, just moments later, at the same event? And it was a hard spanking too. For which he had not even apologized! To raise one's hand to one's mistress was unthinkable. Polyxena couldn't understand why Dieter hadn't gone down on his knees to her the very moment after his unexpected and severe affront to her dignity, claiming momentary insanity or even moon madness, given the season.

And she had not yet ceased to wonder why he had suddenly metamorphosized from the perfect submissive helpmeet into an arrogant young master!

Yes, master, Polyxena thought, or at the very least, an outraged German husband, which amounted to the same thing. But it may be recalled, that Polyxena's latent submissiveness had recently been awakened by Freddie Johanson, who had been the first man to ever spank her. Then it was further inflamed by Michael Flagg, who by flogging her at the party without bothering to first lock the door, had inadvertently started all the trouble with Dieter.

It had been a particularly trying day for Polyxena, what with the beautiful Mrs. Bartlett coming in to dazzle Dieter. Looking at Paula Bartlett was rather like looking in a mirror and this made the spa owner apprehensive in a way she had never felt before with regard to her boy. She looked at him from under her long lashes as he went about the pool stowing equipment and switching the whirlpools off. Now and then he tossed her a stern but disinterested gaze, as though he wanted very much to tell her off but stopped himself each time, in case the attention should further swell her impossible ego.

It had been two whole weeks since he'd clasped her in his arms and she missed him. The whole thing was really ridiculous, she thought. It must be a charade. Perhaps he needed a shock before he would admit it.

"You know if anyone should be angry, it should be me!" she suddenly blurted out when they came face to face at the edge of the pool. "You lay hands on me. Me, your mistress!"

"I know I did. It felt great too," he replied coolly, passing by her to collect more objects for storage. Not thinking of the consequences, but only of puncturing Dieter's newfound pretensions, Polyxena took advantage of her partner's bending down to pick up a pool shoe, to give him a vigorous shove into the pool. Dieter fell in with an enormous splash and surfaced at once, spitting mad.

"That's what you get for being so serious," Polyxena laughed. But her expression changed a moment later when the wiry trainer sprung out of the pool like a piece of film in reverse and seized her by her soft, smooth, bare forearm in a terrible grip.

"What are you doing? Dieter, let me go! Do you hear me?" Polyxena cried to no avail as her partner dragged her out of the pool area, through the showers and into the empty women's locker room, where he sat down on one of the long wooden benches and yanked her face down across his lap. "Stop! Let go! You're getting me all wet!" she protested, while laughing again at her prank. But she stopped laughing when his hard hand began to come down on her voluptuous bottom through the thin cotton skirt.

"You want to play?" he demanded, smacking her hard, then pausing to grab her by her long, white-blonde pony tail, he turned her head towards him. "Okay, we'll play!" He let her hair go and deliberately pushed her skirt up to her small waist, revealing her sheer, white, mesh nylon panties. "You want to go submissive to someone?" Smack! "How about going submissive to me?" Smack, smack, smack! "The one who works for you, cares for you, thinks only of you night and day for seven years!"

"That's a lie! You're any woman's toy!" Polyxena accused, trying to twist off his lap with all her strength. He merely locked his arm on her waist and continued slapping her round, perfect bottom with metronomic rhythm until the white beneath the mesh turned cream pink.

"And you're any man's slut!" Dieter replied, furious afresh at the memory of Michael Flagg whipping her flawless white back at the party. "I'm fed up with you. Do you hear?" Now he yanked her panties down and completely off. "You think you can treat me that way and everything will still be all right?"

"Treat you what way? I did nothing at all!" she protested.

"When you let a man chastise you, in a public place, for all to see, you made a mockery of our relationship and a fool out of me!"

"I don't understand why!"

"I serve dominant women, not submissive ones. You changed your mind about being a mistress? Maybe I changed my mind about being your slave!" Dieter declared, suddenly realizing how enjoyable it was to redden Polyxena's backside while she ground against his raging erection and kicked her beautiful, smooth legs. The clogs had flown off some minutes before and her pretty, small, bare feet, with their pink heels and crimson toenails sawed the air in a kicking frenzy as the European athlete spanked her harder and faster.

"Okay, don't be my slave!" she cried, quite aroused from the rough treatment but just about to cry from the sting of his hand. "Just come back to me and be my man!"

This remark stayed Dieter's hand. He lifted her from his lap and jumped to his feet, grabbing her around her creamy forearm and pulling her out of the locker room and into the free weight room.

"What? What are you doing now?" she demanded, rubbing her bottom as she tried to pull her skirt up and see how pink she was in one of the many mirrors surrounding them.

"Come here," he ordered, dragging her with him around the room until he found a leather padded weight bench of exactly the right height to bend her over. "Spread your legs," he said, pushing her thighs apart and slapping her magenta tinged cheeks a few more times. "Push your bottom up. High!" he commanded, standing behind her and whipping out his rampant cock. Slipping two fingers into her pussy with ease he felt how wet she was. The next moment he was plunging deep inside her. Gripping her girlish waist, he pistoned in hard, filling her damp, velvet sex to the hilt.

Capturing her wrists in his hands, he drew them up to the small of her back and pinned them there, holding her firmly captive until he felt his crisis approaching. Then he let her hands go, took a fresh grip on her hips and let his crescendo burst deep within her throbbing core, which also spasmed in pleasure at the moment of Dieter's release.

He turned her around to look at him, took her face in his hands and kissed her mouth hard. "You want to play games, you see what happens," he told her sternly, then walked out to change into dry clothes before returning to the inn. Polyxena leaned against the bench for some time, reliving what had just happened in her head several times. In spite of the climax she herself had just enjoyed, this occupation sent flutters through her tummy afresh.

After hearing Dieter leave the gym Polyxena wandered back out to the pool, took a mop and began swabbing the deck that her partner's sudden plunge had so violently splashed. Still the darts of pleasure pierced her innermost core as she remembered with a smile being spanked and then taken so fiercely.

"He probably doesn't realize that in America it's quite common to switch," she mused. "I'll have to tell him this when he's in a better mood."

Chapter Eleven

Merry Christmas, Ambrose Bartlett

Ambrose Bartlett was in a vile mood. In the first place, it was the day after Christmas, his most hated day of the retail year, when half the people who'd received lovely gifts from his department store stormed the gilt edged doors of Bartlett's to return them. Bartlett was a man who abhorred disorder and the sight of bargain hunters pawing through sale racks and tables from Shoes to Lingerie tore at the delicate fibers of his soul as badly as did the sight of black socks with white shoes or those partial goatees one saw so many of these days.

To make matters worse, the owner of Bartlett's had been abandoned by his wife on Christmas Day, before even sitting down to dinner. She left because of a look on his part; a glance which offended her deeply, because it was cast at a torte, which she herself had baked.

Ambrose reran the scene twenty times in his head as he stood idly before the bank of security monitors in his office that continuously scanned all the key departments in the store. She had simply stood up, thrown down her napkin and said, "It's over." Without another word she had run upstairs to pack.

Ambrose pursued her, protesting that he hadn't said a thing.

"You didn't have to," Paula replied, marching into her room sized closet. "I could feel the tacit criticism in your expression. I suppose people should eat tofu on Christmas Day!"

"Paula, dear, you're overreacting."

"I'm back up to a size ten and you hate it. Well, I hate living with the pressure of your unrealistic expectations. Our marriage was a terrible mistake." She began carefully packing enough clothes for a few days.

Ambrose stood speechless with indignation, as he thought he'd been doing a marvelous job of concealing his disapproval of Paula's more generous proportions of late. Even if he had looked sharply at her now and then, was that a proper reason to dissolve their union?

"Where are you going?"

"To the inn for now," she replied proudly.

"If you can leave me so easily you must not really care for me," he observed matter of factly.

"Then we're even. You don't really care for me, A.B."

"Paula, how can you say that? You're the only woman I've ever proposed to."

"But I was a size 6 then!" she returned, her blue eyes glittering with tears of humiliation.

She didn't want to leave A.B. He was a virile sophisticate with impeccable taste and a terraced estate. But she hadn't relished being made to feel inferior these past few months, just because of a double digit dress size. The experience of being judged by a man for the first time in her life was a shock to her self esteem.

"I can't believe you're taking on like this," Ambrose exclaimed, tempted to turn her over his knee. "And over nothing!"

She just looked at him and continued packing.

"Paula stop packing this instant. Unless you want the worst spanking of your life!"

"Too late, I'm done!" she said, snapping her valise shut.

"Suppose I was tacitly critical? What husband isn't? On top of which, I'm critical by nature. But I mean nothing by it."

"I'm going away," she said firmly, marching out the door with her bag.

Staring vacantly at the monitors opposite him, Ambrose wondered whether he should have pursued her, shaken her and forced her to stay. He shook his head. Having completely destroyed the mood of the day, he had done well not to conclude it with a Punch and Judy show.

Ambrose sighed painfully, remembering how he had nibbled at the wonderful dinner she'd prepared and eaten a full slice of the magnificent torte.

If his Christmas Day was awful, the night was still worse. As dusk fell he made his way to the inn to reclaim his wife. A light snow was falling on the village when he strode into the lobby and demanded of innkeeper Connie to know where Paula was. Connie nodded toward the Ball and Feather pub and Bartlett marched towards the hall that led to this hearthside room before Connie could warn him that his wife was not alone.

Stopping dead in the doorway Ambrose received the emotional equivalent of a punch in the solar plexus as he glimpsed Paula adorably clad in cream angora and cozily flanked in a corner booth by Michael Flagg on one side and Dieter Brant on the other, There was champagne in a cooler, plates heaped with holiday fare before them and laughter floating up from the table as the three diners amused each other with stories.

Dieter, who was Paula's masseur and personal trainer, beamed on his client as he eagerly refilled her glass. Flagg, who had had his eye on Paula from their first introduction, now seemed to view her as dessert. Thinking of his dignity, Bartlett had turned on his heel and left the inn, convinced that his wife would lie in another man's arms that night.

"If only I had praised her for cooking," he reproached himself, glaring at the monitors and noticing for the first time young Pamela Crane, the leggy beauty who had modeled in some of his runway shows and who now worked in a smart Random Point boutique, shoplifting in Fine Leathers!

"Huh?" he said to himself. "This doesn't make sense!" He dialed the boutique and told the manager to send him the brunette at the glove counter at once. Then he called security and instructed his minions to escort Pamela to him without delay.

In a few minutes Pamela was ushered into Bartlett's office by two uniformed security guards. The door closed behind her. Normally pale as a winter sky, the willowy twenty six year old was blushing as painfully as he had ever seen a girl blush.

"Hi, Pamela," he said, lighting a cigarette.

"Hi, Mr. Bartlett."

"What do you think you're doing?"

"Just checking out the sales," she murmured, not able to meet his eyes.

Bartlett strode across to Pamela, seized her purse, brought it back to his desk and emptied the contents. A pair of cashmere lined ostrich leather gloves with a $100 price tag fell out along with her personal items.

"I saw you put these in your purse," he observed tersely, jerking his head towards the monitors. "I'd just like to know what the hell you were thinking of. Did you do it for a thrill, or is this a habit?"

"I wanted the gloves and knew I couldn't afford them. So I decided to take them."

"But Pamela, I thought Damaris had made you a partner and that the shop was doing so well."

"I have been making more lately, but not nearly enough for my desires."

"Why don't you get yourself a rich boyfriend to buy you things?"

"I don't know."

Now the ordeal commenced, with Bartlett pulling out a straight backed chair and crooking his finger at the girl.

"Normally I'd file a complaint against a shoplifter, but you being you and me being me, we'll settle this between ourselves."

"Me being me?" she hung back reluctantly.

"Come on, dear, don't be coy. I know you were a protégée of Hugo Sands, ergo, you've been spanked before."

Pamela came to Ambrose and let herself be pulled across his lap. She was wearing a full black wool skirt and blue peplum jacket, in the style of the late 1940's. Her body was lithe and her long legs in her high heeled spectator pumps were poems of slender shapeliness, gleaming through black, seamed nylon hose.

"Good taste is expensive," he granted her, stroking her from ankle to hip and in so doing pushing up her full, petticoated skirt. Her narrow, oval cheeked bottom, clad in full, sheer, black panties and girded by a black silk garter belt jutted charmingly, reminding Bartlett that this young woman was intended by nature as well as inclination to be spanked. "However, that's no excuse for you to start boosting, particularly from me!"

He brought down his palm once very sharply on each cheek, causing her to gasp and cry out, "Are they all going to be that hard?"

"Don't worry, I was only going to give you one smack for every dollar," he reassured her, commencing the spanking again, through her sheer panties. Four more excruciating swats fell across her upturned cheeks.

"Ow!"

"Pamela, remember where you are. If you can't help making noise we will have to continue this later, in private," he scolded, inspecting the pink imprints of his palms visible through the sheer mesh.

"Yes!" she cried, ready to say or do anything to stop this spanking. Perhaps it was too early in the morning for a spanking. Or perhaps his hand was simply the hardest she had ever felt across her tender flesh, but this was really not sexy.

"Get up," he told her briskly. "What's the matter, Pamela, can't take it?"

"No, Sir," she murmured, planning the most seductive outfit she could imagine to soften him for the next encounter.

"I'd give you your spanking here and now, but I don't want your cries to alarm my secretary. So, where shall we continue this?"

"My apartment?" she suggested timidly, her mind racing to prepare a tantalizing cocktail and appetizer dish for Bartlett, to further mellow his temper.

"When?"

"This evening? At seven?" she offered, timing it to the closing of the store.

"Write down your address," he passed her a pad.

"Here," she said, handing it back to him with her gracefully gloved hand.

"Take the gloves," he said, cutting off the tag and handing them to her, "you will have earned them by the time I'm through with you."

Pamela gulped, sobbed once, took the gloves and fled the office, her face as pink as her bottom.

Ambrose needn't have worried about Paula spending the night with anyone. But this might not have been the case had Marguerite

Alexander Branwell not joined the impromptu dinner party at the Ball and Feather shortly after it was glimpsed by Bartlett.

"Marguerite, is something wrong?" Michael demanded, the first to notice that his ex-lover's eyes were red behind her glasses. She shrugged off her fur, motioned to Connie to bring a wine list and greeted the others with a sigh.

"Hello Dieter, Paula. Yes, something is wrong. Malcolm has left me!"

"No!" Michael breathed, his heart jumping in his chest. He had loved her for years and had never stopped wanting her. "Whatever for?"

"Oh, nothing that makes any sense!" she cried, running her hands through her thick, russet hair. "Basically he's been in a funk since he lost his business."

"I thought he's gone into the climbing gym business with William," said Michael.

"In his mind that's a mere bagatelle compared with his bookstore chain. He's suffering a crisis of confidence. And it's expressing itself in a desire to dissolve our union." Marguerite's little explanation ended on a sob.

Michael patted her hand and soothingly said, "He'll be back."

"I don't think so," said Marguerite, staring into space until the wine list was put into her hand, at which point she ordered a fresh bottle of champagne. "We quarreled dreadfully on an ill advised trip to Vegas last week. My dears, that's the worst possible place to visit in the company of a frugal male. He didn't even want me to gamble with my own money or buy practically anything."

"Did he pull you out of the casino?"

"No, you don't dare make scenes like that in Vegas, but he tried to stop me from shooting craps in a low cut gown."

"I take it he didn't?" Paula murmured with amusement.

"I should say not. After all, I didn't go to Vegas not to gamble. But he utterly spoiled my luck. And he didn't even feel like dancing! It was a total fiasco. Just like our silly marriage."

"Then why are you crying?" Dieter demanded. He was also Marguerite's personal trainer and worshipful admirer.

"He's in Boston now, divorcing me even as we speak!" she replied.

"Really?" asked Flagg with great interest. "Are you getting a settlement?"

"I wouldn't accept one," Marguerite replied sincerely. "He's lost just about everything except the condo on Boylston Street as it is."

"That should be worth a couple of mil though, huh?" Michael persisted.

"Michael, what do you take me for?" Marguerite cried.

"Well, why were you so excited about marrying a millionaire if you never planned to use his money?" the former-detective wondered aloud.

"Oh, he didn't turn out to be that kind of millionaire," said Marguerite with a sigh. "It's just not in his makeup to be openhanded. Even if he still had his fortune I wouldn't ask him for any of it, because it wouldn't be freely given. Anyway, I was only with him a year or so."

"But isn't it true you sold a half interest in your own shop because you were secure in the knowledge that you husband owned twenty stores of his own?" Michael brought up.

Marguerite smiled and shook her head. "I love sharing the shop with Sloan. It was always too much for me."

"Seems as though you're being awfully understanding," Michael observed.

"Oh, it's not Malcolm's fault," Marguerite said. "He was probably right to leave. But I miss him already."

"You miss someone who doesn't let you gamble in a cleavage gown?" Michael demanded.

"Not that. But other things. You know what I mean. You've been married to someone darling and lost her," Marguerite reminded Michael.

"Because I was running after you," he reminded her. They smiled at each other and clasped hands under the table.

"It's quite a coincidence us all being here like this," said Paula, "because I've just left my husband and Dieter has recently left his mistress."

"I knew about Dieter and Polyxena," said Marguerite, "but you've left Ambrose?"

Paula nodded, "Just today."

"Paula, what happened?" Marguerite was all astonishment and sympathy, for Mr. Bartlett was a true millionaire. Moreover he was the type of one who actually enjoyed spending large quantities of money on clothes, jewels, luxury trips and all manner of delicacies for his wife.

Indeed, the unapologetically decadent Ambrose Bartlett and not the thrifty, frill hating Malcolm Branwell, was always the kind of man Marguerite ought to have chosen to unite with. He would not have raised an eyebrow at a low cut gown in a casino. On the contrary, he would have insisted upon it, handing her a large wad of allowance to gamble with. "He must have done something dreadful for you to abandon all that charm and aesthetic perfection," the sable swathed redhead observed.

"He didn't do anything. I just realized we'll never suit," sighed Paula.

"But why?" Marguerite wondered.

"Because it's just not my nature to be a size six," Paula replied honestly. "He should have married you," she added, for Marguerite Alexander's corset-trained, hour glass figure was one of the marvels of the New England coast.

Marguerite stared at Paula. "But you're a goddess. These boys will back me up."

"That's what I've been telling her," said Michael.

"Her husband is an asshole," added Dieter, with typical German candor. As Paula's personal trainer, the young athlete was justifiably proud of the progress his adorable client had been making. Yes, she was a true size 10, but firm, with an inward curving waist, smooth bottom and upstanding bosom. Dieter was enchanted with the creamy skinned Paula, who so reminded him of those pink cheeked, golden haired 18th century nudes who were so fond of reclining in Arcadian bowers while being fanned by cupids and made love to by virile shepherds. "He wants a stick figure!"

"Oh, I can't believe it," exclaimed Marguerite. "Did you really quarrel about your weight?"

"Not exactly," Paula admitted, suddenly realizing how little her husband had actually said or done to merit her desertion. "But I sensed his disapproval."

"Just sensed it?" Marguerite persisted.

"He gave my Christmas torte a certain look which said more than words."

"Oh, Paula!" Marguerite cried. "Do you really call that a good reason to leave A.B.?"

"You don't think it is?" Paula asked doubtfully.

"Young lady, I think you should go home at once! Believe me, it isn't so nice to be left," said Marguerite feelingly. "And you've done the same thing to your darling Polyxena!" This was directed at Dieter, who started at the accusation.

"I had a good reason!" he replied.

"Oh, I know all about your reason. It's a lot of nonsense. Polyxena misses you. I know she does because she told me so," said Marguerite, to Michael's chagrin. He had been taking magnificent advantage of Dieter's absence at the lighthouse to visit the Dutch gym owner at least once a week. Therefore he had no desire to see her get her live in lover/slave back. "Don't you selfish people know how you've hurt your loved ones?"

Dieter and Paula exchanged glances. Paula was beginning to fully grasp Marguerite's point. Dieter merely shrugged and said, "I'm in no hurry to go back to her. She knows where I am when she wants me."

"What about you, dear? Won't you think about giving A.B. another chance?" Marguerite pressed Paula's hand.

"I will," Paula promised.

In consequence of Marguerite's lecture, Paula did not spend an easy night. The dawn brought a cold, driving rain that washed away the snow of Christmas Day and turned the cobbled streets of Random Point to slush. The Braemar Academy, where she was employed as a guidance counselor, was closed for the next fortnight and Paula realized that if she really planned leave A.B. she ought to spend that time finding a place to live. At the thought of going back to the house to pack, Paula burst into tears. What had she done? Was there any way to undo it and still save face? Her reason for leaving her husband the previous day suddenly seemed absurd.

Confused and depressed, Paula threw a fresh log into the small hearth, lit it and dove back under the cranberry satin coverlet. As she watched the fire crackle and saw the sky gradually lighten to steel grey, she decided the best thing that she could do was stay in bed. The next time she awoke it was eleven. She sat up with a start. The fire had gone out. The rain was still battering the window panes. But now Paula knew what she had to do.

A few minutes after Pamela Crane left Ambrose Bartlett's office, his secretary buzzed him to say that Mrs. Bartlett was on the line. Ambrose lunged at the phone.

"Hi, A.B.," ventured Paula timidly.

Instantly sensing the contrition in her tone, he icily replied, "Oh, it's you, is it? Well, have you come to your senses?"

"Yes."

"Thank god for miniscule wonders!" he snapped.

"May I come back?"

"Don't be ridiculous, Paula. Of course come back! I have to go now. It's the busiest day of the year. I'll be home late." Ambrose hung up with a great deal of satisfaction. His early date with the naughty Pamela would insure his not getting home until at least eight or nine o'clock. This would provide Paula with the maximum amount of anxiety prior to his return. His only regret was that spanking Pamela might take the edge off his spousal indignation. Given his wife's temperate nature, this might be his only opportunity to punish her for willful childishness and he didn't like to waste it.

With Sloan in Boston for a few days, Pamela felt easy entertaining Ambrose Bartlett in her second floor apartment on Main Street. In preparation for the visit of this powerful personage, Pamela had arrayed herself in a sumptuous 50's style hostess gown and prepared a small supper. A good red wine was breathing and a fire had been started in her own fireplace, which along with candles illuminated her bay windowed sitting room. A large and beautifully decorated

Christmas tree added the scent of pine and a holiday warmth. Ambrose was impressed.

Accepting the wine, the favorite chair and a cigarette, he settled back to look at his young and extremely elegant hostess. "I see you know how to soften a man up," he observed. She lowered her eyes demurely, inwardly annoyed that he should have figured her out so quickly.

"Come here," he ordered, putting down his wine and crushing out his cigarette. As soon as she was within reach he grabbed her wrist and pulled her across his lap. Folding the voluminous, stiff, silver grey satin brocade skirt back up to her waist along with a nylon crinoline, he revealed her slender but finely formed bottom, now gleaming through sheer, shiny grey silk mesh panties. These he summarily rolled down and pulled off her long, bare legs, whose slim, dainty feet were shod in grey satin high heeled slippers with jeweled buckles. The full hostess skirt had been paired with a sheer, pale grey georgette blouse with long sleeves and a ruffled deep v neck. Her long black hair was down her back and gleaming like onyx.

"By the way, you look glorious," he added, thinking what a perfect little mistress this one would make, if she could only learn to take a good spanking. "Now, I think we were up to 7 out of a hundred of the best," he told her, continuing the spanking where it had left off that afternoon, smacking one cheek then the other quite hard and repeating the process again and again until each was stained dark rose by the palm of his hand.

This time Pamela knew what to expect and had prepared accordingly by drinking several glasses of wine prior to Bartlett's arrival. She was much more relaxed now than in his office. She had anticipated this meeting all day with an acute mixture of shame and fear. And now that it was finally upon her, it didn't seem quite so bad. Bad enough, but not crying "mercy" bad, which was exactly what it had been in Ambrose's office.

She had never felt quite so hard a hand before. Even Hugo at his most furious, still seemed a very human spanker. And her dear Sloan of course, could never hurt her. But Bartlett had that afternoon been cold, like a machine. It had frightened her terribly. She had wondered if it might not be better to be arrested for shoplifting than taking even one more of those horrid smacks on her bare bottom!

This spanking didn't seem as bad as the first six he had given her at Bartlett's, but even so, by smack twenty five she began to sob, feeling extremely sorry for herself.

"You're making an awful racket over such a little spanking," he observed. "This isn't even half as hard as I spank my wife when she's naughty."

"Well, I don't have as much padding as she does," said Pamela.

"An accurate but somewhat impolite observation," Ambrose replied while continuing the spanking more briskly. "At any rate, this wouldn't be happening to you at all if you hadn't stolen those gloves. You committed a crime and this is your punishment."

"Okay," she whimpered before breaking down in real tears. Pamela in fact began crying so pitifully that Ambrose had little choice but to let her go. Putting her off his lap he handed her his handkerchief and watched her press it to her eyes in shame.

"I'm sorry," she wept, crumpling to the floor and leaning upon a upholstered hassock to continue sobbing uncontrollably. The true humiliation of her position had penetrated her proud mind and this was even more unendurable than his smacks. How had she come to this? She, Pamela Crane, with two degrees in fashion design from prestigious colleges, a season of European modeling, a coffee table book filled from end to end with images of herself, a fine position in a growing business in the village to establish her reputation with and the nicest young man in the civilized world to lean on, what had she been thinking that afternoon?

"All right, that's enough," he told her. "I'm not going to spank you anymore."

She lifted her beautiful, tear stained face to him. "No," she protested. "Please continue! I did wrong and I'm very sorry for it." To impress him with her sincerity she finished drying her face and got back on her feet, ready to go over his knee again. He stood up, laughed at her, pinched her ear lobe and took her in his arms.

"You're a baby, you know that?" he asked, kissing her full on her dark red bee sting lips. She looked up at him wide eyed, never expecting to be made love to by him. "Maybe I should soothe you now?" She only looked at him. "Do you mind?" he asked. She shook her head.

Ambrose led her by the hand into her own bedroom and placed her on the bed. Candles lighted the small room and Pamela's bed was richly draped in a rose satin coverlet. The hard, cold rain continued to batter the window panes but it could not have been more cozy inside Pamela's little jewel box of a bedroom. In a moment he was straddling her, pushing up her skirt, pulling off her panties and yanking down his zipper.

"Raise your hips," he told her, slipping a pillow under her bottom to perfect his angle of entry into her dark curled femininity. Entranced with the flatness of her stomach, the slimness of her thighs and the intoxicating scent of her young womanhood, Ambrose lightly ran his fingers through her silken public curls and very gradually began to introduce one into her moist, glove-like portal.

He lay beside her, stroking her, lightly spanking her Venus mound and penetrating her with first one, then two fingers. Meanwhile, he crushed her lips under his and kissed her deeply while manipulating her to creaminess. When her arms went around his neck to bring him closer to him, he knew she was ready and took her without further ado.

Throughout most of the act he leaned up on his arms to watch the changing expressions of her exquisite face while he possessed her. She closed her eyes but opened them when she felt him looking at her. When their eyes met she felt a serious rush of excitement. A terrible spanker he might be, but as a lover Mr. Bartlett was accomplished. His sizable cock filled her deeply but not harshly. She'd become very wet while he was fingering her and his experienced thrusts caused her tummy to contract with the flutters known and coveted by every submissive woman from almost the first moment of penetration.

"It feels good," she whispered. He brought his mouth down on hers again. Her glamour made him feel romantic. Normally he preferred to take a woman from behind, so he could look at, play with and spank her bottom at will. But Pamela was so appealing he could barely tear his eyes away from her face.

"Do you mean that?" he asked, plunging ever more deeply into her velvety depths.

"Oh, yes!" she cried, overwhelmed when he reached under her to cup her bottom in his hands and thus bring her up even closer against him. "No!" she amended her statement, "Please, that's too deep!" For Ambrose had hit the back wall and there was nowhere else to go. He pulled back a little and felt her untense. But he kept her cheeks in the palms of his hands.

When Pamela felt his crisis approach she suddenly panicked and cried, "Mr. Bartlett, you didn't put a condom on!"

"Don't worry, I've been fixed," he assured her.

Pamela supposed Mr. Bartlett was safe, but felt uneasy about having unprotected sex. She wondered he didn't feel the same and resolved to discuss the matter with him at an appropriate moment. Meanwhile, he had begun to insinuate a finger into her bottom hole. After that, it was a matter of moments until they each expired satisfied.

They lay in each other's arms for a long time without speaking. Finally he looked at his watch. "I have to go. My wife is waiting for me."

Pamela sat up and watched him put himself to rights. After doing so he sat down beside her on the bed. "Would you like to be my mistress?"

"What?"

"I like you," he said, taking her chin in his hand and kissing her lightly on the lips. "And I can give you whatever you need."

"But, why?" Pamela stammered.

"You tell me, girl who never boosted anything in her life before and just happened to choose my store to make her debut. Admit it, Pamela, you wanted to attract my attention today."

Pamela sat up in surprise. "Perhaps unconsciously, I did," she agreed. "But not consciously!"

He laughed and kissed her again. "It's okay. I'm flattered you've selected me to be your patron. You need one."

"Oh, but I couldn't. My boyfriend would never tolerate it."

"Never mind that. I have that all figured out," said Bartlett, lighting a cigarette and looking out the window into the rain washed street. "We'll have a business arrangement for window dressing."

"How do you mean?"

"You and Damaris do beautiful work. But you need to raise your prices and start finding distributors. I'm prepared to offer you space for the line in my store if one of you would like to come and run it."

"You'd do that?"

"I actually thought of it the last time I was in Random Point. Talking to you girls was on my list of things to do after New Year's. Anyway, you can see where the arrangement would allow me to supply you with additional allowance and also see you frequently with neither of our mates being the wiser."

"It's so tempting," said Pamela.

"I can spank lighter," he assured her. "I was just attempting to teach you a lesson."

"But it would be disloyal to both Sloan and Paula to carry on a secret relationship. Wouldn't it?"

"You could look at it like that," said Bartlett. "Or not."

"How would you feel if your wife were carrying on an affair?"

"Oh, that'll happen," he murmured, thinking of Michael Flagg, David Lawrence and Dieter Brant ravening for a taste of his creamy, blonde wife. "It's the way of the world. At least around here."

Pamela walked him to the door, still dazed from the good sex and subsequent promise of an improvement in her finances. "You're a handsome, generous, fascinating man, but I'm afraid of agreeing to anything so wicked."

"Just agree to come to the store with the Damaris line and I'll take care of the rest."

Ambrose kissed her once more and then was gone.

As predicted, he didn't walk into his house until nine that evening, where he found Paula, asleep in front of the fire in the upstairs sitting room. She started awake at his voice and instantly blushed dark pink. While awaiting his return she had found and opened her Christmas presents and was currently well wrapped in one of them, a bronze silk satin Fernando Sanchez dressing gown with rich velvet lapels and tasseled belt. The color picked up the sheen of her straight, cornflower blonde hair just as he'd pictured it would. However, he was disposed to be extremely stern with her after his night of torment.

"So! She returns!" he warmed up quickly, inwardly rejoicing that his darling was back. "Well? What do you have to say for yourself?"

"You were right, A.B., I overreacted yesterday," Paula murmured. Meanwhile, Ambrose had caught a glimpse of himself in the mirror over the hearth and hastened to rub away Pamela's lipstick traces from the side of his smooth shaven face before his wife scrutinized him more closely.

"You're damn right, you over reacted. Didn't I say that exact thing yesterday?"

"Yes," she agreed with down cast eyes.

"And who did you spend last night with?" he demanded.

"Me? No one!"

"You expect me to believe that? I came looking for you at the inn and saw you practically sitting in Michael Flagg's pocket!"

"We did have dinner together, but Marguerite joined us too. Then Michael took her home."

"What about the Teutonic muscle head? I saw him hanging all over you as well."

"If you mean Dieter, nothing about him."

"No midnight massages?"

"Certainly not!"

"I suppose I'll have to take your word for that."

"A.B., I'm so sorry for ruining our day."

"I never dreamt you could be so childish."

"I guess I was just having one of those days. I am a girl, you know," she protested with spirit.

"Yes, a very bad girl!"

"I said I was sorry."

"One apology isn't going to make it right."

"But you're the one who made me feel so insecure."

"You should never feel insecure about us."

"Are you sure you don't regret our hasty marriage?" she demanded.

"Of course, I don't! Don't you see that you've blown a tiny criticism way out of proportion?"

"Yes," she replied with humility.

"I'll tell you what hurt me the most," he continued heaping on guilt with relish, "your saying I don't care for you."

"I shouldn't have said that," she agreed. "Even though you accused me of not caring first."

"That was because you were packing your bags and leaving me. I wasn't packing my bags and leaving you, was I?"

"No."

"You see, it all comes back to your own willfulness, capriciousness and cruelty towards one who only means you well," Bartlett iced the guilt cake.

Paula refrained from answering. The blush was finally beginning to recede from her cheeks but she still had a very high color and Ambrose admired her complexion greatly. Paula's peachy pink cheek tones were especially entrancing when deepened by embarrassment.

"Well, it's been a hell of a day. I'm going to have a bath," he announced, suddenly remembering that Pamela's perfume might be lingering about his person. He would have to be careful about that sort of thing from now on!

When he emerged in a navy foulard dressing gown he found that Paula had lay a little supper out for him by their bedroom fireside. This bit of wifely solicitude brought a smile to his lips. He hadn't paused to eat a bite at Pamela's, for all her trouble and was very hungry.

"You're still getting a spanking," he warned her, sipping a glass of wine and spreading pate on a toast point. Paula was curled up on a loveseat nearby, sipping her own glass of wine. The threat brought her blush up again.

"No, A.B., I'm upset enough!" she protested.

"The hell you are."

"You must want to make me cry!"

"You bet I do!"

"I think you're horrible to want to spank me at a time like this."

"Would you prefer to postpone it until tomorrow morning?"

"If you're really going to be so ungallant as to spank me, you might as well do it now!" she cried, putting down her glass and folding her arms across her full bosom.

"A wise choice. I'm told it hurts more in the morning," he observed, now relaxed enough to find her petulance amusing. The food and wine were having a positive effect. She'd given him a rough twenty-four hours, but that's what spoiled brides were famous for. Even so, there could be but one response. Everyone from Eudora Welty to John Ford knew that a runaway bride must be spanked.

"Get the tawse," he told her, pushing the tray away and walking into the center of the suite to decide where to carry out her punishment.

"The tawse?" she quivered.

"The tawse at once. Unless you want the sole of one of these beautiful Italian slippers you've given me instead."

Paula went to their toy chest, knelt and dug for the tawse. Reluctantly she came to him where he sat on his most impressive, leather bound, brass riveted high backed chair, in his grey pajamas and elegant robe, her Christmas presents to him. She was pleased he thought enough of her taste to actually wear the dressing gown she'd chosen. Perhaps they really did belong together. Still, she feared the tawse in A.B.'s hands.

He took the blue leather strap from her and pulled her down across his lap.

"I can't believe you thought that you could talk me out of spanking you," he marveled, pushing her gown set up to her waist to reveal her bare, bisque complected, heart shaped bottom. "If you don't want to be spanked, learn to behave!"

Gripping her firmly by her waist Bartlett brought the small, split strap down across her bottom, once, twice, and many times more. First he spanked her horizontally, across both cheeks at once. Then he brought the tawse down vertically on either cheek, covering her firm and shapely backside with light red strap marks. It was a small enough tawse to work either crosswise or up and down and Bartlett did both to achieve an even magenta coloration long before stroke one hundred was reached. Little snaps were all it took to make her wriggle and pitch across his lap in an effort to escape the sting. He held her more firmly to his lap and continued applying the tawse to her bottom, methodically and with an ever so slightly increasing severity as he went on.

Paula began to whimper and pant, to grind and sob across his lap. She knew she would cry before he was done. But meanwhile, it felt so interesting to be in reality punished by one's own indignant husband. She had dreamed about such moments as a girl, after reading Frank and I in her maiden bedroom and forming her mature desires forever in her fantasies. Now that it was really happening, and feeling so very erotic, so romantically sexy, she began to wonder whether she hadn't thrown the tantrum on purpose, just to see what her husband would do.

She had hoped he would come to the inn. Now knowing he had come, and seen her with other men, gave her a terrible pang of guilt. She looked up at Bartlett over her shoulder. His profile while spanking her always gave her a thrill. She still felt the impact of the tawse profoundly, but the sensations had suddenly become more stimulating than painful. She would cry or come, but not both.

Smack, smack, smack! Relentlessly the tawse came down, reddening her smooth backside from hip to hip, until a solid field of pink tinged skin radiated heat. Bartlett loved the way she was taking it. The whimpers had become the most endearing little groans and she was grinding ever harder against his thigh. He gripped her more firmly, tossed the strap aside and finished the spanking with his hand, hard and fast enough to insure that she would indeed cry rather than come, as she deserved to do after her scandalous behavior.

"There, there," he said, sympathetically, slowly setting her to rights and pulling her up at last. "I forgive you." He hugged her to him and let her collect herself. "You didn't mean to be so naughty. It was a girl thing. I understand. Just don't do it again."

"I missed you A.B.," murmured Paula.

"Not enough to get in the car and come back to me last night, you lazy slut!"

"I wanted to but it was raining so hard and it was so cozy at the inn," she murmured.

"Keep going, you'll get another spanking!"

Instead he climbed into bed beside her and took her in his arms. "Was it perfectly awful at the store today?" she asked, grinding back against him.

"Could have been worse," he admitted, burying his face in her soft hair and affectionately squeezing her waist.

.

About the Author

In Random Point, everything is linked to spanking and this is true for the author of the Shadow Lane novels as well. Eve Howard has been writing and producing spanking erotica since the 1980's, when she began freelancing for one of California's largest fetish magazine publishers. While editing *Spank Hard* magazine (as Lizzie Bennett) in 1985, she was discovered by the video producer Nu-West and offered a chance to perform in spanking videos. In 1986 she published the first Shadow Lane story and the following year formed the video production company Shadow Lane with her partner Tony Elka. The Shadow Lane novel series, originally published by Eve in serial form in her magazine *Stand Corrected*, was brought out in paperback volumes by Blue Moon books beginning in 1992. There are nine titles in the Shadow Lane series and Eve is currently working on Volume 10.

Since 1988, Eve has written, directed and produced over 140 spanking videos, the vast majority featuring the same male-spanks-female dynamic portrayed in her novels. Female-friendly and designed to make people feel good, rather than guilty, about being into spanking, Eve suggests an irreverent alternative to the all or nothing B&D subculture portrayed in such beloved classics as *The Story of O*. Many spanking fans have discovered the real life spanking scene by following the same patterns of social networking as described in the Shadow Lane novels. And for almost twenty years, Eve's company Shadow Lane has been one of the primary social organs of the real life spanking scene. She lives with her husband Tony and three cats in Las Vegas.

Reader Reviews about the Shadow Lane Series

"I've become addicted to the "Random Point" series so much that I can't wait until the next chapter. I've ordered the first two Shadow Lane volumes and have re-read them over and over. I never tire of them. Eve is the only person I know who can make an enema sexy."

"I discovered Shadow Lane about a month ago via AOL. Prior to that time I thought I could write excellent spanking erotica. Then I ordered, "The Problem with Laura." This is just a note to commend Eve Howard's spectacular talent and to say thanks for an incredible erotic experience."

"I have just completed "Return to Random Point" and decided that I had to write about how much I enjoyed it. I have not been so aroused since reading my first discipline novel many years ago, about a girl raised in England and "coming of age" as I believe they put it. More recently I have enjoyed reading Grant Andrews' My Darling Dominatrix and Ann Rice's "Beauty" series. It seems that women, though, have the right touch when it comes to writing about this subject. Eve, especially, knows how to touch that erotic nerve and bring it to a pure, raw sensuality until one feels that he/she is near bursting with lust."

"I, for one, have always loved (and by loved I mean devoured... breathlessly) Eve Howard's novelettes. To read them... especially when I was just 'coming out'... was to feel completely validated. I truly identified with each and every heroine; the feisty, sassy ones, the shy, demure ultra 'subby' ones... the young ones, and the more mature. I loved the gentle yet firm "taken in hand" nature of the romantic variety of spanking D's that Eve always incorporated into the stories. I loved that the plots were not complicated... but, feasible nonetheless. I loved the depictions of sexual escapades after many of the spanking interludes. I appreciated that the girls were cherished and adored by the affably rogue-ish gents... that the submitting was willing and desired... that it wasn't like 'rape.'

I like the settings... having grown up in New England and living here almost my whole life. I LOVED the idea of the bookstore (which I always find sexy). Then and now. I could cite many passages too, but I fear I've rambled enough. Eve was/is always my favorite spanking author."

www.ingramcontent.com/pod-product-compliance
Lightning Source LLC
Chambersburg PA
CBHW020835260626
47169CB00003B/996